PLOT SUMMARY

A few days before the Kentucky Derby, a rising star jockey is found murdered near Churchill Downs. Louisville homicide detective Laurel Arno's investigation takes her from the private back rooms of elite gamblers, to the ancestral mansions of Kentucky bourbon barons and horse breeders, to the treacherous corridors of the State Capitol. Along the way, she exposes a shadowy world of political corruption, secret societies, and ancient feuds. As she closes in on a hidden killer, she discovers that a killer may also be closing in on her.

Praise for *The Shadow Priest*
"This is a great beach read."
— *USA Today Network*

Praise for *Chasing the Monkey King*
"A compelling read. The dialogue is witty, the plot intriguing,
and the settings enthralling."
Robert Dugoni, internationally best selling author
of *My Sister's Grave*

Praise for *Chasing the Monkey King*
"A brilliant, eye-opening mystery that captures the zeitgeist."
— Elizabeth George, author of *True South*

Praise for D.C. Alexander
"Alexander's characters are complicated, and whether his protagonists are
interrogating suspects or shooting the breeze with one another,
they do it with cocky aplomb."
— *The Kitsap Sun*

BLOOD IN THE BLUEGRASS

ISBN-13: 978-0-578-60127-4

Printed in the United States of America

ACKNOWLEDGMENTS

For invaluable assistance, advice, and encouragement along the way, I owe a debt of gratitude to Holly Pemberton, Kathy Hamilton, Mary King, Judy Pemberton, Diane Quayle, Philip Imber, Allison Imber, Jamie Mingus, Ellen Nason, Peggy Brashear, Mickey Meece, Stacey Wilson, and Amanda Gersh. This story would never have made it to print without their invaluable help.

I am also grateful to many authors and literary mavens for their priceless guidance over the years, including Sue Grafton, J.A. Jance, Kevin O'Brien, P.J. Alderman, Dr. Allen Wyler, Mike Lawson, Jane Porter, David Long, Greg Bear, Mark Lindquist, John J. Nance, Kelley Eskridge, Julie Paschkis, Jennie Shortridge, Dia Calhoun, Nancy Horan, Robert Dugoni, Nancy Pearl, Jess Walter, Stephanie Kallos, Royce Buckingham, Layton Green, and Rose O'Keefe.

For Holly and Haley

BLOOD IN THE BLUEGRASS

Blue moon of Kentucky keep on shining,
Shine on the one that's gone and proved untrue....
—Bill Monroe

ONE

Detective Laurel Arno stared at a two-inch gap—a mere two inches of empty space—that had meant the difference between life and death.

Shortly after 10 p.m. on a humid Louisville night, Laurel and her partner, Detective Trey Hewson, stood in the open doorway of a rickety one-car garage behind an old shotgun house. The body of an unusually tiny man hung before them, limp and motionless, a makeshift noose of sisal rope tight around his neck. The man's face was ashen, his eyes partially open, his mouth agape. Laurel guessed his height at less than five feet. He wore ragged work clothes and boots. His weathered hands were hardly larger than those of a child. But the thing that held Laurel's gaze was the void between the tips of the man's boots and the concrete floor, and it struck her as vaguely unsettling that a human life could end because of two inches of nothingness.

Despite the open door, the air in the cramped garage was tainted with the distinctive, somewhat briny smell of recent death. It was a smell Laurel was all too familiar with. A smell no homicide detective ever forgot.

"You alright?" Laurel asked Trey. "You look a little ill at ease."

"What's that weird smell?"

"The Grim Reaper."

"Well, the Grim Reaper should try a different deodorant."

"Is this your first corpse in a tight space like this?"

"Yeah, I guess it is."

"Death odor can linger, especially when the air is still and humid. You'll get used to it. Sort of."

Half an hour earlier, the call that would change Laurel's life had interrupted a late takeaway dinner of chili dogs and chocolate shakes from Dairy Kastle. Just as the starving detectives were getting back into their unmarked Ford Taurus, mouths watering and stomachs growling, a dispatcher had toned the radio channel to alert all officers to an incoming message. It was a code 10-80—a dead body.

"Report of one deceased Hispanic male, approximately 40 years old, address 112 East Greenfield, caller unknown."

Though the caller had reported it as an apparent suicide, the detectives were obliged to take a look as a matter of departmental policy.

The address was on a quiet street of century-old working class houses and gnarled oak trees a few blocks southeast of Churchill Downs—home of the Kentucky Derby, less than two weeks away. The street dead-ended at what had once been the north-south main line of the long-vanished Louisville & Nashville Railroad—a company that ran elegant, long-haul passenger trains with names like the Hummingbird and the South Wind to cities as far-flung as Chicago, Miami, and New Orleans. Now the track was only used by graffiti-covered freight trains, one of which was sounding its lonely horn from somewhere far down the line, barely audible over the din of crickets echoing across the neighborhood.

Within minutes of their arrival on the scene, they'd learned that the house and the lovingly restored, royal blue 1965 Ford pickup parked in front of it were owned by a man named Javier Cervantes. Having taken a few preliminary photographs, they were now waiting as the medical examiner, Dan Cohen, set up a stepladder to take a closer look before anyone cut the body down.

Laurel, a six-foot blonde with scarred knuckles and a slightly crooked nose, was a veteran detective, Louisville native, and alumna of Sacred Heart Academy where she was a star volleyball player two decades earlier. Trey, buzz-cut and baby-faced, was a newly-christened, twenty-something detective who'd moved to Louisville from his hometown of Portland, Oregon a few years back. The Homicide Unit's lieutenant had paired them up three months earlier so that Trey could learn the ropes from a seasoned pro. They'd been joined at the hip ever since. Happily, they'd hit it off and grown quite close. As both detectives were fair-haired and blue-eyed, their colleagues in the Major Crimes Division had taken to calling them Malibu Barbie and Ken.

Looking for distraction as they waited for Cohen to finish his initial examination of the body, Trey had started asking Laurel her opinions of potential matches presented by the dating application on his smartphone.

"How about this one?" he asked, turning his phone to show Laurel a young blonde.

"Let me see. No. No way."

"No? She's totally hot."

"She has showy jewelry, a fake tan, and gigantic fake boobs."

"And that's a problem because...?"

"She probably has no self-esteem. Women with no self-esteem will cheat on you the minute you hit a rough patch in your relationship."

"What are you talking about?"

"Their sense of self-worth comes from outside instead of inside. Whenever you're not making them feel good, they're going to look for good feelings elsewhere—like from that cute, flirty guy at the office or the gym or whatever.

Do yourself a favor."

"But she's so hot. And who said anything about a relationship?"

"For heaven's sake," Cohen said from atop his stepladder, not bothering to look at the detectives. "How long is this discussion going to last?"

Before Trey's first exposure to Cohen two months earlier, Laurel had warned him that Cohen was a perpetually scowling, panic attack-prone, post-9/11 transplant from New York who had no patience for anyone he considered ignorant—meaning just about anyone other than himself.

"What would you rather we talk about, Cohen?" Laurel asked. "Necrophilia? What topics float a medical examiner's boat?"

"There's a dead man hanging in front of you," Cohen said. "Don't be callous. Maybe even have some respect."

"Cohen, the last homicide I worked with you, I watched you stand over a bloody corpse while gnawing on a fried chicken leg."

"I was starving."

"Oh, I'm sure."

Their conversation was interrupted by the deafening roar of a Boeing 747 climbing out of Standiford Field, outbound from the UPS Worldport air freight facility. Laurel looked up to watch as it passed overhead, wondering where it was bound. Anchorage, Honolulu, London, Shanghai—with UPS, the destination could be just about anywhere on the planet.

"Anyway," Cohen half-shouted from atop his stepladder as the great airliner flew off to the north. "Come check this out. I mean, if you're done with your discussion of women with gigantic fake boobs."

"What is it?" Laurel asked.

"Better call CSU," Cohen said, examining the victim's neck with a magnifying glass. "If this was a suicide, then I'm Dolly Parton."

TWO

"What makes you think this wasn't a suicide?" Laurel asked as Cohen came down the ladder and gestured for her to go up and take a look.

"There are two sets of ligature marks," Cohen said. "One's under the noose he's hanging from, obviously. But there's another that's at more of a horizontal angle across the neck, suggesting that he was strangled from behind. As you can see with your naked eye, the horizontal ligature mark is deep. At first glance, it looks much deeper than the mark under the noose. Also, the victim has dirt and little bits of straw and wood shavings stuck to his clothes and caked on the heels of his shoes. Dirt streaked on his clothes in places that make it look to me as though he struggled. Tried to fight off his attackers. Fought them to the ground. And if that still isn't enough for you, look here," he said, pointing to the bloody end of the victim's right index finger. The nail had been partially torn out. Probably as the man fought for his life.

"Straw and wood shavings on his clothes?" Laurel asked. "Maybe he works at the stables on the backside of Churchill Downs."

"Maybe he's a jockey," Trey said. "But if it's a murder, wouldn't they have closed the garage door?"

"It's jammed, smart guy," Cohen said. "Anyway, I'll be able to tell you more after CSU processes the scene and we cut him down."

"Well, I'm next on the board to catch a homicide anyway," Laurel said. "Who has the scene log?"

"Barret. The patrolman smoking a cigarette over there by the garden shed."

"I suppose we'd better go have a word with Officer Barret, and then have ourselves a look around."

*****

Seeing no signs of a forced entry at the back door to the house, Laurel and

Trey found a key to the deadbolt hidden under an empty flowerpot and let themselves in. The interior was tidy and austere. They passed through an unremarkable bedroom and a circa 1950s kitchen on their way to the front room. There, they found the front door locked from the inside. There was a threadbare couch, a wall of built-in shelving, and an old-fashioned tube television atop a worn wooden cabinet. On the wall above the television, a tin crucifix hung from a bent nail. The built-in shelves held a few dozen books, several framed photographs, and what looked like some sort of personal shrine—complete with a small statuette of the Virgin Mary, dried roses, and Mexican novena candles depicting the Virgin of Guadalupe, the Sacred Heart of Jesus, and two saints Laurel didn't recognize. The shelf above the shrine was dedicated entirely to a large framed wedding photo of the victim, years younger, looking proud but serious next to his beautiful bride. On the shelf below the shrine, there was a well-worn copy of a Spanish language Bible, as well as several books on horse tack and racing technique.

"Hey, take a look at this," Trey said, holding out a framed photograph he'd picked up from an end table next to the couch. In the photo, the victim, in full racing silks and holding a trophy, sat atop a thoroughbred horse, surrounded by men and women in formal racetrack attire. "Told you he was a jockey."

*****

Finding nothing of particular interest in the house, but noting the absence of any evidence of the victim's wife living there, they turned their attention to the immediate neighbors. At a ramshackle shotgun house on one side, a sneering young man with a shaved head opened the door. He wore nothing but a white tank top undershirt and droopy boxer shorts. He reeked of alcohol sweat and cigarette smoke.

"What now?" the man asked, raising his chin and looking down his nose at the detectives.

After being told why the detectives had disturbed his beauty sleep, the man growled that he'd observed nothing out of the ordinary, hadn't noticed anyone coming or going, and knew nothing of the victim's affairs—not even his name. "I don't hang out with wetbacks."

"Well, you must be in the running for friendliest neighbor of the year," Laurel said.

At the house on the other side, an elderly widow came to the door after taking a long time getting out of bed and making herself presentable. She wore a satin sleeping cap and old pink terry cloth robe, her knobby, trembling hands holding it closed.

"I didn't see nothin' funny," she said. "Turned in at 8:30. Right after *The Blessed Life*."

"The what, now?" Trey asked.

"The Gateway Church show with pastor Robert Morris," she said, as if Trey should have known.

After several minutes of getting nowhere, learning only that Cervantes was a "sort of darker skinned but polite man" who kept to himself, Trey asked the woman a very general question. "Is there anything at all you can think of that might be relevant to our investigation?"

"Well, I believe he was sad."

"Sad?"

"A month or two back, they came and took his wife away."

"Who did?"

"The government people."

"Immigration?"

"Yes, that's right. Immigration."

"She was deported?"

"They said she had to go back to Mexico."

THREE

"So you think Cervantes is Mexican?" Trey asked as they walked back to the crime scene.

"Given that he has a Hispanic name, a house full of Mexican holy candles, and his wife was just deported to Mexico, I'd say that's a fair guess," Laurel said.

"You're making fun of me."

"Never."

"Think he could be a drug dealer? A cartel guy?"

"Because he's Mexican? You watch too much cable news, Trey."

"They arrested that one cartel guy on the South End earlier this year, and he was—"

"Trey, have you ever heard of cartel drug traffickers strangling someone and then going to a lot of trouble to make it look like a suicide?"

"I guess not."

"No. If anything, they like to make examples of their victims. Mount their severed heads on fence posts along Main Street. Attach signs to the bodies to make sure everyone knows who did it."

*****

Back at Cervantes's garage, Laurel and Trey watched as the CSU team cut the body down and laid it on a large rectangular tarp. As they began their examination, Trey resumed his consideration of the blonde with the gigantic boobs, having brought her dating profile photo back up on his smartphone.

"Forget the boobs for a second," he said to Laurel. "Look at her eyes. They're mesmerizing."

"Trey, look at the logo on her pressed polo shirt. It says Pastel Inn & Resort."

"Never heard of it."

"It's a pretentious, overpriced beach resort in one of those synthetic little towns of the Florida Panhandle. She's wearing that shirt so everyone knows she stayed there. What does that tell you?"

"She likes the beach?"

"She's status-conscious. So, big picture, despite the mesmerizing eyes, what you're looking at is someone with no self-esteem who is also status-conscious. The worst of all worlds. You'll never keep her happy. And look—it says she has five cats. Yuck."

"What's wrong with cats?"

"Besides their being a species of self-absorbed psychopaths?"

"I love cats," Trey said.

"Of course you do."

"I thought all lesbians loved cats."

"Of course you did."

Trey shook his head. "You're the first lesbian I've ever met who doesn't like cats."

"It's a complicated world," she said as one of the CSU techs handed her the victim's wallet. "But why do you need my approval? If you want to take her out, take her out."

Digging through the wallet, she found a fair amount of cash and a driver's license confirming that the victim was indeed Javier Cervantes, age 38, 4-foot-11, 108 pounds, black hair, brown eyes. Aside from the license and cash, the wallet contained nothing more than a gas station rewards card. No credit cards.

"Can you please run this guy on your MDT for me?" Laurel asked as she handed the license to a nearby patrolman, referring to his mobile data terminal—the computer the officer had in his car that connected to the National Crime Information Center and CourtNet databases.

"You positive this guy didn't kill himself?" Trey asked Cohen, who was bent over the body to get a close look at the fingernails.

"Positive."

"His wife was deported a few weeks ago. Sounds like good cause for depression or whatever."

"Depression or whatever?"

"You sure he couldn't have screwed up his first shot, trying to choke himself at a bad angle, and then gave it a re-do?"

Cohen sighed, stood up, and stared at Trey for a moment before bothering to answer. "The damage under the horizontal ligature marks indicates it wasn't an initial attempt he would have gotten up and walked away from. Plus, killers almost always use the sort of excessive force it would have taken to make deep marks like this," he said, kneeling down again and pointing at the darker, more pronounced of the marks. "He was definitely killed by whatever created this horizontal mark. Just judging by the visible ecchymoses."

"The what?" Trey asked.

"Bruising. When we cut into him, I guarantee we'll find a bunch of focal hemorrhages in the strap muscles around that horizontal mark, but not around the more vertical mark left by the sisal rope. Similarly, there'll be fractures of the cartilage around the larynx."

"What else?" Laurel asked.

"I'm reasonably certain that he wasn't killed *here*."

"Come again?"

"In cases of strangulation, as I would hope you know by now, the sphincter tends to relax such that feces can be released."

Cohen thought Trey looked lost.

"The sphincter, Trey. The little muscle ring—or maybe big muscle ring in your case—that holds in your poop."

"I know what a sphincter is."

"To put it crudely," Cohen said, ignoring him, "a strangle victim often craps his pants, which Mr. Cervantes did. A bowel movement of considerable liquidity, it ran out the bottom of the right pant leg, then onto and off his shoe, as you can see and smell. However, as you'll also notice, there are no feces on the floor beneath where we found him hanging."

"So where'd the poop go?" Trey asked.

"It didn't go anywhere," Laurel said. "He did. Someone moved him."

"Bravo," Cohen said. "So now, with your blessing, I'm going to send CSU over to Churchill Downs to see if they can't figure out where this guy was killed."

"The case of the missing poop," Trey said. "Wasn't that a Nancy Drew mystery?"

Cohen rolled his eyes and headed for his van.

*****

"I don't know what that dude's problem is," Trey said as they got to the car.

"Cohen?"

"He hates me."

"He's a neurotic, native New Yorker. For guys like him, showing open contempt is about the same thing as giving someone a weak handshake. Anyway, don't take it personally. He's like that with everyone."

"Not with you. He loves you."

"Because I throw it back at him."

Trey looked thoughtful. "So you think Cervantes was killed at Churchill Downs and then moved here?" Trey asked.

"Could be. Tomorrow, before dawn, we'll go poke around—"

"Wait, *before* dawn?"

"You can nap in the afternoon."

"Laurel, come on."

"CSU will look for physical evidence on the backside of the track tonight. Unfortunately for us, early morning is when the jockeys and other people we need to talk to will be there, working the horses before the day heats up."

"Great." Trey took a last glance back at the body. "Hey, you think Cervantes maybe got killed because he didn't want to play ball in a race-fixing scheme? Or wanted more money out of it?"

"Or threatened to blow the whistle. Maybe we'll find out tomorrow."

FOUR

After getting no more than three hours of sleep apiece, Laurel and Trey met at Nord's Bakery on the edge of the Schnitzelburg neighborhood. They grabbed a bag of maple-bacon donuts, went next door to Sunergos for large cups of strong, black coffee, then headed for Churchill Downs just as the sky began to lighten in the east.

"Got a voicemail from CSU this morning," Laurel said as they neared the track. "Apparently Cervantes was a well-respected exercise rider who was starting to get to race second tier horses on occasion. This past week, he was working with a horse called Empire Builder. But by the time CSU got to Empire Builder's stable stall last night, it had already been cleaned, its bedding replaced, and all that. In other words, there was no evidence—fecal or otherwise—of Cervantes having been strangled there."

"That's a bummer."

"Yes, it is. But I'm still betting he was killed at Churchill Downs. After their brief initial analysis, CSU is almost certain that the dirt and bits of straw and wood shavings all over him came from there."

The parking lots were already half full when they arrived. The track woke up early in the days leading up to the Derby, with trainers and jockeys exercising thoroughbreds in preparation for the many coming races. By next week, the stables of the backside would house more than a thousand horses, tended to by a multitude of support personnel—hot walkers, stable hands, grooms, and exercise riders—many of whom migrated from track to track throughout the racing season, and some of whom slept in the stables with the horses while in town. They worked ungodly hours, often from 4 a.m. to sundown.

The detectives pulled into a gated driveway off of South 4th Street, flashed their badges at the officer manning the gate, and made their way to a small parking area alongside one of the many long stable buildings. From there, they walked toward the track, looking for anyone who might be able tell them more about what Javier Cervantes had been up to the past few days. As they came upon the track proper, they saw a shallow layer of mist, tinted purple in the predawn light, hanging in the air no more than knee-height above the grass of the infield. It was going to be a sunny, warm morning. The track was in great shape, the landscaping manicured, the buildings all polished up for the Derby.

Laurel loved the Kentucky Derby. Loved its beauty, grandeur, and tradition. To be sure, there was something obscene about so many movie stars and other ultra-rich flying in on their private jets, booking up every restaurant in town, rolling around in limousines, and throwing cash about like sultans among the little people. Something obscene about the excesses of consumption and gambling when nearly one of every five Kentuckians lived in poverty. Still, it was Laurel's favorite time of year to be in Louisville. The city sparkled. For a few days, it felt like the center of the universe.

"Have you been to the Run for the Roses yet?" she asked Trey.

"The what?"

"The Derby. The most exciting two minutes in sports. The longest continuously running sporting event in American hist—"

"I got it. I got it. No, I haven't been. Not yet. I tried to get tickets last year, but they were like $400 for crap seats."

"Just go to the infield. It's cheap."

"I'd run into too many people I've arrested."

*****

The detectives went to an office to learn more about Cervantes's recent activity. It turned out that the horse he'd been working with—Empire Builder—was owned by Barnstone Farm, a legendary thoroughbred breeding and training facility out near the small town of Midway in rural Woodford County. Barnstone Farm had produced half a dozen Kentucky Derby winners in the 20th century, including a Triple Crown winner in the 1950s.

"Empire Builder is set to race in the Pennyroyal Stakes," the desk clerk told them.

"The what?" Trey asked.

"The Clayton Bourbon Pennyroyal Stakes. It's a Grade II stakes race preceding the Derby on Derby Day. Has a purse of $250,000. Three-year-olds."

"What does Grade II mean?" Trey asked.

"Means it has to have a purse of at least $200,000. It's a big-time race. Empire Builder will have long odds. But still, I should think it was a breakthrough opportunity for Cervantes."

"Wait, Cervantes was going to *ride* Empire Builder in the Pennyroyal?" Laurel asked.

"Yes, ma'am."

"He wasn't just the exercise rider?"

"No, ma'am."

"Well, well. Who is Empire Builder's trainer?"

"That would be Guy LaForge. Works with a lot of different thoroughbred outfits, of course. Not just Barnstone Farm."

They got the location of Empire Builder's stable and stall, along with the names of the owners and trainers of the horses using the adjacent and nearby stalls, with the idea that they'd run down all personnel who'd been in the area the previous night. Anyone who might have seen or heard something happening in Empire Builder's stall. According to the desk clerk, one of the adjacent stalls was occupied by Great Flood, a chestnut filly owned by a group of local bank executives. The other was occupied by a black colt named Carbonado, owned by a man named Edgar Clayton.

"Does the name Edgar Clayton ring a bell?" Laurel asked Trey as they left the office.

"Is he related to the Clayton Bourbon Claytons?"

"Very good. Edgar is heir to the Clayton Bourbon empire—the named sponsor of the Pennyroyal Stakes."

"There's a major craze for Peepaw Clayton 21-year-old in bourbon circles right now," Trey said.

"So I hear."

"It's going for like $800 a bottle or whatever."

"$800 a *bottle*? A few years ago it was $85."

"I guess the secret's out."

"Is it worth it?" Laurel asked.

"How should I know? You think I'd be working as a cop if I could afford Peepaw Clayton bourbon?"

"I thought you did it for the love of policing, Trey."

"That's right. For the joy of facing constant hostility from the general public. The joy of living in fear of being unfairly ripped a new butthole by the media, or being thrown under the bus by a chain of command trying to cover its own ass. What's not to love?"

"You're a cynic."

"Please. If I could afford to be drinking $800 bourbon, I'd be living in the Virgin Islands."

A blazing sun had risen in the cloudless sky, illuminating the famous twin spires that towered above the track, giving it its distinctive look. On the far side, a mere handful of VIP visitors were scattered here and there throughout the grandstand. But next week, thousands would be in both the grandstand and the Millionaires Row restaurant at this hour, watching the action in an annual preview event called Dawn at the Downs—a rare chance for the general public to watch the pros exercise some of the most distinguished horses in the world.

The detectives walked to the stable building where Empire Builder had his stall and took a peek inside. The horse was a beautiful, powerful-looking chestnut colt weighing more than 1,000 pounds. Alone in the stall, he was breakfasting on a blend of oats and barley. Laurel had the urge to reach out and touch him, to stroke his muscular neck, his shiny, reddish-brown coat. But she held back, doubting it would be proper.

They spent the better part of the next two hours hanging around in the immediate vicinity of Empire Builder's stall, questioning stable hands, groomers, wranglers, trainers, jockeys, and anyone else they found loitering in the area, asking them the usual battery of questions. Had they seen or heard anything out of the ordinary the night before? Did Cervantes have any enemies? Did they know Cervantes to be in any sort of trouble? Who had they last seen him with? When had they last seen him?

Each person they spoke with claimed to have gone home no later than 8:30 p.m. the previous night. Each denied having anything of value to report. Each was, nevertheless, jumpy. But whatever the reason for the jumpiness, all the detectives learned was that Cervantes was a man who loved the horses, took pride in his work, was diligent, conscientious, and kind.

In addition to Empire Builder's minders, the detectives paid special attention to the people associated with Great Flood and Carbonado—the horses occupying the adjacent stalls. The folks who came and went from the other horses' stalls had nothing of value to report either. However, after questioning a groomer in Carbonado's stall, they came back around the corner to discover a vet giving Empire Builder an injection. He was a squat, middle-aged man in wrinkled green scrubs, his hair slicked down with pomade, a thick gold chain around his neck.

"Excuse me, sir," Laurel said. "We're detectives with LMPD. We're speaking with everyone in the vicinity about something that happened here last night."

"I wasn't here last night," the vet said without bothering to look at them. "And as you can plainly see, I'm busy."

"Well, when you're done, we'd like to ask you a handful of routine questions. Won't take a minute."

The man pressed the plunger on the syringe, withdrew it from the base of Empire Builder's neck, and turned to face them.

"Let's see some credentials," the man said, closing his medical kit.

The detectives presented their badges.

"Laurel Arno," the man said, reading aloud. "And Trey Hewson. Got it."

"Were you here at all yesterday?" Laurel asked him.

"Talk to my lawyer," the man said.

"Sure," Laurel said as she snapped a photo of the man with her smartphone and stepped forward to block his only escape route. "But first let's see some identification from you as well."

Looking profoundly irritated, the man stared at Laurel, then Trey, then Laurel again. He seemed to be deliberating. Then, with a shake of his head, he took his wallet from his back pocket and handed his driver's license to Laurel.

"Mr. Eldon Ridgeway," Laurel read aloud, snapping a photo of the driver's license as well.

"*Doctor* Ridgeway."

"Of course. *Doctor* Ridgeway. I must say, I find it a little odd that you're reluctant to speak with us. Even for a brief moment."

"You must say you find it a little odd? You don't talk much like a cop."

"She was all-honors at Sacred Heart," Trey said.

"Good for her. But I'm busy."

"Of course you are," Laurel said.

As Laurel pondered how she might put some pressure on Ridgeway to cooperate, she detected movement out of the corner of her eye. Glancing over her shoulder, she saw two men approaching who seemed to be eyeballing the detectives with a look of hostile concern. One was tall and portly and wore a black baseball hat bearing the logo of the Austrian gun manufacturer Glock. Next to him was a wrinkled, scowling old man in expensive-looking clothes and shoes. As they made eye contact with Laurel, their pace slowed. The portly one looked down at the ground, muttered something to the old man, then patted his coat pockets as though he'd forgotten his keys or phone. The old man gave the detectives a final acid glare before both men turned around and walked away. Laurel often chastised herself for jumping to incorrect conclusions about people based on their look or vibe. But she had half a mind to chase them down for questioning.

"I have a lot to do here, so," Ridgeway said, interrupting her thoughts, letting his statement hang unfinished.

"We're just asking people—"

"Am I under arrest?"

"No."

"Then you can go pound sand. If you have a problem with that, you can call my lawyer."

Ridgeway picked up his medical kit and walked off.

"Pound sand?" Trey said. "What does that mean?"

"It means get lost."

"A local expression?"

"I have no idea."

"What is with people here?" Trey asked. "Almost everyone we've talked to has been cagey, if not totally hostile."

"Big races coming up," Laurel said, watching as Ridgeway disappeared around the far corner of the stable building. "Pressure is on, I suppose."

"He knows something."

"Does he? Or is he just a jerk? Or does he know something that has nothing to do with Cervantes. Whatever the case, we don't have any way to compel him to talk to us at the moment." She took a deep breath and looked at Trey. "This is a waste of time. Let's go have a word with his Lordship."

"His Lordship?"

"Shelby Beauregard Liddell—better known as the Duke. An all-knowing bookie. Formerly a dentist in Hazard County. Had his license revoked and spent three years in prison for selling prescription painkillers to junkies as a side business."

"They have dentists in Hazard County?"

"Don't be an ass. Anyway, this time of year, you can usually find the Duke holding court in the track's ultra-secret, ultra-exclusive, ultra-swank penthouse facility they call the Mansion."

"That's a lot of ultras."

"Yes. And the people you find up there tend to be ultra-wealthy and ultra-eccentric."

"I'm ultra-curious to check it out."

FIVE

As Laurel and Trey made their way around the periphery of the southwest turn of the track, a pair of massive brown thoroughbreds came racing around the bend at full speed, their manes blowing in the wind, cakes of dirt flying from their hooves, their riders hanging on for dear life. Perhaps it was her imagination, but Laurel swore she could feel a tremor in the earth under her feet, could feel the rush of air as they thundered past barely 40 feet away. No matter how many times she saw Derby Week thoroughbreds run, it always impressed her. Gave her a chill. These magnificent, powerful creatures. The fastest horses on Earth. Forces of nature kept in control by the barest, most tenuous of margins through the extraordinary skill and near extrasensory perception of the sport's finest jockeys.

In a few days, 160,000 people would be crowded around the track to sing "My Old Kentucky Home," sip ice-cold mint juleps, and behold the greatest and oldest of all Grade I stakes races. In the turn where Laurel and Trey now paused, fans would watch a full field of 20 horses and jockeys fly by in a blur. A fleeting glimpse of greatness.

*****

"Where's the Duke?" Laurel asked, flashing her badge at two gorilla-sized men who stood guard in front of an unmarked elevator in the bowels of the Churchill Downs grandstand. The men wore nondescript blue blazers and held small Motorola radios. Their massive, shiny bald heads reflected the overhead light. They could almost have passed for twins.

"The Duke is a busy man," one of them said after a slow blink.

"Is he in the Mansion?"

"I'm afraid I can't—"

"Tell him we need to see him, please. It'll be quick. Then he can go on his merry way."

"Sorry, but I'm not authorized to—"

"Tell him that if he doesn't agree to see us right now, we'll compel him, which will make a lot of unwelcome noise."

After a bit of back-and-forth over the radio, the security gorillas stood aside to let the detectives board the unmarked elevator. Just after the doors shut, they heard one of the gorillas on the other side say, "Man, I'd eat *her* dirty underwear," to which the other said, "She was smokin' hot." At this, out of the corner of his eye, Trey noticed Laurel's jaw tighten and saw her right hand assume the classic bladed shape used for striking the side of someone's neck. He wondered whether it was a subconscious reaction.

"Let me take the lead on this," Laurel said. "The Duke has a lot of powerful friends. If he's going to go crying to the lords of our fair city, let their wrath fall on me instead of you. I have more senior officers who owe me protection than you have."

"You sure?"

"I'm sure."

"You're good people, Laurel."

"Yes, I am."

The elevator doors opened and, after passing two more blazer-wearing security gorillas, they were admitted to the Mansion. It was a vast room of dark wood-paneled walls, leather couches and chairs, and shelves that held Chihuly-esque glass sculptures. There were innumerable granite tables adorned with empty golden vases, ultra-modern chandeliers hanging from the ceiling, and large windows looking down on the finish line. A large square bar surrounded by bright red stools stood in the middle of the room. The atmosphere had that processed, sterile quality of heavily filtered air conditioning.

"This is where you go when you're too rich to hang out on Millionaires Row," Laurel said under her breath. "Rumor has it that it takes about $13,000 per person to get in here on Derby Day."

"Looks like a hotel lobby from the 1970s."

"Nobody ever said the rich had good taste."

As they passed the bar, Trey's eyes locked on a series of large warming trays of forlorn breakfast items. Belgian waffles, browned pork sausages, biscuits and gravy, eggs Benedict on English muffins, and a mountain of thick-cut bacon. It was a huge quantity of food considering the small number of patrons occupying the space. It had hardly been touched.

"Did you see all that bacon?" Trey muttered, his lips wet.

"Try to stay focused."

"With fifty pounds of crisp bacon sitting on the bar? I'll do my best."

Laurel led the way to the far side of the Mansion where a morbidly obese man in a rumpled seersucker suit sat in a wheelchair just outside a glass door on the balcony. He was watching the track through a small pair of binoculars. A cigarette hung from his lips. Laurel wondered if he'd just moved to his remote spot after having been told that detectives were on the way up to see him.

"Is that him?" Trey asked. "That big lump on the balcony?"

"That's him."

"Looks like a human relative of Jabba the Hut."

"Keep your voice down."

The Duke had a green oxygen tank strapped to the side of his wheelchair. A hose led to a breathing mask that sat idle in his lap."

Laurel opened the door to the balcony. "Good morning, Duke."

Without altering his gaze or even lowering his binoculars, he said, in a heavy Southern accent, "Laurel Arno, detective extraordinaire. To what do I owe the displeasure?"

"Hey, now. It's a friendly visit."

"So friendly that you had to threaten unpleasantness in order to have a word with me?"

"Blame the security gorilla. He wasn't having it. Wasn't even going to call upstairs for me."

"Territorial, these security gorillas."

"I see you're still smoking unfiltered Chesterfields."

"Nothin' but."

"I didn't know they still made those in the U.S."

"They don't. I have to order them from Europe."

"Your doctor know?"

"Are you my mother?"

"Just looking out for you, Duke."

"Oh, I'm sure. Now then," he said, lowering his binoculars and turning his motorized wheelchair to face the detectives. "What can I do for you, Laurel and...."

"Trey," Trey said.

"Trey what?"

"Trey the comic relief sidekick," Laurel said. "We need to know whether there are any rumblings about funny business in the coming races. Any rumors at all. I wouldn't ask if it weren't serious."

"What does it do to people's life expectancy when they agree to talk with you, Laurel?"

"Nobody has to know you spoke with us."

"Ha! After you bully your way in here and tramp across the entire venue, in front of everybody, to have this little chat? You're daft."

"Duke, look at yourself. How long do you really think you have left to live, anyway?" Laurel asked.

The Duke went quiet for a second, then burst into the hoarse laughter of a lifelong smoker. "Good gracious, Laurel," he said at last, recomposing himself. "You're one of a kind."

"Come on, Duke. Out with it."

"Rumblings about funny business. Huh. That's rather vague. Is there *particular* funny business you have in mind?"

"Anything that may be related to a homicide."

"Someone's dead?"

"Jockey named Javier Cervantes."

"Oh."

"Ring any bells?"

"I'm sure I've heard the name."

"What do you know about a vet named Eldon Ridgeway?"

"Ridgeway. He's no gentleman. I'll tell you that for free. Grew up in Manhattan and has the consequent blunt manner."

"We figured that out for ourselves."

"A terminal boozehound, he also has a reputation for pushing the edge of the envelope with respect to the use of performance-enhancing drugs. For being willing to stretch the rules."

"Have you heard anything specific about his possible involvement with upcoming races?"

"Can't say I have."

"What about whispers of any funny business with any of the Derby Day races?"

"Laurel, please. Every year there are rumors of Derby Day race rigging. *Every* year. Do they ever find anything?"

"Do they ever look? What about the Pennyroyal Stakes in particular? Any rumors?"

The Duke looked out over the track, picked up his oxygen mask, and took a long, deep breath.

"What would be the point of fixing a second-tier race like the Pennyroyal?" he asked. "Even if you fix it so that a horse you own wins outright—at the most your cut of the purse is going to be, what, $150,000 before taxes? That's chump change to these people. Where's the motive?"

"Don't play me for a hayseed, Duke. They could win from betting on their horse too, with a big payout if the horse has long odds."

"Any big bet on a long-odds horse would draw scrutiny."

"On Derby Day? With all that money flying around? All those people with pockets full of hundreds, drinking mint juleps until horses with 40-to-1 odds start to look good to them?"

"The powers that be are always on the lookout for big bets on long odds, Laurel."

"So then the cheaters have family and cronies make a bunch of smaller bets so that the scheme flies under the radar. Quit playing dumb."

The Duke just stared at her.

"Come on, Duke. Spill it."

The Duke took another long pull of oxygen. "Look, Laurel. Cheating is an inextricable part of all forms of gambling. Anywhere you find gambling, you're going to find people trying to rig things. It's human nature, plain and simple."

"Duke, a man is dead. That means that my need for information transcends any little code of silence y'all have when it comes to gambling shenanigans. I don't care about your general theories on cheating. What I need to know is whether you've heard anything specific, say, about jockeys being approached? Maybe jockeys being offered bribes to rig a race?"

"Nothing specific. No, I have not. And that's the God's honest truth."

He met Laurel's stare.

"But?" Laurel said.

"But. But, but, but." He took a quick look around to make sure nobody was close enough to hear anything he was about to say. "I did hear a very, very non-specific rumor," he said quietly.

"Concerning bribes of jockeys?" Laurel asked, matching his low volume.

"No. Concerning a horse swap."

"A horse swap? What do you mean?"

"You ever heard the name Mark Gerard?"

"No."

"He was a famous thoroughbred veterinarian. The vet for Secretariat, matter of fact."

"So?"

"In 1976, he bought two horses down in South America. One of the horses, name of Lebon, was a dud. But one of them, name of Cinzano, was a champion racer. The thing was, the damned horses looked the same. So what does Gerard do when he gets them to the U.S.? He claims that Cinzano died in an accident, collects $150,000 from his insurance on the horse, then probably buys himself a new Mercedes with the proceeds. But what really happened? It was Lebon that died in the so-called accident. And that clever Gerard, he enters Cinzano in a race at Belmont, posing as Lebon, at 57-to-1 odds. And Cinzano blows away the field."

"How did they catch him?"

"Bless his avaricious heart, Gerard made a huge bet on his long-odds imposter horse and tried to cash in for somewhere in the neighborhood of $80,000—in 1976 dollars, mind you. Around $350,000 in today's dollars. Anyway, officials at Belmont recognized him when he went to collect his winnings, got that proverbial funny feeling, sniffed around, and that was that." The Duke smiled. "Son of a bitch hired F. Lee Bailey to defend him."

"O.J. Simpson's lawyer?"

"The same. That greasy ferret got Gerard off with barely more than a hand slap, despite the magnitude of the scam."

"And now there are rumors that something like that is going to happen here?"

"Unsubstantiated rumors. And I very much doubt their veracity."

"Why?"

"Because in 1988, when you were still eating paste in preschool, there was a serious mix-up here, too. And that mix-up led to a major increase in oversight."

"A mix-up here in Louisville? At Churchill Downs?"

"On Derby Day itself. First race of the day, the winning horse, an experienced thoroughbred with the real name Blairwood, was entered with the name of an entirely different and underwhelming rookie horse called Briarwood. As a consequence, the horse opened the day with 35-to-1 odds. Long story short, Blairwood's trainer claimed it was an honest spelling error. And mind you, nobody ever proved otherwise—despite an eyebrow-raising $20,000 bet having been made on the long-odds horse. Regardless, after that, things really tightened up around here. Now Churchill Downs has a full-time horse identifier provided by the state Racing Commission. Kathy Hammersmith. She inspects each horse before each race to make sure nothing like that ever happens again. Point being, a horse swap would be hard to get away with."

"But not impossible."

"Like I said, at best, we're talking about a vague rumor here. That's really all I can tell you."

"Is it, Duke?"

He took another breath from his oxygen tank. "You should go talk to Kathy Hammersmith."

"And *you* should quit smoking."

"And *you* should quit rocking the boat. Then maybe we'll both live longer."

SIX

"That Duke dude is a weird one," Trey said as they descended in the private elevator.

"You have no idea."

The elevator door opened at ground level to reveal the same two security gorillas gazing at Laurel with lusty, stupid grins on their faces. She didn't bother to make eye contact. But for a brief instant, she visualized snapping the bigger one's pinkie finger if he dared touch her. The thought made her smile.

"Do you think horse racing is dirty?" Trey asked.

"The sport of kings? Bite your tongue, sir."

"Really, though."

Laurel shrugged. "I don't know. I'd like to think it's straight. Of course, over time, if you live in Louisville, you can't help but hear stories. Rumors from a friend of a friend of a friend who works at the track. All of them hearsay. So who knows if any of them are true?"

"What sort of rumors?"

She told Trey rumors of people rigging things for a favorite to lose by stuffing pieces of sponge way up the horse's nose the night before a race to hinder its breathing. Of jockeys putting little button-activated shocker-buzzer things under their saddles to give their horses a little extra adrenaline. Of horses getting caught with illegal performance-enhancing drugs in their blood.

"Matter of fact, one time they even caught the Derby winner with illegal drugs in its blood," she said.

"You're kidding."

"Nope. Back in the late '60s. Horse named Dancer's Image. A Kentucky Racing Commission chemist made the discovery during a blind urine test. But by the time the test results came back, Dancer's Image had already been pronounced the Derby winner. The horse wasn't disqualified until three days after the race. As you can imagine, that led to quite a hubbub."

"Damn. With all the money involved, it was awfully brave of that chemist to report his or her findings."

"Yeah, well, take a wild guess what happened to him?"

"They had a parade down Main Street to celebrate his integrity?"

"He got fired. Blackballed from racing. What does that tell you?"

"Nothing good."

"And get this—even more sinister, some people thought Dancer's Image had been slipped the drug as a means of sabotage. As revenge against the horse's owner for being a major supporter of the Civil Rights Movement and a personal friend of Dr. Martin Luther King."

"Holy smokes."

"Yup."

"I guess things were different back then."

*****

It took them nearly an hour to find Kathy Hammersmith. She was all the way back on the other side of the track near where they'd parked their car.

"Ms. Hammersmith?" Trey asked as they approached. She was in one of the stable buildings, down under a horse, examining the inner side of one of its hind legs.

"Yes?"

"I'm Detective Hewson. This is Detective Arno. Do you have a moment?"

"A short moment," she said, standing up and offering her hand.

"We can make it quick. First off, have you heard any rumors about a possible horse swap in this year's Pennyroyal Stakes?"

"Uh, no."

"Nothing at all? Even, like, totally unsubstantiated rumors?"

"Nothing of the sort. And frankly, nobody could pull that sort of thing off anymore. As I'm guessing you know, it's my job to inspect each horse before each race to make sure they are who they're supposed to be."

"Can I ask how you do that?"

"Well, first of all, each horse has an identification number tattooed to the inside of its lip. I compare the tattooed number to what's in the official records and foal certificates. I also check the horse for identifying colors, markings, and so forth."

"That must be tricky," Trey said. "They all look the same to me. Brown, black, white, or gray. Maybe one has spots. Beyond that, they look like replicas to my eyes."

"Actually, they often have very distinctive markings on their legs."

"Really?"

"So," Laurel said, chiming in, "in doing these record comparisons and so forth, do you ever catch people fielding the wrong horse?"

"Maybe a couple of times a year I'll find that the wrong horse is in the paddock for a particular race. But it's never intentional. Someone just walked over from the stables with the wrong horse. We run a tight, clean ship here, and everybody knows it. Nobody would try to swap a horse. They know they'd get caught."

Trey nodded. "Okay. Thanks for your help."

*****

The air had grown hot by the time they were heading back to their car.

"Now what?" Trey asked.

"I'm not sure."

Turning a corner in the backside stables area, Laurel once again spotted the wrinkled, scowling old man in expensive clothes and shoes. He was shouting to a stable hand a few yards away. He hadn't noticed Laurel and Trey approaching yet. "Have that boy you're with carry the brushes," he said to a female stable hand, appearing to be referring to a full-grown African-American man as *boy*."

"Want to go to Frank's for a sandwich?" Trey asked after they passed the old man.

"What?" Laurel asked, shaking off her stupefaction at the old man's use of the word *boy*.

"Sandwich at Frank's?"

"Is food the only thing you ever think about?"

"Food, women, and college basketball."

"You're a well rounded young man."

"Hey, Laurel. Look," Trey said, pointing at the windshield as they approached the car.

A small yellow Post-it note was held to the windshield by one of the wiper blades. Laurel picked it up. On it, there was a local area code 502 telephone number with a two-word message: "call me."

SEVEN

Fifteen minutes later, they were at Frank's Meat & Produce on Preston Highway, the clerk checking them out with her usual sweet Southern banter. "What do you have, sweetheart? That's $5.17, honey. Have a great day, baby."

They started devouring their sandwiches as soon as they got back to their car.

"That clerk is always so friendly," Trey said between bites.

"Don't talk while you chew."

"You know something funny? When I moved here, people came from up and down the block to welcome me to the neighborhood. Made me pies and cookies and stuff."

"So?"

"People here are really nice. Welcoming. On average, I mean. Besides the criminals."

"You sound surprised."

"Well, I mean, nobody ever brought me pies and cookies when I moved into a new place in Oregon."

Laurel called in on a radio service channel to ask for a trace of the phone number that was left on their windshield at Churchill Downs.

"Man, I love Frank's," Trey said, eyeballing Laurel's towering club sandwich, wondering how she could possibly fit it in her mouth, and marveling that it cost less than $5.

"What did you get?" Laurel asked.

"Liver sausage with Miracle Whip on white."

"You eat liver sausage?"

"It's so good."

"You're insane."

The radio chirped back to life. They were told that the phone number left on the anonymous note came back to a Cecil Robicheaux.

"Wow," Laurel said.

"What?"

"Robicheaux's a big-time jockey. A household name in racing circles."

She gave Robicheaux a call, and he agreed to meet them—but somewhere away from Churchill Downs. He suggested the North Overlook in Iroquois Park in 15 minutes. Laurel started the car.

"By the way, thanks again for trying to protect me back there when we were questioning the Duke," Trey said. "I owe you one."

"Remember me in your will."

"You think you'll outlive me?"

"You eat liver sausage."

*****

Iroquois Park was just one of Louisville's 18 magnificent Frederik Olmstead-designed urban oases. It encompassed an entire forested hill on the southern fringes of the city, and its North Overlook offered sweeping views out over Churchill Downs, downtown, and the mighty Ohio River. As soon as Laurel and Trey parked the car, a short, thin man got out of his own car, gave them a subtle nod of recognition, and headed for a trail that led into the dense green forest. The detectives followed. About 50 yards into the woods, just out of sight of the parking lot, Robicheaux stopped in his tracks and turned to wait as they caught up.

"Mr. Robicheaux," Trey said.

"Yessir," the man answered in an unmistakable Louisiana bayou accent. He had weathered skin, a receding hairline, and a sad face. The detectives introduced themselves, each shaking his small, leathery, calloused hands.

"Thanks for leaving us the note," Trey said.

"Javier was a good man. I'd like to help if I can."

"My first question is how did you recognize our car in the parking lot at Churchill Downs?"

"Who drives Ford Tauruses anymore besides LMPD detectives?"

Laurel and Trey smiled.

"I'm just pulling your leg. I saw you get out of it this morning. Anyway, you probably already know that Javier was going to ride Empire Builder in the Pennyroyal Stakes."

"And that Empire Builder's trainer is Guy LaForge who works with Barnstone Farm, yes," Trey said.

"LaForge used to be something," Robicheaux said. "But somewhere along the way he lost his magic touch. Hasn't had a stakes winner in years. Javier, on the other hand, was a great, up-and-coming jockey. Had a real feel for the horses. He'd been trying to break through into the big time for years, exercising thoroughbreds for the top farms, even getting to ride in some smaller races. The Pennyroyal was a big opportunity for him."

"And?" Laurel said.

Robicheaux glanced up and down the trail. There was nobody else in sight. "Well, here's the thing. Javier and I were shooting the breeze in the paddock on Saturday afternoon. Then, all of a sudden, Javier gets all tense, so I ask what's up. He doesn't want to talk, but he does. You know what I mean?"

"Sure."

"So I drag it out of him. *What's on your mind, Javier? Nervous about the big race? About your big opportunity?* No, he says. It's nothing like that. Then he asks if I remember that he'd been hired to exercise Swizzle Stick during Derby Week last year."

"Swizzle Stick?" Laurel asked.

"Took second in last year's Derby. Won at Belmont. A chestnut colt owned by Oberyn Farm. Trained by George Sills. Auctioned off to Barnstone Farm for breeding when the season ended."

"The same farm that owns Empire Builder," Trey said.

"Right. But what Javier wanted to tell me was that he thought the horse he was exercising this year was Swizzle Stick."

"Wait, he thought Empire Builder was actually Swizzle Stick?"

"Exactly."

"Do you think the horses look the same?"

"Similar, sure. Both chestnut."

"Do you know if Javier checked the number on the horse's lip tattoo?" Laurel asked.

"He did. He said the number matched the records for Empire Builder. And it had different coloring detail on its legs compared to what he remembered of Swizzle Stick."

"Doesn't that settle it?"

"He was still sure it was Swizzle Stick."

"Despite the different tattoo number and leg coloring? Why did he think that?"

"Bunch of reasons. He said it was the way the horse rode. How it responded to him. Where its power was. How it reacted in different situations and at different points around the track."

"Horse behavior is that distinctive?"

"In certain cases. And if anyone could tell, Javier could. He was a natural. Been around horses since he could walk. Had that sixth sense or whatever."

"Any other reasons he thought it was Swizzle Stick?"

"Empire Builder has a distinctive chip in one of its front teeth that Javier remembered being in the exact same place in Swizzle Stick's mouth. That feature wouldn't necessarily have made it into the official records—especially if the horse chipped its tooth shortly before the racing season began last year. But the thing that made Javier most sure that Empire Builder was actually Swizzle Stick was the fact that the horse recognized him. It knew him."

"Knew him?" Trey asked.

"Saw him as an old friend."

Both detectives stood there wondering what to ask next. Laurel wanted to know whether Robicheaux had reported this—even anonymously—to any officials at the track, but figured the answer was no.

"And here's the twist," Robicheaux said. "Swizzle Stick was allegedly killed in a freak accident at Barnstone Farm late last year."

"How?"

"Somehow, the horse jumped its fence and wandered into a neighbor's pasture. Three pit bulls got at him. Mutilated his muzzle so badly he had to be put down.

"Mutilated his lips?" Laurel asked.

"I imagine so."

"To the point where his lip tattoo was obliterated so that it couldn't be read?"

"I couldn't say. But anyway, last night Javier was acting even stranger."

"What do you mean?" Trey asked.

"He was visibly nervous. Way more so than when he was working up the nerve to tell me about Swizzle Stick."

"Where and when was this?"

"Bumped into him on the way to the parking lot off of 4th Street. Asked if he wanted to go for a beer. But he said he still had some work to finish up with Empire Builder. Wanted to be there while somebody was working with the horse's shoes or something. But he looked absolutely spooked. Big eyes looking all around as if he were watching out for someone."

"Did he tell you why?"

"I asked what was up. He just shook his head. Told me he had to get back. I guess it was around 8 p.m. That was the last time I ever saw him."

"Near the parking lot for the backside?"

"Right."

"Did he say who was going to be working on Empire Builder's shoes?"

"No. But I saw him earlier in the day having lunch over at Wagner's when I went to grab a sandwich. He was sitting with Guy LaForge and that new owner of Barnstone Farm—what's his name?—Timmons. Yeah. Lance Timmons."

"Did he look nervous then?" Laurel asked.

"I didn't really look at him. But they were huddled over the table, like they were discussing something sensitive. Unfortunately, that's all I can tell you."

"This is hugely helpful."

"I have to get back to the track," Robicheaux said.

"Of course. We appreciate your help."

"Wish I could tell you more. I hope you catch the son of a bitch who did him in. Javier was a good guy. A straight shooter, if you know what I mean."

Laurel gave him a significant look. "Was he known to turn down bribes?"

All of a sudden Robicheaux looked anxious. "He was a devout Catholic. A straight shooter. That's all I can tell you."

"Understood."

*****

"Here's something I don't get," Trey said, once he and Laurel were back in the Taurus. "If Cervantes was some up-and-coming, red hot jockey, what was he doing living in a shotgun shack by the railroad line?"

"Trey, most jockeys and backside workers make jack squat for income. Unless they win big-purse races, which are few and far between. Matter of fact, until recently, a lot of the tracks didn't even help with their medical insurance."

"With horseracing being as dangerous as it is? That's crazy."

"Yeah. And only a handful of jockeys ever make any serious money doing it. Just the elites, like John Velazquez, Victor Espinoza, and Calvin Borel."

"I guess horseracing isn't exactly the NBA."

"Actually, horse racing generates about three times as much revenue as the NBA."

"You're kidding. Where does all the money go?"

"Not to the jockeys or backside workers, that's for sure."

"Bummer for them." Trey yawned. "So what's our working theory here? That Barnstone Farm bought Swizzle Stick, last year's Belmont Stakes champion and second-place Derby finisher, with the plan to enter it as Empire Builder in this year's Pennyroyal Stakes?"

"That's what it smells like to me. He'll come in at long odds as a supposedly inexperienced horse, then probably blow away the field."

"How could they pull that off? With all the horse inspection stuff they do now? What about the lip tattoo? What about the distinctive markings on the legs?"

"Plastic surgery?" Laurel suggested. "Hair dye? I don't know. Not my area of expertise."

"Would have been awfully stupid of Barnstone Farm to hire a straight-laced jockey who'd exercised Swizzle Stick the year before."

"Maybe they didn't do their due diligence on Cervantes. Didn't check to make sure that he hadn't already had experience with Swizzle Stick."

"So why do you think Cervantes was so nervous the night he was killed?"

"Maybe he was working up the nerve to blow the whistle. Maybe someone threatened him not to. Maybe he'd already blown the whistle and knew he was being hunted."

"But who would he have blown the whistle to?"

EIGHT

They stopped by their offices in the Edison Center at 7th and Ormsby so that Laurel could arrange to get hold of security camera footage from Churchill Downs to see who was at the track the night of Cervantes's murder. As a further measure, she asked Trey to request footage of the surrounding area from the Real Time Crime Center—the City of Louisville's vast 24/7 monitoring system that recorded video via hundreds of cameras all over the city. Cameras with resolution so good you could see the color of people's eyes.

"The RTCC will net us an awful lot of people," Trey said. "A lot of data."

"It's a start. Hopefully, we'll get something else to cross-reference it with."

*****

A little while later, Laurel was leaning back in her chair, staring at the ceiling above her desk and thinking about the case, when Trey strode up.

"All set with the RTCC footage request," he said.

"Thanks."

"We gonna go question folks at Barnstone Farm?"

"Definitely. But first I'd like to get a little background information on these people. Find out what we're going to be dealing with."

"Background? I bet Carmichael's would have a book that mentions Barnstone Farm in its local-interest section."

"I'm sure. But, while I love Carmichael's, I have a live source. Guy named Perry Clark. Docent and de facto head of the Browning Historical Society. Local gossipmonger par excellence."

"A gossipmonger?"

"And major eccentric. You can think of him as a sort of Lord Varys of the Bluegrass, assuming you're familiar with the character from *Game of Thrones*. He knows everything about everything when it comes to so-called society and old-money families from here to Lexington. Makes it his business to be in everybody else's. And, in addition to being a hugely successful estate planning lawyer, Perry was Louisville's undisputed king of drag queens for more than 20 years."

"Isn't that sort of a contradiction in terms?"

"His stage name was Ms. Smoked Brisket."

"But Ms. Smoked Brisket isn't the king of queens anymore?"

"He's 75 years old. Retired."

"I'm picturing a flamboyant male version of Joan Rivers."

"Bullseye. He also says he's a descendant of George Rogers Clark—Revolutionary War hero, founder of the City of Louisville, and elder brother to Captain William Clark of Lewis and Clark fame. I think it's a dubious claim. But I've never had any reason to call him on it."

*****

After stops at three different liquor stores on Oak Street in the heart of Old Louisville, Laurel finally found a pint bottle of Perry Clark's favorite spirit, Martell cognac. The day being beautiful, they decided to walk the five blocks from the store to the Browning Historical Society, admiring the architecture of the many stately brick homes as they went. Passing along the edge of Central Park—one-time site of the great Southern Exposition—Laurel's attention was drawn to a chubby-legged, teetering, smiling girl toddler who held onto the side of a stroller in front of her mother. Her short, fluffy hair was clipped with a purple daisy barrette that matched her purple daisy onesie. She held the stroller until she just got her balance, let go, took three wobbly steps forward, then fell on her face in the soft grass, laughing hysterically. Her young mother, also smiling as she recorded the action on her smartphone, moved the stroller forward a few feet where the little girl grabbed it for support, stood back up, and repeated the process—laughing again as she fell. Laurel guessed these were her very first steps.

The utter joy of the mother and daughter was infectious. But watching them also stirred up an all-too-familiar longing in Laurel. A longing tainted with sadness.

As she watched the toddler prepare to make another attempt, Laurel's toe caught on the edge of a buckled section of sidewalk and she stumbled forward, her arms and legs flailing as she fought to regain her balance. It was enough of a spectacle to make Trey laugh.

"You alright?" he asked.

"I might have pulled a hamstring."

"Watch your step."

"Thanks, Trey."

The Browning Historical Society was housed in a circa 1895 Victorian mansion on Belgravia Court. Functional antique gas lamps lined a walkway that ran between spectacular homes built during a particularly grand era of Louisville's history.

They climbed broad cut stone steps to the Historical Society's tall front door where, eschewing the doorbell, Laurel gave three loud knocks of the heavy, cast iron fleur-de-lis knocker.

"Perry is old-fashioned," Laurel said. "People who choose the electric doorbell over the knocker are instantly low-class in his mind."

"Whatever."

The door swung wide open to reveal Perry "Ms. Smoked Brisket" Clark wearing a fully-buttoned, dark purple velvet dinner jacket with black lapels. His perfect white hair was slicked back with oil. Finishing the look, he wore a black bowtie with a pressed white broadcloth shirt.

"Well, well, well," he said. "If it isn't my favorite cop."

"Hello, Perry."

"And who is your delicious young sidekick?"

"This would be Detective Trey Hewson."

"Trey? Bless your heart. What a name. Who gave it to you? Your dad the skateboarder or your mom the herbalist?"

"Uh...."

"Go easy on him, Perry. He's a neophyte."

"Well, we need to toughen him up then, don't we?"

"Got a minute? We need to pick your brain."

"Did you bring me my medicine?" he asked with a wink.

Laurel drew the pint of Martell cognac from her jacket pocket and handed it over.

"Well, aren't you just a doll?" Perry said. "An absolute doll."

"Why Martell?" Laurel asked. "Why can't you just drink Hennessy or Courvoisier? They're a lot easier to find."

"Hennessy? Don't be damned silly. Hennessy was founded by an Irishman. That means it isn't truly French."

"May we come in?"

"Of course. Of course. Where are my manners?"

The interior of the house was even more spectacular than the outside, with intricate woodwork, stained glass, collectable Victorian-era paintings, and fine antique furniture in every room they passed. The rooms also contained glass cabinets and shadow boxes holding various documents, books, and artifacts of local historical significance. Perry led them down a long hallway and into a lavish parlor in the back where they took seats on Queen Ann chairs upholstered in green velvet. The society's reception room, it seemed.

All of a sudden there was a small snifter glass in Perry's hand. He seemed to have conjured it out of thin air. He placed it on the low coffee table between them, opened the bottle of cognac, and poured himself a generous portion. He closed his eyes as he raised the glass to his nose, took a sniff, then a small sip, seeming lost in ecstasy. "Glory, glory, hallelujah." He opened his eyes. "Can I offer either of you a snifter?"

"We're on duty," Laurel said.

"A cappuccino, then? Tea?"

"Sweet tea?" Trey asked.

"We're both fine," Laurel said.

"Detective Trey is especially fine."

"Easy, Perry."

"Well then," Perry said, sitting back and smiling at them. "Who shall we gossip about today?"

"A high society family of your beloved Inner Bluegrass Region."

"The last bastion of gentility in a world gone insane," Perry said with a wink.

"Barnstone Farm," Laurel said.

"Oh, my!"

"You sound revolted."

"The Barnstones are a revolting family. Positively revolting. No class. They used to be something. But oh, what a fall from grace."

"Enlighten us."

"Their story is like something out of the pages of the *National Enquirer*. Barnstone Farm was established in 1905 by Lee Ashton Barnstone, out in Woodford County, near Midway," he said, referring to a picturesque and quaint hamlet outside of Lexington. "The family owned a big coal mining company in eastern Kentucky, before they sold out to Peabody. Long story short, as I'm sure you know, the farm produced a slew of Derby winners in the 20th Century. Even a Triple Crown winner. But then things started to slide."

He paused to take another sip of cognac and groaned with pleasure.

"What happened?" Laurel asked.

"First, old Lee Ashton passed away in 1965. His son, Lee Junior, took over. Unhappily for the family, he was a lot more interested in raising horses than he was in raising his son and daughter, Channing and Lexy. To be sure, the kids lived rich lives, running with the old-money set of horse country. Everything was handed to them. Fancy clothes, cars, houses, vacations. Every rule was bent for them. Every desire met. But they were essentially parentless, left to raise themselves. Predictably, they grew into spoiled, useless adults with huge holes in their hearts that they tried to fill with drugs, alcohol, and promiscuity."

"Needless to say, it wasn't long before the wheels came off. Lee Junior dropped dead of a stroke in 1980. Six months later, his son, Channing, high on cocaine, ran his muscle car into a big oak tree on Old Frankfort Pike at 110 miles an hour. I don't believe they ever found all the pieces of him."

"After Channing's death, management of the farm fell to Lee Junior's widow, Vivian—an imperious old gorgon. Nicotine-yellowed teeth and hair. Tar-cured skin. Very proper, mind you. Wore tweed and white gloves to the horse races and all that. But a gorgon. And her daughter, Lexy, is a useless twat."

"Perry! Language. Trey's a sensitive young man."

"He doesn't look too young to me."

"Perry."

"Yes, yes. Moving on. Now, bearing in mind that Lexy's real name is Lexy— not Alexis—it goes without saying that she hated her mother. I mean really, who names their daughter Lexy? Sounds like a Dixie Highway stripper."

"I have a good friend named Lexy."

"Of course you do. Bless your heart. Anyway, probably to spite her mother, as soon as she turned 18, Lexy married Lance Timmons. A hayseed-turned-football star recruited to Lexy's private Lexington high school with what seemed no greater ambition in life than to drink cheap beer, watch University of Kentucky sports, and tip cows."

"Old widow Vivian, of course, despised Lance for the lowly white trash that he was—or rather *is* to this day. Needled him. Did her best to humiliate him in front of others. Never, ever let him forget that he was a loser from the wrong side of the tracks."

"So Lance split Vivian in half with a sickle?"

"Worse. He moved in! Started trying to run things at the farm." Perry grinned. "I always figured Lance would turn up dead one day with arsenic in his blood, and then Vivian would end up arrested for the murder."

"Is that the end of the story?"

"Heavens no, dear. Turns out Lance was rather ambitious after all. So much so that society gossips whispered that he was on the make when he married Lexy. In short, instead of self-esteem, Lance has ambition."

"Self-esteem *or* ambition? Are they mutually exclusive?"

"Of course they are. Don't be obtuse." Perry took another sip of his cognac. "Well, by 1987, old widow Vivian had lost enough of her marbles to be declared mentally incompetent. So management of the farm fell to Lexy—which really meant that it fell to Lance. And here's where the fun begins. The first thing Lance does is take a loan of $12 million to renovate the farm, to make it more to his liking. Installs an indoor gun range, of all the silly things. A home theater to rival IMAX. An enormous swimming pool in the shape of a horse."

"Classy."

"Next thing you know, he's throwing huge parties, leasing luxury motor coaches to take the parties mobile—from the farm to UK basketball and football games and so forth. He even leased a private Gulfstream jet. Spent $40,000 a month on that. And all he ever did with it was fly his party crew to Montana for steak dinners."

"What about the racehorses?"

"Sorry. I was getting sidetracked. Lance did make a sincere if misguided effort on the racehorse front. Wanted to make his mark, you might say. Over the next few years, he bought more than 300 young racehorses to the tune of more than $38 million. He funded his buying spree by mortgaging the farm. The bankers probably didn't think twice about it. Barnstone Farm had always been profitable. It was one of the biggest names in horse racing history."

"Anyway, you can guess where things went from there. Lance's judgment with respect to quality racehorses wasn't what we would call learned. And what would you expect? He didn't grow up working with horses. Never availed himself of any sort of formal training. He was just some guy who suddenly found himself in the driver's seat of a legendary horse farm. So the quality of the Barnstone horses dropped dramatically. The number of stakes race wins, of course, dropped as well. And before long, customers started looking elsewhere, to places like Zayat Stables, WinStar Farm, and Reddam Racing. Lately, Barnstone Farm has been hemorrhaging money. By all accounts, it's in tremendous debt."

"How tremendous?"

"I've heard whispers in the neighborhood of $45 million."

"My, my."

"Yes. And just in the past year, in a desperate play, Lance somehow squeezed another $9 million out of a shady Florida bank to buy last year's Belmont Stakes champion, Swizzle Stick. His plan was to charge $400,000 a pop in stud fees."

"A 3-year-old horse put out to stud?"

"Medical retirement. Some sort of chronic injury. I don't know the details."

"So Lance was asking $400,000 for a romantic night with Swizzle Stick?"

"Yes. Among the highest stud fees in history. Unheard of for an initial stud fee."

"Initial?"

"Before any of its foals have proven to be winners. Well, guess what? Nobody wanted to pay Lance's ludicrous fee. So he dropped it to $300,000, then $100,000, and finally settled at around $35,000. Bad news for Lance. Then last fall, on top of everything else, Swizzle Stick had to be put down after an *alleged* freak accident. For the first time in its history, Barnstone Farm somehow let a horse—a $9 million horse—escape its stall, its stable, and the farm's vast surrounding grid of fenced pastures and tracks, only to end up on a neighbor's land where its muzzle was mauled by a trio of pit bull terriers."

"Lance can't seem to catch a break," Laurel said.

"Ah, but there's a twist."

"Don't tease us."

"Remember the level of debt the farm was rumored to have?"

"Around $45 million."

"Good! You're listening. Now guess what Swizzle Stick was insured for."

"Around $45 million?"

"Bingo!"

"What a remarkable coincidence."

"Oh, indeed."

NINE

"So, what does your gut tell you about Barnstone Farm?" Laurel asked when they were back outside.

"That they led a Swizzle Stick lookalike into a pasture full of crazy pit bulls in the middle of the night, collected the insurance on Swizzle Stick, then somehow rebranded the real Swizzle Stick as Empire Builder. Cervantes figured it out, so they killed him. What do you think?"

"I think I'd like to have a word with Lance Timmons and Lexy Barnstone."

"We hardly have enough information to book them in yet."

"That's more of an issue in an interrogation. We'll play this like a casual witness interview, but get them to commit to an alibi."

Laurel's phone rang. It was Cecil Robicheaux, calling to let them know that he'd just watched Empire Builder's trainer, Guy LaForge, walk into Wagner's.

*****

To many native Louisvillians, Wagner's—a combination restaurant and turf goods shop across the street from the track, selling everything from pork chop sandwiches to racehorse liniment since 1922—was as iconic and as much a part of Churchill Downs as the twin spires. Trey was struck by its unique character as soon as he walked through the front door. It was like stepping back in time. An old-fashioned lunch counter ran half the length of the restaurant. The walls were adorned with framed photographs of Kentucky Derby winners of old. Proud jockeys atop horses draped with blankets of roses. Legends, some of them household names, memorialized. On any given day, a customer at Wagner's might bump into a world-famous jockey, a billionaire stable owner, or ordinary backside stable hands.

The detectives spotted LaForge in the white seersucker suit and pink silk tie Robicheaux told them he was wearing. He sat at a corner table with two other men who looked like backside workers, dressed in somewhat grubby work clothes. A server was taking their order.

"Let's talk to him outside when he leaves," Laurel said.

"Then we might as well eat."

"You're nothing if not predictable."

As they took stools at the counter, they heard a man behind them ask his server for the dessert menu, pronouncing it dee-zert, with emphasis on the first syllable.

"There are so many different accents in this town," Trey said. "In one neighborhood, everybody sounds like H. Ross Perot. Two neighborhoods over, they sound like Tom Brokaw."

"Louisville's a crossroads. It's the Upper South or the Lower Midwest, depending on who you talk to."

"So what's good here?"

"I usually get the Pam & Jack's omelet. Bell pepper, tomato, onion, ham, sausage, bacon, and lots of gooey cheese."

"That's your usual? How do you stay so, you know, shapely?"

"Boundaries, Trey."

"Seriously, though."

"Trey."

"Alright, alright."

Forgoing the omelet, Trey went with the special—a Derby week sampler. It included a taste of some traditional Kentucky Derby picnic foods—tiny sandwiches filled with Benedictine or pimento cheese spread, a cup of burgoo, and cheese grits. Laurel ordered two buttermilk biscuits with sorghum syrup. When their food came a few minutes later, she tore one of the hot, golden-brown biscuits open, revealing a steamy, flaky interior. She buttered each half, then drizzled sweet, dark sorghum syrup all over them.

"What are you pouring on your biscuits?" Trey asked, licking his lips, looking as though he might bite Laurel's hand.

"Sorghum. Tastes sort of like a light molasses. It's as Kentucky as Kentucky can be."

"Can I try it?"

"I got an extra one with you in mind."

"Marry me."

Trey ate the biscuit, his entire sampler plate, and then—because LaForge was still holding court at his corner table and showed no sign that he intended to leave anytime soon—got two more biscuits with sorghum syrup.

"You better slow down there, Trey. You'll give yourself a bolus."

"What's a bolus?"

"A food block that can perforate your esophagus. Then you'll aspirate biscuits into your own lungs."

Trey paused for half a second, then resumed chewing. "It's worth the risk."

"Suit yourself."

"Hey, you want to go see some live music tonight? Supposed to be some good bands at Iroquois Amphitheater."

"No. I'm going to go hit the MADE gym for some ground fighting practice."

"You just go until you drop, don't you? What in the world do you need more ground fighting practice for?"

"Complacency kills, Trey."

"You sound like one of those neurotic instructors at the academy. Come on. The weather's perfect. It'll be fun. We'll get some cold beers. Kick our feet up."

"Another time."

"What about WFPK's Waterfront Wednesday thing. We could sit on the big lawn down on the river. Listen to some good live music while the coal barges cruise by."

"When's that?"

"Wednesday."

"I was kidding, Trey. Anyway, got a SCERS class on Wednesday."

"A what?"

"Seized Computer Evidence Recovery Specialist class. I'm building new skills."

"You need to have more fun in life, Laurel."

*****

Trey was just stuffing the last buttery, flakey bit of biscuit into his mouth as LaForge rose from his table. They intercepted him just outside the front door.

"Mr. LaForge," Laurel said. The detectives displayed their badges. LaForge turned white.

"What's this about?"

"We have some things we need to clear up, and we think you might be able to—"

"Am I under arrest?"

"No."

LaForge turned away from them and set a brisk pace for the parking lot.

"We just have a few questions about your relationship with Barnstone Farm," Laurel half shouted.

At this, LaForge stopped in his tracks.

"You're the trainer for one of their horses, are you not?"

LaForge turned and stared at Laurel. She thought his face betrayed a sudden change of heart, and she wondered at its cause.

"Yes," LaForge said at last. "Empire Builder. Look, I've only been involved with Barnstone Farm for a few months."

"You knew Javier Cervantes."

"I did. A good man. I mean that sincerely."

They asked LaForge the usual questions. He claimed to have no idea why someone might have wished Cervantes dead. Laurel eventually guided the conversation back to the subject of Empire Builder.

"I have a really good feeling about that horse," LaForge said with genuine enthusiasm. "Definitely underrated. Been flying under the radar because he hasn't been in enough races for the experts and odds compilers to get a firm idea of his abilities. But he has tons of potential. Could surprise everyone."

"Why have you only been working with him for a few months?"

"He had a different owner and different trainer before. Then, after Barnstone Farm bought him, his mouth was injured and he had to have surgery. So he was out of commission for a little while. I didn't start working with him until he was healed up. That was just a few months ago."

"What happened to his mouth?"

"They said he got into a little brawl with another colt, got bit on the lip, and the bite got infected. Not a big deal, I guess, but enough to keep him off the track for a few months."

"How familiar are you with Barnstone Farm?"

"Oh, I trained a few horses for them years ago, back when Lee Barnstone Junior was still alive and running things. But this is the first time I've worked with them in—I don't know—probably 30 years."

"So now you deal with Lexy Barnstone's husband, Lance Timmons?"

"Yup," LaForge said with a conspicuous lack of warmth. Laurel stood quiet, waiting for LaForge to offer more. When he didn't, she prompted him with another question.

"What can you tell us about Timmons?"

LaForge took a breath. "Don't really know him. Don't really know what's going on out there these days."

"But you've heard rumors?"

"Well, you know. I don't much like to gossip about folks."

"We're detectives, Mr. LaForge."

"Right. So, I mean, financially, I guess Barnstone Farm is supposedly in dire straits."

"So we've heard."

"To be honest, I'm not even sure where Lance got the money to hire me. That being said, I don't know Lance from my Great Aunt Fannie. I've only interacted with him a handful of times."

"He keeps you at arm's length?"

"I keep *him* at arm's length."

"Why is that?"

"Don't like him. And you know what? I'll tell you why. I care about the horses I work with. I care about their welfare, their comfort, their happiness. And it's obvious to me that Lance doesn't. To him, the horses are just assets— not living, feeling creatures. The man's heart is cold."

"I see. Is there anything else you think might be relevant to our investigation?"

He paused, looking reflective. "Are you bourbon drinkers?"

"Yes."

"Have you ever had Peepaw Clayton 21-year-old? Some people, once they've tasted it, they'll do damn near anything to get more."

"And?"

"Lance Timmons has developed a taste for Peepaw Clayton."

TEN

Laurel fell into bed after returning home from her ground fighting class, burrowed into her soft comforter, and was asleep within minutes. But shortly after 3 a.m., she woke from a nightmare in which she'd been struggling to swim against the current of a swift, cold river that was pulling her downstream toward a deep canyon, the far reaches of which were cloaked in darkness.

As she blinked to clear her vision, a vague anxiety pricked at her insides. It was enough to make her sit up in bed, click on her reading light, and look around her room. Nothing seemed amiss. Her door and windows were shut. All that surrounded her were the same dresser, nightstand, and reading light that had been in the exact same spots in her room for years.

She lay back on her pillows and stared at her ceiling, trying to recall more of the dream—how, for example, she'd come to be in the river in the first place— when a deeper sense of fear washed over her. She grew hyperconscious of the sound of her own breathing. Her heartbeat began to pound in her ears. Her chest seemed to tighten. In all, it was a feeling not unlike one she'd had as a teen when she thought she'd overslept on the day of her college entrance exams.

Then, as if it had always been there waiting for her to take notice, a troubling but not altogether unfamiliar question materialized in the forefront of her mind: *Is this all there is?*

She sat upright again and took several deep breaths. It wasn't the first time she'd woken in the dead of night with the same question on her mind. Wasn't the first time it had made her feel this way. It seemed to start a couple of years ago. But were the episodes becoming more frequent? More intense? She wasn't sure.

She got out of bed and went to the kitchen for a glass of water. After drinking it down, she stood in the darkness of her living room and did a series of stretches targeting her hamstrings, calves, neck, and shoulders. Wide awake, she took a seat on her couch and began clicking through cable channels, waiting, hoping, for drowsiness to return. She ran through the entire progression of channels twice, never finding anything that interested her in the least, before giving up and turning the television back off, returning her condo to a state of oppressive quiet. Back in bed, she switched her reading light on and began a biography of Amelia Earhart in order to keep her mind occupied. To keep herself from revisiting *the question* until, nearly an hour later, she fell back to sleep.

ELEVEN

The next morning, Trey picked Laurel up at her place in east Louisville since it was more or less on the way to Barnstone Farm. She lived in a sprawling community of uninteresting, low-rise condo buildings that looked like they'd been built during the architectural nadir of the 1980s. Close to the intersection of interstates 64 and 264, they struck Trey as uniformly dark and unappealing. Her unit was on the bottom floor, alongside a dense stand of trees, which made it that much darker.

Her door was open a few inches, so he gave it a couple of knocks and let himself in. The acrid smoke of burned toast hung in the air. "Yoo-hoo? Laurel?"

"Come on in," she shouted from somewhere in the back. "Help yourself to some carbon toast."

"My favorite. How'd you know?"

Trey took in the scene. It was his first visit to Laurel's place. Given the look of the community as a whole, it had exactly the interior he'd expected—complete with the beige walls, faux oak cabinetry, and cheesy, dated fixtures typical of the saddest sort of bachelor pad. In the living room, there were three tall shelving units packed with books. Hardcovers and paperbacks of all sizes. Fiction and nonfiction both, jammed into every available space in a seemingly haphazard way.

There was almost no decoration in the room, save for a team photo from Laurel's days as a Sacred Heart volleyball player, as well as a framed poster advertising an NCAA Final Four basketball tournament in Indianapolis years earlier. A photograph was taped onto the lower corner of the poster. It was of a smiling teenage Laurel and an older man—presumably her father—standing to either side of a freakishly tall North Carolina Tar Heels basketball player, the three of them in front of the old Hoosier Dome. Laurel was lanky and awkward-looking and had a mouthful of braces. But she looked exceptionally happy. Her face beamed. The photo stood in stark contrast to the rest of her condo, which, in Trey's opinion, was a gloomy, lonely looking place.

"I like your Final Four poster."

"Thanks," she said, emerging from her bedroom, heading for the kitchen. "My dad used to take me every year they had playoff games in the region. Good times."

Used to? "Did your dad pass away?"

A pause. "No."

Trey waited for more. But nothing more came. "How long have you lived in this place?"

"Let's see. I think twelve years as of last January."

Trey followed her into the tiny galley kitchen and leaned against the countertop. A stack of opened mail drew his eye. On top, there was a large envelope with a return address for something called Oak Leaf Adoption Services. Sticking out from under that, he could see the upper half of a letter from a Wilcox Adoption Agency, thanking Laurel for her submission of an initial application package and asking that she contact the office to set up an interview. He opened his mouth to ask about it, but a gut feeling held him back.

Laurel took a tall glass from a cabinet, filled it half way up with orange juice, opened a plastic jar on her counter, and then added two spoons full of its sawdust-looking contents to the orange juice. She stirred the concoction, then drank it down with a frown of disgust.

"What's that stuff?" Trey asked.

"Psyllium."

"Psyllium? Is it good?"

"You mean is it tasty? No. It's awful."

"Why do you eat it then?"

"I'm a woman, Trey. A woman who does a lot of sitting as part of her job." Trey looked perplexed. "Ask your mother. Let's get rolling."

*****

Having driven an hour east of Louisville—after a brief delay near Laurel's condo, where Trey insisted on stopping traffic to allow a mama mallard and her seven ducklings to cross a road fronting Brown Park—the detectives were turning off Interstate 64 near Versailles. Trey was giving Laurel the rundown on background information he'd gathered on Lexy Barnstone and Lance Timmons.

"Lexy has two arrests for driving under the influence. One for reckless driving. One charge for possession of cocaine, dropped. And one charge each for vandalism and public urination, also dropped."

"Sounds like she was protected from on high by her family's money and connections, at least early on," Laurel said. "Just like Perry told us."

"No schooling beyond high school. Nothing to indicate that she has an aptitude for anything. Oh, and her driver's license was suspended until last January."

"What about Lance?"

"Also has two arrests for drunk driving. A citation for driving without insurance. A misdemeanor for marijuana possession. A misdemeanor for possession, use, or transfer of a device for theft of telecommunications serv—"

"Wait, what?"

KRS 514.065. Possession, use, or transfer of a device for theft of telecommunications services."

"That's a new one for me," Laurel said. "What did he do, try to get free cable?"

"Probably. And here's an even better one. Just after he married Lexy, he was arrested for trafficking in stolen property. At age 20, of all the stupid things, he was selling cigarettes he'd stolen from a corner grocer in Lexington out of the trunk of his Plymouth Barracuda in the parking lot of his old high school. But the charges were dropped because the only witness, the shop owner, was arrested a few days later for overstating the quantity of stolen property when he filed his insurance claim."

"Selling stolen cigarettes in the high school parking lot. Cheeky."

"Or just stupid."

"Yes. And what else does Lance's record tell us about him?"

"That he's a jackass?"

"That he's willing to cross the line. That he doesn't think the rules apply to him."

*****

They lowered their windows as they turned onto Old Frankfort Pike to enjoy the fresh air of the sunny spring morning. The road was lined with massive, ancient oak trees. Limestone rock walls enclosed bright green pastures of the many horse farms flanking their route. The terrain rose and fell in gentle gradients. Magnificent horses of every color—black, bay, chestnut, dun, gray—foraged, trotted, or galloped in small groups. Some stood with their awkward and spindly-legged little foals.

"This has got to be one of the prettiest roads I've ever been on," Trey said. "All these farms and horses. It's like being inside a painting or whatever."

"They call it Thoroughbred Alley, if that tells you anything."

"Thoroughbred Alley," Trey repeated in a tone of wonder. "Center of the racehorse universe."

"Actually, you see that building on the right?" Laurel asked, pointing to an old, whitewashed wooden building on the corner of an intersection they were passing through.

"Yeah."

"Used to be called the Black Horse Tavern. Built in the 1700s. One of the oldest intact dwellings in the state. But what makes it really cool to us law enforcement types is that it was the childhood home of Zerelda James."

"Who's Zerelda James?"

"Mother to Frank and Jesse."

"You're kidding."

"Cross my heart."

"How do you know all this stuff? Derby history, Louisville history, Kentucky history?"

"Sacred Heart honors program, baby."

"Of course."

"Plus, I grew up reading the Courier-Journal. It was always on our kitchen table."

"Huh. Zerelda James. A lady who mothered not one, but two psycho murderer war criminals. What an accomplishment."

"Come on, Trey. Everybody always wants to point their fingers at mothers as the root cause of male sociopathy. What about the abusive alcoholic fathers?"

"For your ordinary criminals, maybe. For the serious head case crazies—the mass murderers and scrial killers and so forth—it's always the mother."

"Whatever. Though I'll grant you Zerelda probably didn't read Dr. Spock."

TWELVE

They turned onto a drive at a break in one of the longer limestone walls and drove through a tall wrought iron gate that bore a giant letter B at its apex. The drive, lined with white four-board fences and Yoshino cherry trees, wound across a vast, 3,000-acre property encompassing at least a dozen lush horse pastures, little stone bridges, limestone creeks, and several ponds.

"This is a long driveway," Trey said.

"Nothing gets by you, Trey."

The drive led, at last, to a cluster of buildings surrounding a circular drive of mosaic pavers. There were two stables, a barn, a garage with six parking bays, what looked like a guest house, two smaller utility buildings, and a faux antebellum mansion that had to have been at least 12,000 square feet. A bright red Camaro convertible sat in one of the garage bays. A black Ford pickup with oversized tires and a pair of decorative rubber testicles hanging from the rear bumper occupied another. The other four bays were empty. Around the side of the mansion, they could see half of the infamous horse-shaped swimming pool. It was empty too.

"Welcome to Tara," Laurel said.

"Tara?"

"The O'Hara plantation in *Gone with the Wind*."

"I don't remember seeing any trucks with rubber testicles in *Gone with the Wind*. Are they supposed to make the truck look like a bull?"

"God knows."

The stables were long, side-gabled structures topped with cupolas. Aside from the mansion, all the other buildings were painted white, with black metal roofs and cobalt blue trim around the windows—the cobalt blue of the farm's famous racing silks. Two workers at the far end of one of the stables were busy rolling up hoses.

"Should we start with them?" Trey asked.

"No, let's go for the main house. And remember, play it casual. We don't want Lance to think he's a suspect. Not before he at least commits to an alibi."

The landscaping to either side of the front walk didn't look as though it had been mulched in several years. At the cobalt blue front door, paint was peeling from the surrounding trim. Laurel reached out and cracked a piece of flaking paint off a Romanesque column with the nail of her pinkie finger. Then she pressed the doorbell. A deep bell ring sounded from some distant point in the interior of the house.

"Do you think a butler in black tails will answer the door?" Trey asked.

"An old guy named Jeeves. I'm certain of it."

A moment later, the door opened to reveal a gaunt, late-middle-aged woman in heavy makeup, with bleach-blonde hair, lips stretched shiny by too many collagen injections, and colossal breast implants that looked ridiculous attached to her petite, bony body. She looked glazed. Disengaged. Laurel thought she might be on Xanax or some other benzodiazepine.

"Yes?"

"Mrs. Barnstone?" Trey asked.

"Yes?" she repeated, sounding as if she weren't quite sure.

Both detectives produced their credentials. But Lexy Barnstone was preoccupied with a large imperial topaz set in a cocktail ring on one of her fingers.

"Do you go by Barnstone or Timmons?"

"Barnstone," she said with a hint of bitterness.

"Okay. Well, as you can see, we're detectives with the Louisville Metro Police Department."

"Yes?"

"We have reason to believe that you and your husband might have information that would really help us out in a case we're working."

"Yes?" she said again, her gaze shifting from her ring to something out in the distance behind the detectives.

"May we come in for a quick word? Won't take long."

"Yes."

She turned and disappeared into the house without another word, leaving the detectives standing in the open doorway. Laurel glanced at Trey, shrugged her shoulders, and entered the house. The foyer was a circular room with a marble floor, an oversized crystal chandelier hanging from the high ceiling, and cobalt blue equine-themed wallpaper adorning its walls. Twin curving stairwells with elaborate railings ran in mirror images of each other to either side of where they stood, up to the second floor. To their right, a wide opening led to a trophy room, full of the gold and silver cups, medals, ribbons, photographs and other memorabilia of a glorious period in the farm's increasingly distant past.

"She went down there," Laurel said, gesturing to a hallway on the far side of the foyer. They followed the passage to a large open area organized as a living room on the right and a dining room on the left. The dining room had a long wooden table that could seat at least 20. The living room had a pair of sectional couches of dark brown leather, a brick fireplace, and, mounted above the mantle, the biggest flat-screen television Laurel had ever seen outside of a stadium. On the walls hung a dozen portraits of horses, each with the horse's name on a brass nameplate attached to the bottom of the frame. Lexy was sitting on one of the couches, her glassy eyes locked on the television as if she'd forgotten that the detectives were there. She was watching a reality court show with litigants arguing over ownership of a barbeque grill.

"These are beautiful paintings of your horses," Laurel said.

Lexy turned, looking startled to have heard Laurel's voice. Gathering herself, she turned back to the television. "I hate horses."

Apart from the horse paintings, the only other thing on the walls was a large portrait of Lance Timmons himself, dressed in his high school football uniform and helmet, posing in a three-point stance as if he were about to surge forward. His name, position, jersey number, and a column of statistics—including how many tackles, tackles for loss, and sacks he'd had that season—were all stenciled near the bottom of the portrait. At the top, in large block letters, *Class of the Commonwealth—Honorable Mention.*

"Is your husband home, Mrs. Barnstone?" Laurel asked.

"Probably with the horses. Everything is always about the damned horses."

They heard a heavy door close in some other part of the house. A moment later, Lance Timmons walked in, pulling work gloves from his hands as he gave the detectives a concerned look.

THIRTEEN

Lance wore a flannel shirt, faded jeans, and steel-toed work boots. He was a heavyset but not quite obese man. He'd probably been handsome once, long ago, before his hedonistic adulthood. Now, in late middle age, he looked, like his wife, as though he'd lived intemperately for a very long time—and his body had paid the price.

Laurel assumed one of the farm employees told Lance of their arrival. He looked perplexed.

"Do you have an appointment?" he asked as Lexy, clearly irritated at having her television show interrupted, turned it off and slipped from the room.

"No appointment, Mr. Timmons," Trey said. "We're detectives with LMPD. We're working a case that we think you might be able to help us with." They each held their credentials out and open so that he could eyeball them. He didn't bother. A look of surprise and anxiety flashed across his face. But he mastered himself quickly, assuming a face that spoke of appropriate, innocent concern.

"This is quite a portrait," Laurel said, pointing at the large framed picture of Lance the football star.

"Lettered three years in a row at Crittenden," he said.

"Crittenden?"

"Crittenden Preparatory Academy," he said in a tone suggesting that anyone would know that.

"Ah. Right."

"All conference D-tackle my senior year. Honorable mention for the Commonwealth team."

"Wow. Isn't Crittenden on the far side of town from here?"

"There are closer high schools. But they aren't Crittenden."

"Got it."

"Do I need a lawyer?" he said with a chuckle that was a tinge too loud.

"A lawyer?" Laurel said, smiling as if they were sharing a joke. "Well, I mean, not that I know of."

Trey laughed, right on cue.

"No," Laurel said. "As I mentioned, we just think you might have some information that could help us in a case we're working over in Louisville. We're making our way down a long list of people. Gotta check all the boxes to keep the bosses happy."

Lance gawked, hesitated for a split second, then said, "Right. Sure. More than happy to help. But I don't have a whole lot of time."

"Why don't we sit by your dining room table here," Laurel suggested. She let him pull out a chair and sit down first. Then she pulled a chair out for herself and placed it so they'd be sitting face-to-face, barely two feet apart, with no objects between them. Trey grabbed another chair and took up position about six feet to Lance's right and slightly behind him.

"You have a beautiful farm," Laurel said.

"Thanks." Lance was tapping both his feet.

"Well, let's get this over with, and we'll get out of your hair."

"Okay."

"We're investigating a crime involving the Churchill Downs racing community. So of course, our boss is making us talk to anyone involved in horse racing on any level in the entire history of the track."

"Your boss, the Chief? I hear he's a major political suck up. No offense."

"We probably shouldn't comment," Laurel said with an even bigger grin. "Anyway, since Barnstone is such a major farm, we have to ask whether you have any horses slated to race at Churchill Downs this Derby week."

"Probably," Lance said, casual as could be. "We have so many horses in play in so many different places, it's hard to keep track."

"Do you happen to know a jockey named Javier Cervantes?"

Hearing this, Lance's eyes opened wide. He crossed his arms and slumped forward as if to protect his abdomen from a punch.

"Javier—what was the last name?" Lance asked.

"Cervantes. Like the author of *Don Quixote*."

"Hmmm. Sounds familiar. But to be perfectly honest, I have a hard time keeping Mexican names straight."

Laurel and Trey waited, letting the silence hang. Lance pretended to think hard.

"Actually, now that you mention it, I think we *may* have worked with a jockey with that name. Last year, far as I can recall. Our trainers handle all of that stuff, of course."

"You don't deal with the jockeys directly?"

"No. Unless they're posing for pictures in the winner's circle. Then, of course, I magically appear by their side," he said before bursting into laughter.

"How many trainers do you work with?"

"Right now, uh, I think five."

"You wouldn't happen to know whether Mr. Cervantes had any enemies, or interactions with criminal elements on any level? Drug dealers? Loan sharks? Gamblers or bookies?"

At gamblers or bookies, Lance began pulling at his earlobe.

"Or," Trey added, "whether he might have been mixed up in any love triangles or affairs that might have pissed off a boyfriend or husband?"

"Well, I mean, like I said, I'm not even 100 percent sure we've ever worked with the guy. The name rings a bell. But I swear to God I don't know anything about him. What did he do?"

"He didn't do anything," Trey said. "He was murdered."

Lance went still. He looked more confused than worried.

"Murdered? How?"

"He was strangled the night before last."

Lance leaned forward as if he were genuinely interested in learning more. "Do the police have any leads?"

"We aren't allowed to discuss ongoing investigations."

"Oh. Well, I'm sure that if this Cervantes guy was going to be riding for us, the trainer would have told me if he'd been killed."

"Who is the trainer?" Trey asked.

"Guy LaForge," Lance said, even though they hadn't told him that Cervantes was slated to ride Empire Builder—the specific horse LaForge was training. "He's a legend. Tremendous trainer. Fantastic."

"Got it. Now, we have to ask everyone this question, and it has nothing to do with any specific suspicions, but can you tell us, with as much detail as possible, where you were and what you were doing the night before last?"

"Night before last. Let's see. Had dinner here. Leftover ribs. Couple of Bud Lights."

"With Lexy?"

"No. She was at the nail salon. Then I drove to the feed store down in Versailles to get a bunch of salt licks."

"What time was that?"

"After dinner. Around 7."

"Which feed store."

"Zane's."

"Where did you go from there?"

"Home. Watched a rerun of 'Jersey Shore,' then went to bed."

"Anyone who can vouch for you being here that night?"

He looked thoughtful. "I doubt it."

"Lexy?"

"We don't sleep in the same room."

"Did she see you before you went to bed?"

"I don't think so. No."

"Any other employees here?"

"The only ones here that late would have been in the stables, so they probably wouldn't have seen me."

"We'd like to talk to them."

Lance started tapping his feet again. "Why?"

"The more people who can vouch for you, the sooner we can put a checkmark next to your name and move on."

Lance appeared to give serious consideration to their request. "Not today, I don't think."

"May I ask why not?"

"Sure."

"Why not?"

"They're busy. I'm paying them. They have work to do."

"Wouldn't take a minute. We'd appreciate the cooperation."

"No. Another time. They're too busy."

*****

As the detectives rose to leave, they asked to have a quick word with Lexy—who didn't seem terribly busy. But she'd already left for "the club" in her Camaro.

"What club is that?" Laurel asked.

"Bootless Day Country Club," Lance said. "We're members. It's on the far side of town, too. And yes, there are clubs that are closer. But they aren't Bootless Day."

FOURTEEN

As the detectives walked from the Barnstone Mansion back to their Taurus, Trey called the Lexington Police to let them know that a woman in a red convertible Camaro was heading toward the Bootless Day Country Club from Barnstone Farm, probably driving under the influence of too many tranquilizers.

"That guy Lance is an arrogant ass," Trey said.

"It's just an act."

"An act?"

"The pretension. It's just a cover for his feelings of inadequacy, like with every other arrogant person on earth."

"Whatever."

As they reached the car, Trey put a hand on Laurel's arm to stop her.

"What?"

"Look at that," Trey said, pointing at a pair of horses that had come over to the fence to get a better look at them.

"What about them?"

"The one on the left. Is that chestnut? Or just brown?"

"I'd say Chestnut."

"Look at its lower lip."

The horse's lip hung down as if it had been injured, as if its nerves had been damaged, leaving its big lower teeth exposed. It made the horse look as if it were mocking them with an ape-like underbite, baring its Halloween costume hillbilly teeth.

They stared for a minute, then got in the car.

"What do you think is wrong with that horse?" Trey asked.

"Maybe a plastic surgeon used it for practicing lower lip surgery."

"To replace its tattoo? As, like, practice for replacing the tattoo on Swizzle Stick?"

"Anything is possible."

"Do you want to go question some of the employees?"

Laurel gave the question a few seconds' thought. "No. Not today. We'll let Lance go ahead and try to compel them to lie. Then later, we'll get them to turn and admit that Lance is orchestrating a cover-up of some sort."

*****

Back on the road, they headed to Zane's Feed Store in Versailles to check Lance's alibi.

"So what's the deal with the Bootless Day Country Club?" Trey asked. "Lance made a big point of mentioning his membership."

"It's an old Lexington golf club with a $60,000 initiation fee."

"Holy smokes. It must have an awesome course."

"No. As a matter of fact, it's vastly overrated. And it didn't have a single African American member until 2007."

"2007?"

"Afraid so."

"But doesn't Lexington have, like, tens of thousands of African American people?"

"It sure does."

"Wow. That's...." Trey shook his head in lieu of finishing his statement.

"So tell me," Laurel said. "What do we know now that we didn't know this morning?"

"That Lance is dirty."

"And a liar."

"He was lying like a no-legged dog."

Laurel looked at him. "A what?"

"A no-legged dog. Now that I live in Kentucky, I'm trying to be more Southern. To fit in."

"Is that a Southern expression?"

"Isn't it?"

"I have no idea. But I'll tell you something, Trey. Southern character is like cayenne pepper. A little is nice. A little adds flavor. Too much will send you running for the toilet in the middle of the night."

"I like cayenne pepper."

"Uh-huh. So anyway, yes, Lance was lying. As if he wouldn't remember that he has a horse in a stakes race on Derby Day, or who its jockey is. The odd thing is, when we told him Cervantes was dead, he almost seemed to relax." She thought for a moment. "Maybe Lance thought we were there for something else."

"Something else? Like what?"

*****

Fifteen minutes later, they were coming out of Zane's Feed Store, having learned that Lance had lied yet again—that he hadn't gone to the feed store at 7 p.m. on the night Cervantes was killed because the store had closed at 6. In short, the relevant parts of his alibi were either impossible to corroborate or entirely false.

"I'm starving," Trey said as they got back in the car.

"Of course you are. But you're in luck. There's a place we can hit just up the road called Wallace Station. They make the best hot brown and best chess pie in the world."

"Best in the world?"

"In the entire world."

"We'll see. Incidentally, what is a hot brown? I see it on menus all over town."

"You've lived in Kentucky for three years and you've never had a hot brown? You, a gluttonous foodie?"

"Well, what is it?"

"It's a broiled, open-faced sandwich with roasted turkey, ham, smoky bacon, and tomato, all covered with a creamy, bubbly, gooey, cheesy Mornay sauce. It's the sandwich they serve in Heaven."

"And chess pie? What's that?"

"A pie filled with the four greatest things in the world: eggs, vanilla, butter and sugar. It's the pie they serve in Heaven."

"Do they serve liver sausage in Heaven?"

"They serve liver sausage in Hell."

"Well," Trey said, breaking into a smile. "I'll be damned."

"Probably."

FIFTEEN

At their office, Laurel and Trey were standing in Laurel's cubicle, looking over a list of employees of Barnstone Farm that Trey got from income tax officials at the Kentucky Department of Revenue.

"The guy I talked to said to keep in mind that a lot of these horse farms employ undocumented aliens for the harder, dirtier jobs that other people don't want, so this probably isn't a complete list," Trey said.

"Is that the Ken doll I hear?" a booming voice asked from an open doorway across the room. It was Detective Sergeant Isaiah Turner, their boss. "Is Barbie with you? You two come in here for a minute."

"What's up, big guy?" Laurel asked as she and Trey entered.

Turner was an imposing figure of a man at six-foot-five and 250-some pounds—much of it solid muscle. A broad scar ran the length of his left forearm. He referred to it, without elaboration, as a souvenir that he brought back from the Middle East.

Turner's office had a wall of high windows that looked out onto the same railroad line that ran down past Cervantes's house, two miles to the south. It was decorated with framed commendations, an autographed team photo of the 2013 Louisville Cardinals men's basketball team, and a desktop model of the U.S.S. Okinawa—an amphibious assault ship that transported Turner and his beloved 1st Battalion/4th Marines landing team to the Persian Gulf in the run-up to Operation Desert Storm. The detectives could still make Turner's blood boil whenever, just to be jerks, they reminded him that the Navy had sunk the Okinawa for target practice in 2002.

"Hey, look," Turner said. "Trey's wearing real shoes instead of Jesus sandals. Did Laurel take you shopping for grown-up people clothes?"

"Please," Trey said. "What's that clearance sale carwash towel-looking thing you're wearing?" Turner wore a plaid flannel shirt with more clashing colors than Trey could count. "I'll bet the ladies all come running when you go clubbing in that."

"Trey, I haven't been to a club in a quarter century. Unless you count Sam's Club."

"I prefer Costco."

"So do I. Now, one of you give me a thumbnail of this Cervantes thing."

"Trey?" Laurel said. "Want to take this opportunity to practice your briefing skills?"

"We spent yesterday morning talking to every Tom, Dick and Harry we could find at the Churchill Downs backside. Picked up on some very vague rumors about racing fraud. Nothing solid yet. Most of the people there weren't enthused to be talking to us."

"I'm sure," Turner said.

"Anyway, given the medical examiner's opinion that Cervantes might have been killed at Churchill Downs and his body then moved, we're going over security video from the usual sources. We'll let you know as soon as we have any worthwhile leads."

"Who have you talked to so far?"

"Mostly backside workers. One very hostile vet."

"Anyone with standing?"

"Standing?" Laurel asked, jumping in.

"You know what I mean."

"It's an odd question."

"Laurel."

"We spoke with the Duke," she said.

"Oh, great."

"And the owner of Barnstone Farm, the outfit that owns the horse Cervantes was going to ride on Derby Day."

"Hmmm," Turner said, turning and looking out his window.

"Why?" Laurel asked.

Turner turned back around and looked at Laurel. "Well, here's the thing."

"There's a thing? I hate it when there's a thing."

"You can talk to the backside people. But the Duke and the Barnstone family are off limits."

Laurel stared for a moment. "Tell me you're joking."

"Ah, Laurel, you know how it is."

"I do?"

"I'm sure there are political considerations here."

"What political considerations exactly?"

"I don't know. Take your pick. City Hall wanting to sweep dirt under the carpet for Derby Week. Maybe campaign contributions influencing policy. Favors owed. One of the usual things, I'm sure. I didn't ask. Anyway, it's not my idea."

"Whose idea is it?"

"I don't know."

"Come on."

"Laurel, don't give me a hard time. This is coming from on high. It's Derby Week. You know how much money is flowing into this city right now? We don't want to rock the boat."

"Rock the boat? We aren't talking about some celebrity visitor who got caught with half a gram of blow. You're telling me to lay off witnesses, and even potential suspects, in a homicide investigation."

"I know. But like I said, it's coming from on high. We're to lay off."

"On high as in who? And don't say *I don't know*."

"The message came to me through a major."

"Our major? The major of the Major Crimes Division?"

"No. Dale Mecklenburg."

Laurel found herself at a momentary loss for words. "You're kidding," she said at last.

"Who's Dale Mecklenburg?" Trey said.

"Major of the Special Investigations Division," Turner said. "But Mecklenburg said the order comes from higher up."

"How high?" Laurel asked. "The Chief?"

"Laurel, I told you—"

"The mayor's office?"

"Laurel!" Turner said, louder.

"What the hell?" Laurel asked, matching Turner's volume.

"I know. But let's just toe the line here, okay? We don't want any trouble from the overlords."

"I could take this to the union."

"Bad idea, Laurel."

"Don't be such a f—"

"Hey, hey, hey!" Trey half shouted. "You guys want to hear a joke? What did the Zen Buddhist say to the hotdog vendor? Make me one with everything. Get it?"

Turner and Laurel both turned and looked at him, irritated, but also, thankfully, distracted and speechless.

*****

Standing in the elevator as they descended, Laurel's body was rigid, her fists clenched, her face contorted with rage.

"You alright?" Trey asked.

"Depends on what you mean."

"I've never seen you get angry like this."

"Well," she said, her mind drifting twelve years back to another time when one of her investigations was interfered with. It was a case in which the entitled, worthless son of a regional gas station chain magnate—and big-time donor to the mayor's election campaign—assaulted a young man who was out on a date with his girlfriend because the young man refused to vacate a table the entitled son wanted to usurp from him at an overpriced downtown steak house. The young man ended up with permanent brain damage after the entitled son hit him over the back of the head with a wine bottle. For reasons that were never given, Laurel was ordered to drop the case entirely. Furious, she'd taken the matter all the way up to her division major and had been told in blunt language to shut her mouth, stand down, and obey her chain of command—or else. The entitled son got off without so much as a slap on the wrist. The case just went away. Laurel had given serious thought to quitting over the matter. But after several desperately conflicted weeks, she managed to convince herself that it had been a one-time thing—an anomaly in an otherwise exemplary and ethical department. Managed to convince herself that her efforts still mattered. That the thankless work of LMPD's officers and detectives wasn't being undermined by politicians or their wealthy cronies. Yet here was just such a situation once again.

Neither Trey nor Laurel spoke again until they were back out in their Taurus. Laurel pulled her door shut with a bang. "Things just got weird," she said.

"Spooky even. What do you think is up?"

"Somebody with political power is calling in favors. Pulling strings."

"The Duke? The Barnstone people? Some bigwig at Churchill Downs?"

"Good question."

"The murderer?"

"Maybe. Certainly someone who has a big reason for not wanting us poking around."

"How are we going to solve this case if we can't talk to these people?"

"I don't know."

Trey sneered. "They always win, don't they?"

"They?"

"The rich. The powerful. The well-connected, or whatever. They always get away with things the rest of us get locked up for."

"Don't give up just yet, young Trey. The dice are still in the air. And remember, the backside people are still inbounds."

"Lot of good that'll do us."

"We'll see. But I'll tell you what—I'll be damned if some son of a bitch is going to get off the hook in one of my cases again because of some rotten apple venality at city hall."

"What are you talking about? Sounds like there's a story there."

She took a breath. "Never mind."

A silent moment passed.

"I'm hungry," Trey said, starting the car.

"Again? What is with you? Do you have hyperthyroidism? A tapeworm?"

"Boundaries, Laurel," Trey said with a wink. "By the way, I have a date with the fake boobs girl tonight."

"The one from the dating app? Vice president of the UK sorority council or whatever?"

"Former vice president."

"Oh, Trey."

"She could be cool."

"She isn't."

"You don't know that."

"Trey, didn't you have any female friends growing up who you could talk to about girls? Didn't you at least have one sister in that big Catholic family of yours?"

"Three brothers."

"Older?"

"Yes. But not wiser in the ways of ladies."

"Brutes?"

"Let me put it this way. Whenever we're all sleeping in tents after a brotherly night of camping, drinking beer, and eating chili around the bonfire, their idea of the funniest thing in the world is to unzip my tent just enough to stick one of their butts in, shout *Remember the Alamo*, fart as loud as possible, and then zip my tent back up and hold the zipper pull so I can't escape. Not just once, but over and over again through the night, each of them taking turns."

"Remember the Alamo?"

"I've never claimed that anything they do makes sense."

"Sounds like they were some silly boys."

"Oh, no, no—they still do this to me as adults."

"Huh. I think that tells me just about everything I need to know about you and your whole family."

They went quiet again. Then Trey said, "I think I'm in need of a lesson here. What do we do when local rich folk are calling in favors to government or police department brass, blocking our progress?"

Laurel turned and looked him in the eye. "You know what? I'll tell you what we do. We call in a favor of our own," she said, taking out her phone and dialing.

Trey listened as she spoke to someone she called *Uncle E.B.*, asked if he were busy, gave him a thumbnail of their situation, then asked him to get alongside the employees of Barnstone Farm as soon as he could. She read him names and associated birthdates from the list Trey had obtained from the state tax people, told him that she loved him, then hung up.

"Uncle E.B.?" Trey asked.

"My favorite relative. Retired detective from Bullitt County. Now a private investigator. Loves me. Does things for me off the books."

"And he isn't under the same political command structure that we are."

"Exactly. The local blue bloods don't have any power over him."

"Not entirely ethical to share investigation details with him, I'm guessing."

"Less unethical than quitting on a homicide investigation because of political pressure."

"You may have a point. So we aren't giving up then?"

"Take a wild guess, Trey."

SIXTEEN

That same evening, while she and Trey were leaving Safai Coffee after stopping in for double-shots of the velvety rocket fuel they called Espresso Especial, Laurel got a call from Uncle E.B. She put it on speaker phone so that Trey could hear what he had to report.

"I hit pay dirt," he said in a heavy country accent.

"Already?" Laurel said. "That was quick."

"I got lucky. Second guy I approached gave me what I'm guessing you're looking for."

"Just like that?"

"Well...."

"Well what?"

"I may have applied a little bit of good old fashioned pressure."

"And how did you manage to do that, Uncle E.B.?" she asked, smiling at Trey.

"Sometimes people just make it easy for you."

"What does that mean?"

"Don't ask. Let's just say the man has a green card."

"That's all you're going to tell me?"

"Fragile immigration status makes a man vulnerable to leverage if you can catch him on video pulling a definite no-no."

"You're an evil man."

"Be that as it may, this guy, who is a general stable hand at Barnstone Farm, says a special doctor made several visits to the farm over the past few months."

"Special doctor?"

"Not the regular vet. Some other guy. Slick. Tanned. Well-dressed. Each time he was there, he'd spend several hours with one of the horses, sequestered in a special barn they use for medical treatments. As far as my guy was aware, nobody besides the slick, tanned doctor and Lance Timmons himself were allowed in or knew what went on in there. The horses would recover in the barn for several days, hidden from view. Finally, when they were let back out, he said they had swollen, stitched up lower lips. None of the horses that had the stitched lips were allowed to race for several months. Not until they were fully healed."

"And not until they were so fully healed that nobody could tell they'd been worked on," Trey surmised.

"So who is this slick, tanned, mysterious doctor?" Laurel asked.

"I was going to look into it this afternoon. Shouldn't be hard to run down. The guy I leaned on told me the doctor drove a black Maybach sedan."

"A Maybach? How many of those could there possibly be in the entire state of Kentucky?"

"Not many."

"Well, that narrows things down."

*****

As soon as she hung up on Uncle E.B., Trey called in a DMV request for a list of all black Maybach sedans registered to doctors. It didn't take 30 seconds to learn that there were only two. One was owned by an anesthesiologist who lived in Paducah—in the far southwestern corner of the state. The other was owned by a Dr. Vikash Patel who had a home address in Lexington, not terribly far from Barnstone Farm. He owned a Maybach 62S. An absurdly expensive, ostentatious, yet technologically antiquated car that probably cost the good doctor a cool $400,000 new.

"Bingo!" Trey said as he looked at his follow-up Google search results. "Dr. Vikash Patel, MD. A plastic surgeon specializing in face lifts, nose jobs, boob jobs, and, let's theorize, horse tattoo replacements or lip grafting."

"Let's go have a word with the good doctor, shall we? But first, let's go back to Churchill Downs, grab Kathy Hammersmith, and have her join us to take a close look at Empire Builder's lip and leg markings. That should thoroughly ruin someone's day."

*****

Back at the Churchill Downs backside, passing through the stables area on the way to their rendezvous with Kathy Hammersmith, Laurel and Trey found themselves walking head-on toward a Hispanic exercise jockey who was staring straight at them, his eyes unblinking. The distance between them was closing quickly. For a short moment, both his stare and his stride wavered. But then he stood up straight, met their eyes once again, and strode forward until they came together.

"Can we help you?" Trey asked.

The man looked all around, checking the faces of everyone in the area. Then he gestured to an open door that led into a vacant horse stall. Once they were all three inside, the jockey closed and bolted the door. "I see you talking to people here. You police?"

"Yes. What can we do for you?" Trey said.

"I think I maybe just see the big man with the black hat. One of the men Javier tells the police about."

"What men?"

"The men Javier overhears. The ones he tells the police about."

"The ones he told the police about?" Laurel said. "What police?"

"The one Javier talks to that night. The night he is killed."

"The *police officer* Javier Cervantes talked to the night he was killed?"

"Si. Yes. By the gate. The police who takes Javier's, ah—como se dice declaración?"

"Statement?" Laurel offered.

"Si! Yes. Statement. I maybe just see the big man in the black hat."

"What's your name, sir?"

"I just see him now, this way," the man said, instead of giving his name.

The exercise jockey—who with obvious fear and reluctance finally told them his name was Miguel Martinez—led the detectives at a fast walk all the way across the backside to the quarantine stable. By the time they got there, they were all short of breath and sweating. There were horses and workers and visitors walking every which way. Looking desperate, Martinez peered all around, scanning everyone in the area, looking for a black hat. But the man was gone.

SEVENTEEN

After learning that Miguel Martinez had been a good friend and colleague of Cervantes for many years, and that Cervantes had possibly given a statement to a patrolman the night he was murdered, the detectives took as much useful information from Martinez as they could. Martinez said that Cervantes was clearly scared the night he was killed. He thought he'd overheard two men discussing a murder they'd committed. Cervantes heard them talking in a nearby stall when he was caring for Empire Builder that evening. At some point, Cervantes saw the men. Martinez wasn't clear on when or how. All Cervantes had told him was that they were both big, tall fellows, and that one of them wore a black baseball cap. Spooked, Cervantes went to give his story to a uniformed police officer working at the north security gate off of 4th Street. It was the last time Martinez ever saw him.

It turned out that Martinez's entire basis for rushing the detectives to the quarantine stable was that he saw a big man in a black baseball hat. Given that the quarantine stable was far from Empire Builder's stable, and given that there were hundreds, if not thousands of people roaming the backside just then—a good number of them wearing black hats—Laurel decided that they'd probably been led on a bit of a wild goose chase. All the same, she thanked Martinez.

*****

Having indefinitely postponed their meeting with Kathy Hammersmith, the very next thing the detectives did was call around to find out which LMPD officers were assigned to the north gate area of the backside on the night Cervantes was murdered. As it turned out, there were two off-duty officers working security there that night in an unofficial, private-hire capacity. And one of them, Officer Tony Bradley, was there again today.

"Are you Bradley?" Laurel shouted as they approached the only officer standing near the north gate. The young officer looked concerned. His face struck Laurel as bizarrely flat, as though he'd repeatedly run face-first into a wall during his formative years.

"Yeah, I'm Bradley."

"Let me ask you something. Did you ever plan to send us a copy of the statement you took from Javier Cervantes the other night?"

"What?"

"Cervantes. The jockey who was murdered the same night you took his statement."

"I know who Cervantes is. Was."

"Did it ever cross your mind to send us a copy? Did you ever think, hey, I should let homicide know that I took a statement from a *victim* the same night he was killed?"

"Whoa—hold on," Bradley said, turning red. "I emailed a copy right to you as soon as I heard about the murder, and as soon as I saw that you caught the case. I assume you're Arno and Hhh…."

"Hewson," Trey said.

"Yeah, Hewson. You both have copies in your email."

"You sent it to both of us?" Laurel asked.

"What did I just say?"

"You sure you hit 'send'?"

"Yeah, I'm sure I hit 'send.'"

"Well, neither of us got it."

"Yeah, you did. You emailed me a response. That's why I didn't follow up with a call."

"I did not email you a response."

"Yeah, you did."

"What did my response say?"

"It said *thank you.* So case off."

Laurel wiped a hand down her face. "Look, Bradley, I'm one-hundred percent positive—"

"Here," Bradley said. "I'll show you." He took his smartphone from his pocket, opened his email account, and began scrolling through emails, looking for the one he claimed Laurel sent him. "Well, maybe I deleted it," he said after taking a second look. "You know what? I'll show you in my out box or sent messages folder or whatever it's called." He switched folders and began scrolling again. "Here! See? Right here. Sent to you Sunday night."

He turned his phone so that Laurel could see the notation for a message that appeared to be from her. The subject line said 'Cervantes, Javier: Statement.' But when Bradley tried to click it open, he got an error message saying that the content of the email was unavailable.

"That's weird," Bradley said.

Trey and Laurel gaped at one another.

"Alright, alright," Laurel said. "Let's back up for a second. Just in case

Cervantes's statement disappeared into the ether, can you just send us the footage from your body cam?"

"I wasn't wearing it that night."

"Why not?"

"I wasn't on duty. I was moonlighting. Doing security for Churchill Downs, like I am right now, for extra money. You know how it is."

Laurel sighed.

"Hey, look," Bradley began to protest.

"No, no," Laurel said. "It's alright. Sorry to come at you like that. It's just the way this case is going."

A pause. "It's cool. You guys really didn't get the statement I emailed?"

"No. Look, can you at least tell us what Cervantes told you?"

"It's been a couple days. I didn't try to commit the details to memory because I typed them out for you."

"Understood."

"So I was on security at the gate here, and Cervantes approaches me all hesitant, looking all around, like he's scared of something. Comes up and says he was in a stable stall working with a horse when he heard two men in the next stall over talking about the Paul Taylor homicide—you know, the guy who got shot at a liquor warehouse he worked at the other night near 11th and Broadway."

"Two men talking about the Paul Taylor homicide how, exactly?"

"Talking about the steps they were taking to make sure nobody figured out that they did it."

"*They* being the guys who were doing the talking? The two guys in the stall next to Empire Builder's?"

"Empire Builder?"

"The two guys in the stall next to the one Cervantes was in."

"Right. Anyway, at some point Cervantes left the stall he was working in to go find a cop. Unfortunately for him, the guys who were talking next door exited the stall they were in at the exact same time. Long story short, they saw Cervantes. And I'm guessing that Cervantes froze or had a scared look on his face. Whatever the case, Cervantes thought that the guys he overheard realized he'd overheard them. So he was worried."

"I should think so. What time did Cervantes talk to you?"

"Around 9 p.m. Just before I went off my shift."

"Did Cervantes describe the two men?"

"Both tall. One, heavyset. Sort of muscular. Wearing a black baseball cap. The other was big too. Chubby. Wearing nondescript work clothes. Maybe Carhartt or Dickies brand duck pants. Too clean to have ever been put to real use. Like the guy was just pretending to be a genuine working-class type because it's cool or whatever."

"Was that Cervantes's assumption, or yours?"

"His. I mean, sort of. He used the Spanish word *maniquí*, for manikin. Or poser, I think. Unfortunately, since Cervantes was running scared and didn't linger to get a better look at the two men, his descriptions were pretty thin. That's really all I have for you."

"Did you take notes during the interview?"

"My pen ran out of ink."

"What patrol division are you with?"

"The Fourth."

"Did you send a copy of the statement to the detective running the Paul Taylor homicide investigation too?"

"Of course. I think his name is Rueff."

"Detective George Rueff"

"That's him. He was copied on the same email I sent to you."

"Is the Cervantes statement on the computer in your car?"

"No. It's at the office."

"Are you going back to your offices tonight?"

"I wasn't planning to. But I can swing by there and send you another copy of the statement.

"We'd appreciate it."

*****

"Maybe we've been chasing the wrong people," Trey said as they walked away.

"Maybe."

"Maybe Cervantes was killed because he got caught overhearing two guys discussing their murder of this Paul Taylor kid. Not because he was going to rat out the Barnstone people about race fixing."

"Maybe."

"The Barnstone people are definitely dirty."

"Yes, they are. But because of Cervantes's murder, or because of something else?"

"Maybe the Barnstone people had a hand in the murder of the Taylor kid *and* Cervantes. Maybe the cases are connected in some way we aren't seeing."

"Maybe, maybe, maybe."

"What do we do now?"

"We reassess. But I do have one interesting thing to mention. Remember the other day when we were talking to people around Empire Builder's stable?"

"What about it?"

"There was a tall, heavyset, sort of muscular guy with a black Glock baseball cap walking our way with a mean-looking old man. They turned on their heels the second they saw us."

EIGHTEEN

The detectives went to their office the next morning to catch up on paperwork for other cases. But when Laurel got there, the first thing she did was listen to a voicemail from Bradley telling her that he couldn't find the Cervantes statement on his computer. That he'd looked everywhere.

Laurel began to wonder whether the case was jinxed.

*****

A few hours later, the detectives sat at an outdoor table at Royals Hot Chicken in Louisville's NULU district—a buzzing neighborhood of unique restaurants, bars, galleries, and shops. Trey, his face pink and his hairline developing a fine dew of perspiration, was in the middle of devouring an early lunch of crispy fried chicken with a level of spiciness the menu described as *gonzo*, along with a side of creamy pimento cheese grits. Laurel was content with a cucumber salad and a single fried chicken taco that she was dipping in pepper jelly.

"Is that all you're getting?" Trey asked.

"I'm saving room for the fried sweet potato and marshmallow pie."

"Oh, my, my, my. You'll give me a bite, right?"

Laurel nodded, smiling. "Trey, I don't know that I've ever met anyone who loves eating as much as you do."

"This is the best fried chicken I've ever had," he said, licking his fingers. "Damn, I love southern food."

"You should check out Dasha Barbour's Southern Bistro if you like southern food. I mean *real* southern food. Not *Garden & Gun* southern food. Not that Royals isn't legit."

"Dasha what?"

"Dasha Barbour. Just off of Bardstown Road in Buechel. You'll think you died and went to deep-fried heaven. Fried pickles. Fried green tomatoes. A sweet potato casserole that's so good you'll slap your mama."

"Slap my mama?"

"That's a genuine southern expression you can add to your lexicon."

"Must be some damned good sweet potato casserole. But hey, we've been partnered for three months. Why haven't you taken me there yet?"

"You have to earn it."

"So much great fried chicken in this town."

"And bourbon. And tobacco. It's what makes us all so healthy."

"Someone should do fried chicken tours. Just like they do bourbon distillery tours." Trey paused to take a few cooling gulps of his sweet tea. "Okay, then. Where do we find these tall, somewhat muscular guys with the black baseball cap and the too-clean work pants?"

"If Cervantes overheard them from Empire Builder's stall, then they were probably in one of the adjacent stalls. With any luck, they're affiliated with the folks who own one of the horses in those stalls."

"One housed a horse owned by a group of bank executives, right?"

"From Bond & Karman Bank. Right."

"And on the other side, the horse was owned by the Clayton Bourbon people."

"Right. Sponsors of the Clayton Bourbon Pennyroyal Stakes. An old bourbon family."

"But we don't know which group our mystery suspects belong to. Or if they're affiliated with any of the owners in the first place. They could have just been using one of the empty stalls to have a private conversation."

"True. But the other murder victim, Paul Taylor, was killed at a liquor warehouse where he worked. And the Claytons are, of course, in the liquor business. That's a commonality worth looking into."

"Yeah, but I mean—you throw a dart in this town, you're going to hit someone in the liquor business."

"Never disregard a commonality, Trey. Anyway, I'm pretty sure I'd recognize the big guy who was wearing the black Glock baseball cap if I saw him again—even if he changes hats."

"Should we go camp out at Churchill Downs and watch for him?"

"I think I'd like to see what the video footage reveals first. Maybe we can spot him getting into a car and get the plate number. Then we could get his name and run him through NCIC and everything to find out who we're dealing with before we go charging in."

"It's a lot of work, sifting through all that video."

"Well, option B is to lurk at Churchill Downs, maybe for days, maybe forever, hoping he shows up, and not knowing a damned thing about him if and when he does."

"Yeah, alright. On a related note, what do you know about the Paul Taylor homicide Bradley was talking about?"

"Just the same stuff we've all heard. He was some young guy who worked at a liquor warehouse near 11th and Broadway, which is also where he was shot. We'll call George Rueff to get the details, and to tell him about the possible crossover of our cases."

*****

After lunch, Laurel called Detective Rueff.

"You're on speakerphone George, and I'm in the car with my young and innocent apprentice, Trey Hewson, who is still wet behind the ears. So don't use any cuss words."

"Well, shit. What the fuck can I do for you, Laurel?"

"I need a copy of the Javier Cervantes statement that our wunderkind patrolman, Tony Bradley, put in your case file."

"Bradley? I'm not sure I know what statement you're talking about," Rueff said.

"You didn't get a statement from Bradley the morning after the Cervantes killing?"

"Don't think so."

"Check your email."

"I've checked it twice in the past half hour."

"Just check it again. Look at messages received at around 10:30 p.m. on Sunday."

"You're a pain in the ass, Laurel. Hold on. Mmmmm. Okay. Nope. The only departmental email I got that night was a reminder that I'm overdue for recurrent training at the range."

Laurel and Trey gave each other a look. "So can you tell us what you've learned with the Paul Taylor case?" Laurel asked.

"Fella in his early 20s. Married. No children. Was a National Merit Scholar alumnus of Saint Xavier High School. You probably heard that already."

"Some of it."

"Captain of the soccer team. President of the St. X Young Republicans Club. Vice president of the Future Business Leaders of America Club."

"Did he sell Amway and subscribe to GQ magazine too?"

"And Maxim, I'll bet. Anyway, by all accounts a go-getter of a kid, bright future, making it happen. Until he was shot to death just after 9 p.m. last Friday at a liquor distribution warehouse he owned down on 11th, south of Broadway, about a block from that Indi's fried chicken place."

"Indi's!" Trey said. "Another great chicken joint. Love their extra spicy keel."

"Wait, wait," Laurel said. "A liquor warehouse the Paul Taylor kid *owned?*"

"Yup," Rueff said. "Looks like a simple street robbery gone bad. Took the guy's cash, left the rest of his wallet. Probably a psycho junkie. Or someone who had a major craving for Indi's fried chicken but was short of cash."

"I'm still trying to wrap my head around this," Laurel said. "A kid in his early 20s *owned* a liquor distribution warehouse?"

"I know. Weird, right?"

"Where did his money come from?"

"Not from his family, that's for sure. His parents are semi-retired social workers. His wife, Mimi, grew up in Radcliff, raised by a single mother—a bank teller at Fort Knox."

"Drugs?"

"Guy had no record at all. Pure as the driven snow."

"I'm sure. So where did his money come from, then? You don't start a liquor distribution business with money you saved from busing tables at Jack Fry's."

"There's probably an invisible partner or partners," Rueff said. "I'm working on running that down. On paper, the warehouse is owned by a Kentucky limited liability corporation that is itself, in turn, owned by an out-of-state limited liability company that has no public record of ownership interests. I just subpoenaed the registered agent for the owners' contact information. Still waiting on his response."

"Did you recover any bullets or casings?"

"One slug and three casings. Still waiting on the report."

"We do a lot of waiting in this job, George."

"Don't I know it?"

"Keep us in the loop on this one, okay?"

*****

"Things just got even weirder," Laurel said as they headed for the office to read the Paul Taylor casefile.

"So Rueff doesn't have Cervantes's statement either?" Trey said. "What the hell is going on?"

"Two serious possibilities. One, Bradley is a moron who doesn't remember deleting the Cervantes statement from his computer, *and* there's a mysterious and unbelievably selective quirk in our email system that made Bradley's emails to us disappear. Or two, we got hacked and someone deleted the Cervantes statement and our emails."

"Hacked you, me, Rueff, and Bradley? All four of our email accounts *and* Bradley's computer? Hard to believe."

"Maybe they did it some other way."

"What other way?"

"I don't know, Trey. I'm not a computer geek. But we managed to put people on the moon all the way back in 1969. I'm sure someone out there has the knowhow to make some emails and a document disappear."

"To cover something up?"

"Is that still so hard for you to believe? We already have it from Sergeant

Turner's own mouth that Major Mecklenburg of the Special Investigations Division came at him with orders—from the Chief, from the mayor's office, or who knows where—that we lay off the horse people."

"But why would the Duke or the Barnstone people give a damn about a homicide involving some liquor distributor who's barely out of St. X High School?"

"Maybe the pressure to lay off the horse people didn't actually originate with the horse people. Or maybe the pressure doesn't have anything to do with someone making our emails disappear."

Laurel wondered how they were going to find out.

NINETEEN

Sitting in his undecorated cubicle, Trey started reading the Paul Taylor file while Laurel called Officer Bradley to get his help in setting a trap. She asked Bradley to send her another email at 10:30 p.m. that night—roughly the same time Bradley supposedly sent his email containing Cervantes's statement on Sunday night. In his email, he was to say that he had another hard copy of the statement and that he would swing by Homicide around midnight to put it in the Cervantes case file. In the meantime, from an anonymous throw-away email address she used for online shopping, Laurel would email Bradley a document she'd just composed that was formatted to look like a genuine statement from Cervantes, but which, after a few lines of fake but authentic-looking content, said, "Hey, dumbass. Tampering with evidence is a felony under KRS section 524.100." She'd filled the rest of the page with a bunch of random text copied and pasted from an online advertisement for generic Viagra. After swinging by his patrol division office to print out the fake Cervantes statement, Bradley was to drop in at the Homicide office around midnight, put the fake statement into the Cervantes file, and then go home and keep his mouth shut about it forever.

"What's going on?" Bradley asked her, sounding troubled. "You smelling a rat in LMPD?"

"Don't worry about it. Just don't discuss it with anyone. Not with your closest drinking buddies. Not with your girlfriend. Nobody. Got it? This won't come back on you, I promise. And another thing; whenever you're working security at Churchill Downs, I need you to keep a lookout for a grumpy old drunk of a veterinarian named Eldon Ridgeway. I'll email you his DMV picture along with a close-up I took with my smartphone camera."

"This isn't really my job."

"Don't be a chump. If you see him, call me right away."

*****

"Want the gist of the Paul Taylor case so far?" Trey said, striding into Laurel's cubicle.

"Lay it on me."

"There isn't much more than what Rueff already told us. Last Friday, at 9:09 p.m., ShotSpotter caught the sound of five rapid-fire shots, a pause, and then one more shot in the 800-block of South 11th Street," Trey said, referring to Louisville's system of cutting-edge listening devices set up throughout the city to instantly pinpoint the exact location of gunfire. "Units arriving on the scene found Taylor already deceased. No witnesses. Despite the six shots fired, Taylor was only hit twice. Both bullets hit him from behind. Body was found sprawled and face-down in front of his business, Bacchus Distribution. Maybe he has a business partner named Bacchus."

"Bacchus is the Roman god of wine."

"Right. I knew that. And I went to public school."

"Sounds like Taylor was running for it."

"Yeah. One bullet severed his spinal cord at the second lumbar vertebra and then blew out part of his large intestine. The second was a close-range shot to the back of his head. Probably the finisher. Anyway, the bullet fragments they recovered were found on the ground beneath his face, among remnants of his cheekbone and cerebellum. Informal comments say it looks like .45 caliber."

"What do we know about him?"

"Like Rueff said, Taylor was a golden boy at St. X. Grew up in the Bonnycastle neighborhood. Had a vision of offering Kentuckians greater choice in booze, wine, and beer. Fell in love with wine after taking a side trip to Napa while his parents were visiting family in San Francisco. Drove him crazy that he could get so few California wines here. The guy only turned 21 eight months ago."

"What 21-year-old falls in love with wine?"

"Well, I mean, sounds like he was an unusual kid," Trey said.

"And more importantly, how on earth had he already broken into the alcohol distribution business in a state where that's supposed to be about as easy to do as climb Mount Everest."

"What do you mean?"

"I mean alcohol distribution in Kentucky is allegedly controlled by a small de facto cartel of old money families and companies. It's one of the reasons there's so little variety of alcoholic beverages available here compared to other states. The existing distributors don't abide new competition, to put it mildly. Or so says the rumor mill."

"How hard could it be to get a distributor's license here? This is still America."

"I'll tell you a little story. What do you think is the biggest beer company in the country?"

"I don't know, probably Budweiser?"

"The makers of Budweiser, also known as Anheuser-Busch InBev. You are correct, sir. Matter of fact, Anheuser-Busch InBev is the biggest beer producer in the world. The *entire* world, Trey."

"Okay."

"Now then, a few years ago, the folks at Anheuser-Busch InBev decided they wanted to run their own distribution in Kentucky. Makes sense, right? They have the trucks. They have the drivers. Why not cut out unnecessary middleman distributors to cut costs? To enable higher profits, cheaper retail prices for their customers, and so forth?"

"Sure. Capitalism at its best, or whatever."

"Right. But guess what happened."

"The Kentucky distributors blocked them?"

"Very good, Trey. The old gang of Kentucky distributors supposedly blocked the world's largest beer producer—a company that makes billions of dollars a year—from setting up its own distribution network here. Can you imagine the political influence it takes to do something like that? And can you imagine what that influence costs? The distributors are known to have a small army of lobbyists constantly crawling around the halls of the capitol. A mercenary platoon of overdressed, glad-handing busybodies up to who knows what."

"Handing out under-the-table goodies to our awesome legislators?" Trey asked. "Cases of 30-year-old bourbon? Season tickets for UK basketball?"

"Or maybe big reelection campaign contributions," Laurel said. "Your guess is as good as mine. Maybe they just chat about the weather."

"Doesn't blocking new distributors violate some sort of fair competition law?"

"I'm not a lawyer. But you'd think so."

"So, bottom line, it's weird that Taylor—a 21-year-old kid—got a liquor distribution business going."

"It's beyond weird."

"What does it mean, big-picture wise?"

"Maybe nothing. Maybe, like Rueff theorized, Taylor was shot in a simple street robbery gone wrong. But maybe there was more to it."

TWENTY

Just before midnight, with the help of one of their more tech-savvy colleagues, Laurel and Trey propped up Laurel's smartphone on top of a random desk so that its camera had a commanding view of the file cabinet containing the Cervantes file. The camera was set up to transmit a live image of the area to a laptop computer that Laurel and Trey were watching in a windowless room just down the hall, between the file cabinet and the elevators. The homicide office was mostly dark and largely vacated. All but two of the detectives who were on duty were already out in the field.

After sitting and waiting for a few minutes, they watched Officer Bradley arrive, open the cabinet, pull the Cervantes casefile, take the fake Cervantes statement from a small folder he carried, and insert it into the casefile.

"Good boy," Laurel said as they watched Bradley replace the casefile, close the cabinet, and depart. "Now let's see if we can get a bottom feeder to rise to the bait."

"Bottom feeders don't rise to the bait, Laurel. That's why they're called bottom feeders. Still, thinking about it makes me want to eat some fried catfish. With tartar sauce and malt vinegar. Maybe a side of hot, salty fries."

Laurel pulled a plastic-wrapped, half-eaten chocolate chip cookie from the inside pocket of her jacket and handed it to Trey. "Here. Eat this and try to stay focused."

Half an hour went by with no activity.

"This is boring," Trey said.

"Patience," Laurel said, doing her best impersonation of Yoda.

"This chair is uncomfortable."

"So stand up."

"I'm too tired."

"Why don't you tell me about your date with Fake Boobs?

Trey smiled and closed his eyes, staying silent.

"That bad?"

"So I pick fake boobs up at her place, and as we're approaching my car on the sidewalk, I cut behind a shiny black Land Rover. Thinking it was mine, her face lights up and she grabs the passenger door handle. But when she sees that I'm going to my dented old Buick, her face falls. It just completely *falls*, Laurel."

"Bummer."

"Wait. There's more. Her pulling on the door handle makes the Land Rover's car alarm go off, and then some bug-eyed psycho in nothing but briefs comes flying out of his apartment with a Louisville Slugger bat ready to crack me over the head. Fake Boobs takes off running down the street, screaming, and breaks the heels off of *both* her shoes in the process."

"Ouch."

"Yeah. And it went downhill from there."

"It got worse?"

"At FABD barbeque she ordered—and I'm quoting here—*a cosmo with your best vodka.* The server gave me a look like she wanted to ask if Fake Boobs just stepped off a flying saucer."

"I tried to warn you."

"You did."

"You should listen to me."

"I should."

Ten more minutes went by with both detectives more or less twiddling their thumbs as they kept an eye on the laptop screen.

"So tell me, my young apprentice," Laurel said, by way of killing more time. "How are you liking detective work so far?"

"There's a lot of sitting."

"Really, though."

"I like the work okay, I suppose. But the hours are long. Doesn't leave much time to pursue other interests."

"You aren't allowed to have other interests."

"Sounds like a hollow existence."

"I'm starting to realize that myself."

"Just now?"

Laurel took a deep breath. "I mean, I love the work. I always have. But I suppose I wonder what my life would be like if I'd made other choices. Made time for other things."

"Now remember, you're a woman. You aren't allowed to have it all."

"Right."

"Do you want to start a family?"

"You saw my adoption inquiries, didn't you?"

"They were in plain sight on your kitchen counter."

"Yeah, well. I don't know. It's been on my mind. But I'm sort of running out of time for all that."

"You're nowhere close to running out of time."

"I'm getting old, Trey."

"My mom didn't have me until she was, like, 35 years old."

"I'm 40."

"Yeah, right."

"Four-zero."

"No way."

"Yes way."

"You don't look a day over thirty-nine and a half."

"Good one."

"Really though, you look way younger than that."

"Thanks."

"Huh. Well. Forty *is* a big one."

"So they say."

"Now that you're officially middle-aged, are you starting to wonder what it's all about?"

"What *what* is all about?"

"Life. Are you starting to have little late-night freak outs, sitting there in the dark, wondering if this is really all there is?"

Laurel's eyes went wide for a second. "Shut up."

"That's what's happening with my oldest brother. And he's only in his mid-30s."

"Let's just change the subject."

"Hey, look," Trey said, pointing to the computer screen. "A mysterious visitor."

From the direction of the elevators, a man in blue long-sleeve coveralls was slowly walking toward the file cabinets, taking furtive looks all around as he went. Out of 32 available drawers, he opened the exact one that held the Cervantes file. He appeared to examine the tabs, then grabbed a file from the general area that Laurel knew the Cervantes file was in. He opened the file, removed a document, shoved it into his pocket, replaced the file, and closed the drawer. Then he headed straight for the elevators.

"Let's see who he takes it to," Laurel said.

The detectives stepped into the hallway just as the elevator doors closed. They watched the elevator floor indicator until they could see that the man had gone all the way to the first floor, then raced down the fire stairs to catch up. Opening the stairwell doors on the first floor just a crack, they spotted the man standing by the exit as he tossed the fake Cervantes statement into a random trash can. Then he took out an antiquated cell phone and began dialing. He was short, middle aged, and had a lopsided haircut. His mouth hung open. He looked up as Laurel and Trey approached and his face froze in an expression of sheer terror.

"Hey, buddy," Laurel said. "Are you police?"

Trey went straight to the garbage can and retrieved the fake Cervantes statement, now stained with coffee and ketchup. "Well, well. What have we here? Should have used the shredder, pal."

The man was speechless.

"Who are you calling?" Laurel asked him, taking the phone from his unresisting hand only to see that he hadn't gotten beyond entering the digits of Louisville's area code. "How about we see some identification?"

After a couple of jerky-arm false starts, the man pulled a badge from a chest pocket of his coveralls and, with obvious reluctance, handed it to Laurel. It gave his name as Stuart Donnelly. A janitor.

"Well, Mr. Donnelly. What brings you to the Homicide Unit at this hour?"

The man continued to stand there speechless, though he appeared to be thinking hard about a possible response.

"Mr. Donnelly, I'm going to take a wild guess that your fingerprints are all over the document my partner just pulled out of that trash can. And I'm sure I don't have to tell you that you're in big trouble. But you probably don't have to be, because I'm guessing someone else made you do this. Am I right?"

Donnelly stared, then nodded weakly.

"Okay. Now, if you want to take the blame for the creep who made you do this, that's fine. We'll just slap the cuffs on and take you to jail right now. But if we're going to help you out of this jam, the first thing you need to do is tell me who sent you to get that document."

"Stealing it is a class D felony in the state of Kentucky," Trey added. "So you'd probably only be in prison for five years."

"And Blackburn Prison is supposed to have a great colorectal reconstruction surgeon on staff," Laurel said. "

"That's the kind of doctor who repairs your butthole," Trey said. "Handy, right?"

"Mecklenburg," Donnelly mumbled, sounding miserable.

"Excuse me?" Laurel said.

"Mr. Mecklenburg."

"Dale Mecklenburg? The major of the Special Investigations Division?"

"He made me. Said if I didn't help him, he'd say I stole a gun that went missing from one of the cop's desks last week. It's bullshit. This is *all* bullshit. I never stole nothing from nobody."

"Don't worry, Mr. Donnelly. You're a victim here. Nobody is going to give you any trouble as long as you cooperate and then never tell anyone that you met with us. Not Major Mecklenburg. Not even the chief. Nobody. Ever. Understand?"

Donnelly nodded.

"If you do tell anyone, we'll send you to prison. Got it?"

Donnelly nodded again.

"I want to hear you say that you've got it."

"I got it. I got it. I won't tell nobody."

"If Major Mecklenburg asks what you found, just say there was nothing in the file."

"Okay. Nothing in the file."

"Did Major Mecklenburg make you take something out of this file earlier in the week too?"

"Yes."

"Do you know what it was?"

"No. Piece of paper."

"What did you do with it?"

"He told me to throw it away."

"Where'd you throw it away?"

"Same garbage can."

Hearing this, Trey took another look in the can. It was empty but for two used coffee cups, an expired parking pass, and a half-eaten bowl of wedge-cut fries.

"Did Mecklenburg have you delete any emails from the server?"

"Did he have me do what now?"

"Never mind."

*****

Having sent Donnelly on his unhappy way, Laurel and Trey went back up to their conference room to ponder the implications.

"We still don't know who deleted the emails," Trey said.

"We can figure that out later. The important thing is that we know Major Mecklenburg is actively destroying evidence. Whoever deleted the emails probably did it on his instruction."

"What's his story?"

"Mecklenburg? I remember him being a mediocre 3rd Division lieutenant I crossed paths with in a case I was working down near Iroquois Park a few years back. A seemingly decent guy. Always volunteered for the LMPD Foundation's Christmas Shop with a Cop program for needy children."

"You mean the non-religious *holiday* Shop with a Cop program."

"See, I knew you were a closet liberal," Laurel said.

"If Mecklenburg's mediocre, why is he a major now?"

"How does anyone without brains or talent get that high up the chain, Trey? He's probably a bootlicking suck-up."

"So Mecklenburg is monkeying with our case *and* Rueff's case. Two separate homicides. What's his motive?"

"I doubt he has any direct, personal motive. He's probably just a lackey. A fixer who makes stuff go away whenever his masters in the chain of command tell him to."

"Do we confront him?" Trey asked.

"Not yet. Like I said, I doubt he's acting for his own purposes. He's too far down the food chain to be pressured by outside money. Ideally, we want to figure out who the puppet master is first."

"Who do you think it might be? The chief? The mayor?"

"I don't know. But whoever it is, they're awfully clever. I mean, think about it. Under normal circumstances, if we caught a cop destroying evidence, who would we report it to?"

"Special Investigations Division."

"Exactly. The very unit that Mecklenburg commands."

"SID reports directly to the deputy chief, who reports directly to the chief, who reports directly to the mayor. And everybody knows the chief is the mayor's puppet."

"Diabolical, isn't it?"

"It stinks to high heaven," Trey said.

"Worse, with respect to that whole top of the pyramid chain of command, we have no real clue as to who would want that evidence destroyed. Or why."

"What should we do?"

"We should be careful, that's for sure. We cross the wrong person, and we'll find ourselves demoted or fired on some trumped up nonsense like insubordination or one of the other lies they use for getting rid of cops who won't play ball."

"Good cops always get shafted by crooked politicians."

"Not always. Not if they're clever. And lucky."

"So who do we turn to then?" Trey asked. "The union?"

"Maybe."

"What about the FBI? Don't they investigate this sort of thing?"

"They investigate public corruption, certainly."

"Great."

"But the Bureau usually leaves state law and local incidents to us. Plus, it's always a matter of resources and priorities with the feds, right? And they're still consumed with their mandate to find Kentucky-based Islamic terror cells that don't exist."

"So we're on our own."

"For now. Anyway, let's keep this under our hats until we learn more."

"Okay. But in the meantime, how are we going to move this case forward if someone out there is monitoring and obstructing us?"

"It's a pickle."

"Speaking of pickles...."

"You're still hungry. Of course. Let's get you some treats before you go all hypoglycemic."

TWENTY-ONE

The next morning, Laurel and Trey paid a visit to Paul Taylor's childhood home in the Bonnycastle neighborhood. It was a small bungalow that stood at the back of a tiny, tree-shaded lot, barely a block off Bardstown Road. Humble, but well-maintained. As the detectives approached the front door, songbirds chirped away in the surrounding trees, oblivious to the sorrow of the depleted family they serenaded.

Paul's parents were both at home, their faces dark and sad a mere day after burying their son—their only child. The detectives politely declined an offer of chamomile tea. Having promised to make their visit as short as possible, they asked a few questions to address parts of George Rueff's report that begged for follow-up or reiteration.

They confirmed that Paul had no known enemies. Nobody they could think of who might have had a problem with him. He was a good kid. Honest. Conscientious. Respectful of others. They couldn't imagine why anyone would hurt him.

As for the financial backing for Paul's liquor distribution outfit, Bacchus, the detectives learned that the money had supposedly come from a business partner. His parents had no idea who the partner was, which struck Laurel as odd. But the thing that really piqued her interest came when she asked how things were with Paul's marriage to Mimi. There was a notable pause before Paul's mother emphatically insisted that the marriage was just fine—as far as she knew. Paul's father said nothing.

As they got back in the car, Laurel asked Trey if he'd noticed the pause when the subject of Paul's marriage had come up.

"I did. But people of that generation are always weird about that sort of thing. I mean, if I were married, and if my parents witnessed an argument between my wife and me, I'm sure they'd feel weird about discussing it with anyone else—let alone total strangers. Regardless of the circumstances, they'd regard it as private."

"Maybe. But my gut feeling is that there's more to it."

"Want to go question Mimi?"

"Not yet."

"You're the boss," he said as he watched a woman being pulled down the sidewalk by a trio of hyperactive Jack Russell terriers. Then he turned to Laurel. "My kingdom for a donut. And coffee. What's near here?"

"Fante's. Outstanding coffee."

"Will it make me slap my mama?"

"Let's find out."

*****

On their drive back to the office, Rueff called to let them know he'd received the forensic report on the bullet and casings recovered from the Taylor murder scene. Laurel put him on speakerphone.

"Did you get a trace?" she asked.

"No such luck. A clean gun. No previous record of bullets recovered. But we at least were able to determine the make and model."

"Lay it on me, George."

"First off, the bullets were Hornady brand. .45 caliber, 185 grain, from Hornady's Critical Defense series."

"Expensive bullets," Laurel said.

"Damned expensive. And they were fired by a Sig Sauer P226 Legion Series."

"Expensive gun, too."

"How can they tell it was a specific series of the P226?" Trey asked.

"PFM," Rueff said.

"Huh?"

"Pure f-ing magic."

"George is referring to basic forensic ballistics," Laurel said. "General rifling characteristics. Land and groove impressions."

"I'm not a moron. But don't all P226s have the same barrel? Wouldn't they have the same rifling characteristics?"

"Maybe they figured it out from the brass casing," Rueff said. "Maybe the Legion Series leaves unique breech marks, or extractor marks, or firing pin impressions. I don't know. Not my department."

"So what is the Legion Series?" Trey asked.

"It's an extra-fancy, $1,400 version of the P226," Laurel said, "with a special finish and a special grip with a Legion Club medallion embedded in it so that everyone knows you're cool. The important point here is that this pulls another leg out from under the theory that the Taylor killing was just a street robbery gone wrong."

"I don't follow."

"Hornady Critical Defense bullets are rich, paranoid white boy bullets, and the P226 Legion Series is a rich white boy poser's gun."

"Shooter could have stolen it from a rich white boy poser," Trey said.

"True. But rich white boy posers usually have gun safes where they lock away their toys when they aren't carrying them."

"Could the gun owner be the same sort of rich white boy poser who would wear a black Glock baseball cap or work pants that are too clean to have ever been used for actual work, like the two big guys Cervantes saw at Churchill Downs?"

"Now you're thinking like a detective."

"Hey, listen," Rueff said. "If you two want to take the lead on this Taylor business for a couple of days, I'd welcome your help. I'm up to my neck in paperwork for the Smith case."

"Smith case?" Laurel said.

"Dismemberment of that hairdresser in the St. Matthews neighborhood yesterday."

"Oh, right. What happened there?"

"Perp was a new customer who turned out to be a mentally ill stalker already wanted for murder in Texas. They caught him trying to bury pieces of the hairdresser near the railroad tracks by Trinity High School."

"Maybe he didn't like his haircut."

TWENTY-TWO

Having been summoned to the dark, windowless headquarters interview room Trey had been using as a makeshift video lab for the past two days, Laurel stooped over Trey's shoulder to watch a grainy, black-and-white clip from the night vision security camera footage they'd been given by Churchill Downs. It was from a camera that covered the area between Empire Builder's stable and another building. At what the video clip recorded as 9:27 p.m. on the night of Cervantes's murder, a black Cadillac Escalade entered the field of view and, with more back-and-forth maneuvering than should have been necessary, backed up to a stall door very close to Empire Builder's. It could have been Empire Builder's, it could have been that of the bankers' horse, Great Flood, or it could have been the stall housing the Clayton's horse, Carbonado. It was impossible to tell from the perspective of the security camera. But it was certainly one of the three.

"Now watch right here," Trey said, pointing at the driver's side door of the Escalade. It opened, and a tall, portly man in work clothes stepped out of the vehicle, opened the tailgate, and disappeared into the stall. "Is that your man?"

"Could be. Hard to tell at this distance."

It was clear that a man had gotten out on the passenger side, too. But he kept to the far side of the car from the security camera, so the video footage didn't provide a good look at him. It *was* clear, however, that the man was wearing a dark baseball cap.

"I've watched this clip 20 times," Trey said. "It looks like they're loading something into the back of the Escalade. But I'll be damned if I can see what it is. Or even how big it is."

"Did you get the plate number?"

"Kentucky vanity plate that says Peepaw1."

"Like Peepaw Clayton Bourbon?"

"That's how it's spelled."

"And I trust you already ran the plate?"

"Comes back to an Edgar Clayton. Address of registration has him off Longview Lane in the Glenview neighborhood. And here's his driver's license photo," Trey said, clicking open another file to reveal a fat-cheeked, round-faced, dopey-looking 30-year-old man with a receding hairline. He was 6-foot-2, 245 pounds, with brown hair and brown eyes. Judging by his appearance, Laurel figured the man would have full-blown jowls by age 40. An archetype of a spongy-tissued dolt. And something about him struck Laurel as sad. He had a face that seemed to express a premature disappointment with life.

"That's not the guy I saw in the black Glock baseball cap," she said.

"Maybe the baseball cap guy was his passenger."

"Maybe." She took a breath. "Very good, young Trey. Now you know what car to look for in all that RTCC video footage from the surrounding area, and the area of the Taylor crime scene."

"Oh, man. Come on. I'm already going cross-eyed from all this."

"I'll help."

Trey stretched his arms and yawned. "So, you think we're looking at a rich white boy poser here?" he said, gazing at the photo of Edgar Clayton.

"Could be. One of two."

"But who's the other?

TWENTY-THREE

Laurel's cell phone rang as the detectives were taking a break after two long hours of video review. It was Officer Bradley calling to let Laurel know that the veterinarian, Eldon Ridgeway, was at Churchill Downs, making the rounds at that very moment. Officer Bradley thought Ridgeway looked drunk.

"Perfect," Laurel said. "We'll be right there. We owe you a beer."

"Yeah, you do."

ılılılılıl

At the Churchill Downs backside, Laurel and Trey split up to cover a wider area, each taking position where they could keep a lookout over the busiest entry and exit points of each of the two main clusters of stable buildings.

"Got him," Trey told Laurel over his handheld radio. "Looks like he's headed for the parking lot by the chapel that backs to 4th Street."

"Stay with him. I'll grab the car and meet you there."

Trey watched Ridgeway get into a maroon Pontiac Grand Am and back out of his parking space. As Ridgeway drove off, Laurel raced up in the Taurus, picked up Trey, and turned to pursue. They caught up with him just as he was exiting onto 4th Street, then followed him north at a discreet distance. It didn't take long for them to see what they were watching for. Ridgeway's Pontiac was drifting from side to side as he drove along.

"He's weaving," Trey said.

"Big time. Set up the lights," Laurel said, referring to the portable dashboard police lights they kept under the passenger seat.

Trey put the police lights on the dash and turned them on. Ridgeway drove for another two blocks, not seeming to notice. Laurel flashed her high beams at him, then gave a series of short honks of the horn. At that, Ridgeway pulled to the curb, running his tires up against it so hard that Trey was amazed the sidewalls didn't rupture.

Laurel and Trey approached Ridgeway's car from opposite sides.

"License and registration," Laurel said as Ridgeway opened his driver's side window and tried to look composed while Trey looked on from the far side of the car.

Ridgeway struggled to focus on Laurel's face. "You're that woman," he said, his eyes glassy and bloodshot. "At the, at the Barnstone's stall."

"License and registration, sir."

"What are the charges?"

"Sir?"

"Charges. What are the charges?"

"There aren't any charges, sir."

"Cause I didn't do what they—then how come you...." Ridgeway lost his train of thought.

"You didn't *do what they* what?" Laurel asked. But Ridgeway just stared, trying so hard to keep it together. "Alright. Step out of the car, please, Dr. Ridgeway."

*****

As expected, Ridgeway failed all three phases of the field sobriety test— blowing the one-leg stand in spectacular fashion by closing his eyes, losing his balance, and falling backward onto a large pile of dog crap in the grass flanking the sidewalk. Realizing something was amiss as he struggled to his feet, he reached a hand around his hip to feel the back of his pants, then brought it around to see that it was smeared with excrement. He stared at it with a drunkard's intensity, then gave a weak moan.

"Dr. Ridgeway, you were driving under the influence in violation of KRS 189A.010," Laurel said, showing him the citation form she'd filled out while Trey was administering the FST. "Having run your driver's license, I can see that you probably already have that statute number memorized, since this is your third offense." Ridgeway leaned against his car with his hands in his pockets, slouching, looking dejected, stinking of dog crap. He didn't say anything. "But today could be your lucky day."

Ridgeway looked up at her. "Right."

"Tell you what. I'll tear up this citation, and we'll let you off the hook this one time if you just answer a couple of simple questions for us. But you have to be completely honest. If I find out you lied to us, I'll file this citation and we'll suspend your license, fine you, and throw you in the can. Are we clear on that?"

"What questions?" Ridgeway asked.

"You work with the Barnstone people. With their horse, Empire Builder."

"So what?"

"You know their jockey, Javier Cervantes, was murdered."

"I don't know anything about that."

"You know he was murdered."

"Yes. But I didn't...I don't—"

"Did you have occasion to interact with Cervantes at any point in the week before he was killed?"

"Occasion to interact?" Ridgeway asked in the slow voice of a drunk. "Who are you supposed to be, William F. Buckley?"

"Did you talk to him?"

Ridgeway paused and looked at the ground. "No.".

"Did *he* talk to *you*?"

Ridgeway continued to stare at the ground.

"Dr. Ridgeway. Did Cervantes talk to you?" she asked again.

"Yes."

"About what?"

"I don't know. About the horse. I talk to lots of people about lots of horses. I don't remember all of what the hell they tell me."

"Did Cervantes mention a horse named Swizzle Stick?"

At this, Ridgeway locked eyes with her for a split second. "What horse?" he asked, sounding more surprised than unable to hear.

"Swizzle Stick. Last year's Kentucky Derby runner-up. Winner of the Belmont Stakes. Auctioned off to Barnstone Farm."

"Yeah. Yeah, he did."

"What did he say?"

"He wanted to know if I'd ever worked with Swizzle Stick before."

"And had you?"

"No."

"But...."

"But then he wanted me to look at Empire Builder's lip. To look at where its identification number was tattooed on," he said, slurring the word *identification*.

"And did you notice anything noteworthy about Empire Builder's lip?"

"Had what might have been a thin scar that ran the length of it. Couldn't say for sure."

"What did you make of it?"

"What could I make of it? So the horse might have had a scar on its lip. So what?"

"You didn't have any suspicions?"

"Of what?"

"What else did Cervantes say?"

"Nothing."

"Did you ever mention this conversation to the Barnstone people? Be straight with us, or you go to jail right now."

Ridgeway stared at her, his watery eyes bitter. "No. I didn't mention it to the Barnstone people. I didn't mention it to anyone. Why would I have?"

*****

The detectives called a taxi for Ridgeway and sent him home. As the cab rolled away, Trey said, "Do you believe him?"

"To a point. He harbors his own suspicions, clearly. But I don't think he told anyone about his conversation with Cervantes. Still, that doesn't get the Barnstone people off the hook. If anything, Cervantes's conversation with Ridgeway tells us that Cervantes was asking around about Swizzle Stick. Maybe he talked to other people. Maybe it got back to the Barnstone people. Maybe it provoked them."

TWENTY-FOUR

George Rucff called again as the detectives sat in a traffic jam on their way back to the office.

"What's the word, Georgie boy?" Laurel asked.

"Got a new suspect to add to our list."

"Don't we have enough already?"

"Just interviewed a colleague and *former* friend of Paul's widow, Mimi Taylor, down at Humana. This lady was all too eager to dish the dirt. Turns out Mimi is having an affair. Has a boyfriend, name of Chad Brody. Ten years her senior. Priors include one count each for third-degree assault, first-degree stalking, second-degree stalking, and driving under the influence. Has three months of parole left for the second-degree stalking charge."

"Third-degree assault can mean attacking a police officer."

"Or various other public officials. In this case it was his high school PE teacher. I guess Chad didn't want to do any more pushups. That got him expelled a mere two months short of graduation."

"And probably kicked out of MENSA."

"Yes. And he'd just turned 18, so he got to spend 16 fun-filled weeks in Metro Corrections before being granted pretrial diversion. But—and I know this will shock both of you—despite Chad's heartfelt promises to adhere to the terms of the pretrial diversion, the experience failed to rehabilitate the young man."

"Goodness gracious," Laurel said.

"I'm afraid so. Six months later, he was back in for the first stalking charge. And here's something else worth thinking about. Apparently Paul told his dear wife, Mimi, that he was funding the startup of Bacchus Distribution with a big pile of money he inherited from a great uncle who died in Phoenix, Arizona in February."

"February?" Laurel said. "Bacchus Distribution opened in March. So probate only took a month? I don't think so."

"But he told his parents the money came from his business partner," Trey said. "Why would he tell his wife something else?"

"Good question," Rueff said, promising to email his interview report as he hung up.

"So which story is true?" Trey asked.

"Well, I imagine Paul's parents would have known if a relative had just died and left Paul money," Laurel said.

"Still, if this Chad guy believed the inheritance story, then he had motive to bump off Paul so that he and Mimi could get their hands on the money."

"Good point. Turn the car around. Let's go have a word with Mimi Taylor."

TWENTY-FIVE

Roses seemed to be blooming in every yard they drove past as they wound their way down toward the Taylor residence. Roses of all sizes and colors. Laurel had her window down, trying to catch their scent.

"Sounds like Mimi is a bit of a tramp," Trey said, reading Rueff's interview report on his smartphone. "According to her coworker-slash-former friend at Humana, our grieving widow is a kiss-ass of a personal assistant who is happy to commit unladylike acts for the sake of promotion or getting to go on fancy trips with upper-level management."

"Lovely."

"And let's not forget that that's in addition to her running around behind her late husband's back with this Chad Brody guy."

The Taylors lived near Lakeside Swim Club—a magnificent aquatic facility of sapphire water set up in an old rock quarry. Laurel and Trey pulled to the curb in front of a small, brick, mid-century home with two small dormers and a tiny well-kept yard. The air smelled of newly mowed lawn. It was a cute little place where you'd expect to find the archetypal all-American young family—but for the dirty, dented, sinister-looking black muscle car parked in the short driveway.

As they approached the front door, Laurel could see that a television was on, displaying what looked like a reality show set in a beach house full of scantily-clad 20-somethings. Opposite the television, a pair of hairy male legs rested on a coffee table that held an empty pizza box, five beer bottles, a baggie of something green, and a tall red bong.

Laurel gave the door a loud, annoying knock. There was a commotion inside—falling beer bottles and cursing. For half a minute, nothing happened. Laurel pictured Chad standing just on the other side of the door, deliberating over whether to open it—not wanting to, but sure that whoever was at the door had heard his commotion and knew he was there. Knowing that if he didn't open the door, it would seem suspicious. It was a dilemma that his drunk and stoned brain was probably having trouble sorting out.

She gave the door another hard, compelling knock. At last, Chad opened it a few inches and peered out with bloodshot eyes. He had a three-day beard and thinning, unkempt, dirty black hair. His threadbare T-shirt said *Saint X Football*.

"What?" he asked.

"Is Mimi here?"

"What do you want?"

"Is Mimi here?"

"No."

"And you are?"

"I are busy."

"Busy?"

"Yeah. I have to go," he said, making a show of digging car keys out of the front pocket of his jean shorts. As he opened the door a bit wider, Laurel could see that he was out of shape, with a distended, hanging belly of the sort she associated with people who drank more beer than water.

"You taking that fast-looking black car in the driveway?"

"Yeah. Gotta go."

"Where to?"

He stood silent.

"You're Chad, aren't you? Chad Brody. Making yourself at home on Mimi's couch one day after her husband's funeral."

"Husband? That dandelion was no husband to her. Anyway, what difference—"

"Tell me something, Chad. Are violations of KRS 218A.1422 cool under the terms of your parole? Or would that get you sent back to jail, you think?"

"I don't know what you're talking about."

"I'm talking about the bag of weed and the big red bong you were sleeping next to, sitting in plain view on the coffee table, dumbass."

"It's not mine."

"Right. Tell you what. You can answer a few quick questions, or we can come in and seize your paraphernalia. And you."

He glared at them. "Shit. Shit. Fine."

"Where's Mimi?"

"With her boss."

"Who is her boss?"

"I don't know his name. He's some corporate dickhead at Humana."

"Where are they?"

"How should I know? They fly off in a private jet all the time. Off to another fancy hotel. Maybe D.C. Maybe New York."

"She isn't in town?"

"Left this morning. Back in two days."

"Okay. Let's talk about you."

"What about me?"

"Where were you at 9 p.m. last Friday?"

"Last Friday? Out."

"Out where?"

"Chuck E. Cheese, on Hurstbourne Parkway."

"Chuck E. Cheese."

"Yes."

"You were at Chuck E. Cheese."

"That's what I said."

"What were you doing at Chuck E. Cheese?" she asked, trying not to grin, half wondering whether Chad might be a pedophile.

"What do you think? I was playing video games."

"And someone can vouch for you being at Chuck E. Cheese at 9 p.m. last Friday?"

"My friends, Dwayne and Ricky."

"Dwayne and Ricky who?"

Chad gave their full names and numbers without hesitation. It probably wasn't the first time he'd had to provide police with an alibi.

"So when my partner here calls these numbers while you and I continue our chat," Laurel said, "Dwayne and Ricky are going to tell him that the three of you were playing Pac-Man at Chuck E. Cheese the other night, right? Because if they don't, you know how this is going to go."

"Yes. Shit. Yes."

"What do you know about Paul's liquor distribution business?"

"Nothing."

"Do you know where he got the money to start it up?"

At this, Chad's face changed. He went from looking irritated and nervous to looking utterly bitter.

"Chad? Did you hear my question? Where did Paul get his money?"

"Why don't you ask his partner," Chad said, affecting an exaggerated lisp.

"Who was his partner?"

Chad was fuming. It was clear that he didn't want to answer the question. Perhaps he had violent plans for Paul's partner.

"Chad, I'll ask you one last time before we take a very different course here," Laurel said, taking out her handcuffs. "Who was Paul's partner?"

Chad glanced at the cuffs Laurel held in her hand. His face was as flushed and hateful as could be. "His partner was Benjamin," Chad said with the same lisp. "Sweet, sweet Benjamin."

"Benjamin who?"

"Sweet Benjamin Clayton. Paul's very special friend."

*****

"Looks like Chad's alibi holds water," Trey said, ending a call as they drove away from Paul and Mimi Taylor's house. "Dwayne and Ricky both confirmed that the three of them were at Chuck E. Cheese the night of Paul's murder."

"Bummer. Part of me really wanted to arrest Chad. Or better yet, have him resist."

"Then why don't we just bust him for the dope?"

"Might still need that leverage on him down the road, depending on what we find out."

"What do you suppose Chad's malfunction is?" Trey asked.

"Usual story. He didn't get enough love as a child."

"You're probably right. I'm starting to think that people should have to get a permit to be allowed to have children,"

"And you should be in charge of the approval process."

Trey smiled. "So did Chad mean that Paul Taylor and this Benjamin Clayton guy were partners, or that they were *partners*?"

"Maybe both. It could explain why he told his wife that he came into his startup money via inheritance instead of a mysterious, hidden partner."

"Do you think Benjamin Clayton could be related to the Clayton Bourbon Claytons?"

"Let's find out. I know someone at the Courier-Journal who's plugged into all things bourbon and booze around here."

"Food first."

"Of course. Where to?"

"We're close to Morris' Deli, up on Taylorsville Road," Trey said. "Good smoked tuna sandwiches."

"I like their egg salad."

"Mmmm. Maybe I'll have both. And then we should swing by The Café on Brent Street for a big to-go slice of their Italian cream cake. Or the bread pudding."

"They closed at 4. And you're insane."

TWENTY-SIX

After devouring their sandwiches from Morris' Deli, Laurel and Trey drove to the downtown offices of the Louisville Courier-Journal—a venerable, Pulitzer Prize-winning newspaper, struggling to continue providing the region with a reliable source of local news in an era when many traditional American papers were defunct or sliding toward oblivion.

"You know what?" Laurel said as they approached the front door. "Don't mention the Claytons just yet."

"Got it."

After being offered coffee, the detectives were ushered back to the office of Joy Brashear, a well-informed staff writer to whom Laurel had turned for insider information on local goings on many times in the past. She was behind one of those trendy stand-up desks, her legs and feet pumping up and down on an under-desk, mini elliptical exercise device.

"Laurel!"

"Hello, Joy. This is my current Tonto, Trey Hewson."

"Trey," she said, coming out from behind her desk to shake hands. "Pleasure." She directed the detectives to a couple office chairs, leaned against a file cabinet next to her desk, picked up a well-worn tennis ball, and began bouncing it against one of the walls. "So, what can I tell you?" she asked.

"We're wondering if you've heard any rumors of criminal shenanigans in the bourbon circles," Laurel said.

"Is this about the Paul Taylor murder?"

"What makes you say that?"

"Give me a little credit."

Laurel smiled and looked at the floor.

"You don't have to tell me if you don't want to," Brashear said. "I'll help, regardless."

"Well. Off the record?"

"Off the record," Joy said, still bouncing the ball.

Laurel waited for Joy to stop bouncing the ball. She didn't.

"Forget to take your Ritalin today?" Laurel said.

Joy caught the ball, held it, and smiled. "Is it obvious?"

"Not at all. And yes, we're investigating the Taylor murder."

"I thought that old off-season Santa Claus-looking detective—what's his name—George Rueff caught that one," Joy said, giving the tennis ball one final bounce off the wall before setting it on her desk and starting to tap her right foot.

"He did. Turns out there may be some crossover with another case we caught a couple days later."

"Related cases. Juicy. You going to give me an exclusive when you break it open?"

"We'll see, Joy."

"Okay, then. To answer your question, yes, there are loud rumors in the bourbon circles that young Paul Taylor was using underhanded methods to get himself admitted to the ultra-exclusive club of Kentucky liquor distribution."

"What do you mean by underhanded methods?"

"Nobody seems sure what he was up to. But the most persistent rumors involve either bribes or blackmail."

"Taylor was 21 years old," Laurel said. "If he was bribing people, where did he get his money?" she asked, declining to mention Taylor's possible invisible partner, *sweet Benjamin Clayton.*

"Exactly," Brashear said. "That's why I favor the blackmail theory. Plus, I would think that in this day and age, if you can find even a half decent hacker, you can probably pull some good blackmail material off the computer or smartphone of one of our state liquor control officials without too much trouble."

"That complicates things," Trey said. "Maybe Taylor tried to blackmail the wrong legislator or liquor control officer."

"Blackmail doesn't usually bring out the best in people," Laurel said. "Have you heard any rumblings about particular officials who Taylor may have been trying to manipulate?" she asked Brashear.

"Sorry. Nothing specific. But I would start with the person who granted Taylor his distribution license, and work your way up the ladder from there. Because I'll tell you what—given the stranglehold the old-school distributors supposedly have on the state capitol, whoever made the decision to grant Taylor a license probably did it under duress."

TWENTY-SEVEN

The next morning, after a monotonous 50-mile drive from Louisville, and having been given cups of scorched coffee from the communal office coffee pot, Laurel and Trey sat across a faux oak desk from Ernie Trotter IV—commissioner of the Kentucky Alcohol Beverage Control Board—at his office in a nondescript, low-rise building just off of Interstate 64 on the outskirts of the state capital of Frankfort. Laurel thought Trotter's taste in clothes looked to have stopped progressing when the 1980s hoity-toity golf course clubhouse look was still in style—if it ever was. His blue blazer, with its padded shoulders and gold buttons, was too big for him. Underneath, he wore a permanent press white button down with an oversized collar and no tie. He also had a large, showy watch of some kind, and a gigantic high school class ring with a fake ruby. To Laurel, he looked like a two-bit used car salesman or a church usher.

Having offered no advance warning as to the reason for their visit, Laurel went straight for the jugular. "Commissioner, did anyone—and I mean anyone at all, from inside or outside of the state government—direct or in any way pressure you to approve the liquor distribution license for Paul Taylor or his company, Bacchus Distribution?"

Trotter went rigid. "No. No, of course not."

"You're sure? Not even a hint of pressure?"

"No."

Laurel locked eyes with Trotter.

"Your office is in charge of approving such licenses, correct?"

"Yes, but I—"

"And as commissioner, you have the final word on license approval?"

"I serve at the pleasure of the—what, I mean, what is this about?"

"We're investigating Paul Taylor's murder."

"He was murdered?"

"You hadn't heard? He was shot to death last week at his new distribution business in Louisville. So here we are."

Trotter paused before saying anything else. "I don't have to talk to you, do I? I mean, you can't compel me."

"That's an odd thing to ask," Laurel said, still staring at him. "To answer your question, no, we can't compel you to talk. At least not yet. And Mr. Trotter, you are, at this point, in no way a suspect. But you did just tell us, clearly and unequivocally, that you were neither directed nor pressured to approve that license. So I'm now obliged to tell you, as I tell everyone I interview, that it's a crime to make false statements to the police. In other words, whenever we have a situation where, somewhere down the road, we find out someone told us something false, then we have to charge them. Our state prosecutors don't take lying to the police lightly. I don't say this because I suspect you. I'm just pointing out how things work. The flip side, of course, is that even if people make false statements, if they retract them before we rely on them in our investigations, then all is forgiven. You follow?"

Trotter had turned white. He was staring through his desk.

"I...."

"Follow?"

"I think...."

"You think?" Laurel suppressed a smirk. Trotter remained quiet, so she went on. "Sometimes people will lie to police thinking they're doing the right thing by covering for a friend. Or they do it because they're afraid of retaliation from superiors at their place of work. It's understandable. I mean, people fear for their friends. Fear for their livelihood. They have families to feed. Kids to send to college. But, Mr. Trotter, the truth always comes out at some point. And then the ones who lied are the ones who take the fall. Lose their jobs. Go to jail. Face humiliation with their family, friends, and colleagues. The good news is, at least in the workplace, there are laws that protect you from retaliation. Whistleblower laws. You probably heard about them in your new state employee orientation seminar back when—"

"McKittrick," Trotter whispered as he exhaled.

"Pardon?"

Trotter's eyes met Laurel's. He looked surprised, as though he couldn't believe what he'd just said. But then his face hardened.

"Riley McKittrick," he said with a look of disgust.

"Who is Riley McKittrick?"

"Senator from the 26th District. Vice chair of the Kentucky Senate Standing Committee on Licensing, Occupations, and Administrative Regulations. Self-righteous, power-tripping son of a whore."

"Senator McKittrick asked you to approve Paul Taylor's liquor distribution permit?"

Trotter looked out the window and scowled. "Asked? No. Told. Comes in one day, slaps the permit application on my desk, and tells me to sign it right then and there. I tell him, no, Riley. That isn't how we do things here." He looked at Laurel. "I try to run a clean ship, you know? I want you to know that. Despite all the crooked sons of bitches who try to twist my tail, who try to corrupt us to make us do what they want—the distributors, the liquor store chain owners, the distillers, the restaurant guilds, and all their greasy, well-dressed, BMW-driving lobbyists—I try to run a clean ship. I just want people to follow the rules. Have an even playing field. I hate it when people try to cheat. And all for what? The almighty dollar."

"Well, Mr. Trotter," Laurel said. "Some of us appreciate your efforts. Personally, I despise the idea of back-door dealing." She shook her head. "Rich and powerful people always pulling strings and getting their way."

Hearing this, Trotter's frown eased a bit. He took a deep breath before going on. "Senator McKittrick, being the vice chair of the committee that oversees us, has a lot of power. And he's good friends with the governor who appointed me and has the power to fire me. I serve at their pleasure, as McKittrick reminded me. Twice."

"We understand. Nobody needs to know we spoke. In fact, we'd *prefer* that nobody knew. And if someday it gets to the point where you have to give sworn testimony in court, I don't think you'll need to worry about Senator McKittrick anymore."

TWENTY-EIGHT

Trey, who had never been to Frankfort, wanted to take the long way down to Senator McKittrick's office and see a bit of the town, so they drove around and came in from the far side of the city. Away from the fast food and sprawl of the main roads between the Capitol and I-64, it was a beautiful place, with magnificent old trees and quaint, quiet neighborhoods of well-kept 19th and early 20th century houses. Pink and white dogwoods were blooming in many of the yards.

Eventually, the detectives came to an old business district that looked forgotten by time, with stately brick office buildings and warehouses, some of which had been repurposed as restaurants and coffee shops. As they turned onto an old bridge over the wide, meandering Kentucky River, the Capitol Building came into view dead ahead.

"The new Capitol Building was built in 1910," Laurel said.

"That's the *new* one, huh? There weren't even 50 states in 1910."

It was a majestic structure—all the more impressive the closer they got—built of granite and marble, in a sort of hybrid of the French beaux arts and neoclassical architectural styles. It had tall pillars and pediments reminiscent of the grand federal buildings of Washington, D.C., along with a striking 190-foot dome at its center. But Laurel and Trey weren't going to the main Capitol Building. Senator McKittrick's office was housed in the Capitol Annex office building across the street. And the back side of *it*, where they had to park, had a dull, utilitarian face of pale brick and uniformly square windows that to Laurel's eye made it look an awful lot like a 1950s-era mental hospital. This struck her as entirely appropriate given her opinion of its occupants.

Inside, the air smelled of cheap coffee, dust, and furniture wax. There was also a trace of an odor that reminded Laurel of dirty ashtrays—probably from off-gassing residues in air ducts that hadn't been cleaned since before the smoking ban.

When the detectives arrived at the senator's office suite and explained who they were, an exceptionally polite old secretary in his waiting room showed them right to his private office, explaining that the senator would be back from his meeting with the Judiciary Committee in just a minute or two. They took seats in two enormous, reproduction wingback chairs that faced the senator's vacant desk. The desk was bare but for a well-worn Bible in one corner and a gold, 8-inch tall desktop Christian cross that stood on a small pedestal in the other. The front of the cross had the stars and stripes of the American flag painted onto it. On the wall behind the desk, in a large gilded frame, was a curiously amateurish airbrushed painting of Golgotha—the hill of three crosses where Jesus Christ was crucified—with a biblical psalm quoted alongside it. It read, *For the Lord loves the just and will not forsake his faithful ones. Wrongdoers will be completely destroyed; the offspring of the wicked will perish.*

"Doesn't exactly give you the warm fuzzies, does it?" Laurel asked Trey, gesturing to the painting.

"Maybe it just means he's a good, honest man."

"Did you bump your head on something? Number one, he's a politician. Number two, in my experience, the more in-your-face a person is with their self-righteousness, the more skeletons they have hiding in their closet. You could almost call it a law of nature."

"Don't be so cynical."

"Gentlemen, sorry to keep you waiting," a deeply-accented country southern voice said from behind them.

They rose and turned to see Senator Riley McKittrick walking into the room.

"Oh, gentleman and *lady*. My apologies."

He had a full head of silver hair, conservative wire frame glasses, and a politician's practiced smile.

"These committee meetings can really drag on," he said, taking a seat behind his desk. "Everyone wants to get their name in the transcript, even if they don't have anything useful to add."

For Laurel, his voice brought to mind Foghorn Leghorn, the dimwitted southern gentleman rooster from the classic Warner Brothers cartoons. "No worries, Senator," she said. "We just got here."

"What can I do for you?" he asked, looking at Trey, even though it was Laurel who'd addressed him.

"We're investigating a homicide," Laurel said. "And we think you might have knowledge that could help us out."

"A homicide?" he asked, still looking at Trey instead of Laurel.

"Did you know a man named Paul Taylor?" Laurel asked.

"Paul Taylor," McKittrick repeated, as if searching his memory. "I don't think so. I mean, the name sounds familiar. But I can't put a finger on why. Of course, there *are* a whole lot of Taylors out there."

"He was a newly-christened liquor distributor in Louisville. By all accounts a fine young man, barely out of high school."

Laurel thought McKittrick's expression changed just a hair when she said the words *fine young man*. Just a passing twitch of scowl.

"I take it he's the victim?"

"He was shot to death in Louisville last Friday night."

With the flip of some probably oft-used internal switch, McKittrick put on an outraged face. "Oh, that's terrible. Just terrible. Whether I knew him or not, I'm sorry to hear that. My heart goes out to his family. These are violent times."

"They are, indeed."

"Now, of course, if I'm a *suspect*," he said with a sudden hint of a conspiratorial grin, "I can assure you that I was at a town hall meeting at the American Legion Post in La Grange that night. At least two dozen witnesses can confirm this."

Laurel forced a chuckle. "No, sir. I can assure you that isn't necessary."

"Then how can I help you?"

"It's just a case of certain information in the file leading us to believe that you might have known Taylor, or might have known something about his affairs that could prove useful to us."

"What sort of information? If you give me a hint, it might help jog my memory. At my age, the brain starts to resemble Swiss cheese, you know. I need all the help I can get when it comes to recall. Ha-ha."

"Unfortunately, we aren't at liberty to disclose anything from the case file, senator. Suffice it to say, something one of our detectives found in Louisville prompted our chain of command to send us out here to ask you about things."

McKittrick leaned back in his chair. "Huh. Well, I'm stumped."

"But you said the name Paul Taylor sounded familiar. Could you have been acquainted through his involvement in liquor distribution?"

"I don't think so."

"Or socially?"

"I doubt it. I'm 62 years old. Don't get out much. The wife wouldn't tolerate it. And even if she did, I don't have the energy. Ha-ha."

TWENTY-NINE

After a quick stop for awful gas station coffee and a long drive back to the office, they divided up tasks. With a list of license plates observed by Real Time Crime Center cameras in the vicinity of the Taylor murder scene on Friday night, Trey was searching for a registration match for Edgar Clayton's black Cadillac Escalade, as well as any associated video footage. Meanwhile, Laurel did what she could to find out what business and social ties Senator McKittrick had in the Louisville area. Church and club memberships. Property holdings. Court filings. Anything that might help paint a picture of his life. Anything that could give them an idea of the universe he ran in, and whether there was any apparent crossover with Paul Taylor's universe. She made calls. She queried databases. She scoured the internet. But nothing jumped out. McKittrick had been married for 43 years. His wife was a homemaker. His two daughters were grown—one living in Pensacola, Florida, the other in Reno, Nevada. He attended a shrinking Disciples of Christ congregation in east Oldham County. He was a member of the celebrated Valhalla Golf Club. He owned several Burger King franchises. He had no criminal record. No civil court record aside from a long-settled suit involving a property drainage dispute with a neighbor. No bankruptcy filings. Nothing to indicate that he'd be susceptible to bribery or blackmail.

However, barely two hours after getting back to the office, Trey arrived at Laurel's cubicle with a big grin on his face.

"You're looking self-satisfied," Laurel said.

He put his laptop on Laurel's desk and showed her a video capture of Edgar Clayton's Escalade driving west on Broadway at 8:58 p.m. on the night of the Taylor murder.

"That's great, Trey. Now show me the Escalade at the actual crime scene," she said, meaning the 800 block of South 11th Street, just *south* of Broadway. The street fronting Bacchus Distribution.

"Yeah. Here's the thing. The RTCC doesn't have a camera covering that exact block. It's a minor side-street."

"Can you at least put Edgar's Escalade right at 11th and Broadway?"

"Ah, well, no."

"No?"

"Turns out some hoodlum shot the lens out of that particular camera a few weeks ago and it hadn't been fixed yet. The closest footage we have is what I just showed you, covering Broadway, just about four blocks east of 11th.

With a little more searching, they found footage from the same camera showing the Escalade leaving the area, eastbound on Broadway, at 9:11 p.m.— roughly two minutes after ShotSpotter recorded the sound of the gunfire that killed Taylor.

"I think Edgar Clayton and his unidentified henchman killed Paul Taylor," Trey said. "And then, after they realized that Javier Cervantes overheard them talking about it at Churchill Downs two nights later, they strangled *him*, moved the body to the poor guy's garage, and did a crap job of trying to make it look like a suicide."

"Could be," Laurel said. "I wish we had enough evidence to request Edgar's cell phone location records. I bet they'd put him right in the 800 block of 11th Street that night."

"We don't have enough evidence yet?"

"The Claytons own a horse in a stall next to Empire Builder's, so Edgar has a perfectly good excuse for being there the night of the Cervantes murder. And if our RTCC footage only puts him within four blocks of the Taylor murder, that's a radius that might cover 200 people that night. No, we don't have enough evidence yet."

"Well, probable cause aside, why would Edgar Clayton and his henchman want to kill Paul Taylor? Clayton is from a bourbon family, and Taylor was a liquor distributor. Wouldn't it be in their mutual best interest to get along? Was it a business deal gone bad?"

"Good question. Let's go learn more about Edgar Clayton and his clan."

"Where do we go to do that?"

"Back to Perry Clark, dummy."

Trey smirked. "I should have known better than to ask."

THIRTY

Back in the green velvet chairs, facing Perry Clark across the coffee table at the Browning Historical Society—the usual bottle of Martell cognac having been handed over—Laurel and Trey asked for background on the Clayton family.

"Oh, the Claytons!" Perry chirped with delight. "Louisville's own version of Falcon Crest or Dynasty. Wealth, ambition, and conquest!" he cried. "Scandal, crime, and ruin! Mental illness, suicide, family feuds!"

"Intriguing," Laurel said.

"Oh, honey. You have no idea. It all starts with a local legend involving Carter "Peepaw" Clayton himself. Make yourselves comfortable and cast your minds all the way back to April, in the year of Our Lord 1865."

"Wait a second," Laurel said.

"No, no, dear. Indulge me. April, 1865. It's the waning days of the Civil War. Robert E. Lee's battered Army of Northern Virginia is encircled by Grant's Union forces near the tiny Virginia town of Appomattox, having fled the Confederate capital of Richmond. According to the legend, General Lee's last hope involves a fortune in Confederate gold and an attempt to bribe a corrupt Union colonel who has promised to accidentally-on-purpose move his entire brigade out of position for several hours, opening a two-mile-wide gap of Virginia forest through which Lee's army could escape southward in the night to join with General Joseph E. Johnston's army of 89,000 soldiers down in North Carolina. Incidentally, it seems Confederate generals were very proud the middle initial *e*."

"Perry," Laurel said. "I'm sure this is a great story. But time is of the essence."

"Don't be a killjoy, my dear. And remember, the past is the key to the present. We are each of us, for better or for worse, influenced by our ancestors' character. Going all the way back to the Garden of Eden."

"Please, just the condensed version."

"In brief then, the Confederate gold disappeared, two of the three soldiers delivering it to the corrupt Union colonel were found with their throats cut, General Lee was forced to surrender, and a year later, Carter Clayton, a carpetbagger nobody had ever heard of—a man with no verifiable backstory—arrived in Louisville with an inexhaustible bank account. I only say this because there was a persistent rumor that Carter was the third soldier. The murderous deserter and trickster who made off with the Confederate gold. The rumor was enough to eventually cause a schism in the family that persists to this day, between the offspring of Carter's scoundrel sons, Lucian and Carter Junior. Now then, Carter Senior's wife, Minerva, was a real upper-crust Louisville socialite and dimwit with a penchant for drinking too much absinthe and then dancing without wearing a—."

"Perry. I'm begging you."

"Fine." Perry took a sip of cognac. "It ruins the story. But I'll do it in bullet points. One, Carter opens the original Clayton bourbon distillery on the Kentucky River, out in Port Royal, in 1886 and starts calling himself Peepaw. In a few years, Carter "Peepaw" Clayton is running one of the biggest distilling and distribution operations in the U.S. Builds himself a big mansion in Glenview. Buys his way into all the clubs that matter. Never mind that he's an infamous drunk, philanderer, and knave, rumored to have murdered his two partners in the bourbon business after things got rolling. Still with me? Okay. Two, the King Lear phase. Peepaw divides his empire between his two equally horrible sons, Carter Junior and Lucian, with Lucian getting the distillery and Carter Junior getting the distribution business. Then Peepaw promptly kicks the bucket. Three, Prohibition hits in 1920. Lucian has to shut down the distillery. He's ruined. But Carter Junior thrives, turning the distribution business into a bootlegging outfit working with Al Capone. In the meantime, Lucian has an affair with Carter Junior's wife. Four, Prohibition ends in 1933, and Lucian asks Carter Junior for money to restart the old Distillery. Carter Junior, aware of Lucian's dalliance with his wife, tells him to stick it. Five, a few years later, Carter Junior, being a good brother, offers to buy the mothballed family distillery from Lucian for pennies on the dollar. Desperate, Lucian agrees, getting just enough money from the sale to set up a cigarette factory in Louisville. Six, rumors surface that, while clearing the ruble of one of the distillery buildings that burned down after being hit by lightning, Carter Junior found, in the hollow of an old wall, a fortune in gold ingots stamped with the seal of the Confederacy. Seven, the great flood of 1937 destroys Lucian's cigarette factory. He comes to Carter Junior again, cap in hand, having heard the rumors about the gold. Carter Junior once again tells him to stick it, infuriating his dear brother. Eight, Carter Junior builds an entirely *new* Clayton Distillery, in South Louisville, in 1938—really rubbing it in Lucian's face." Perry paused for another sip of cognac.

"And the point of the story is?" Laurel said.

"The point," Perry said, "is that the two sides of the family hate each other going all the way back to Peepaw and his two scoundrel sons."

"Great. So where do things stand now?

"As of now, in addition to being a retired but legendary philanderer in his own right, grumpy old Carter IV is an uber-rich bourbon baron who is grooming his dope of a son, Edgar, to take over the business. Carter IV's oldest daughter killed herself at age 23, his middle daughter is estranged, living in a crumbling monstrosity of a Queen Anne house in Old Louisville and enjoying life as a plein air painter of some repute, and his youngest daughter is a resident of Central State Psychiatric Hospital. On the other side of the family, Lucian's last living heir, Benjamin, is the proverbial aging bachelor, trying to figure out how to salvage the legacy of his side of the family."

Laurel and Trey shot each other glances at Perry's mention of Benjamin.

"So, not that it matters, but Carter IV is Carter Junior's grandson, while Benjamin is Lucian's grandson?" Laurel asked.

"Correct."

"This is like *Game of Thrones*," Trey said.

"And the two sides of the family *still* hate each other," Perry added. "My heavens, how they hate each other."

*****

"Do you think the Benjamin of Perry's story is *our* Benjamin—Paul Taylors partner and/or *partner*?" Trey asked as they strode toward their car, down a sun-dappled sidewalk, under the partial shade of ancient magnolia trees.

"I'd say that's a pretty good bet."

"So Benjamin and Carter Clayton IV hate each other because of a never-ending family feud. Fine. But that doesn't explain why Edgar Carter would want to kill Paul Taylor."

"The old man sure sounds like a creep."

"Carter IV?" Trey asked.

"Let's just call him Carter, to keep things simple. Definite creep."

"Yeah, but there are creeps, and then there are *creeps*."

"I think we should go back to Joy Brashear at the Courier-Journal," Laurel said.

"This time can I mention the Claytons?"

"You can ask her specifically about the Claytons."

THIRTY-ONE

It was just getting dark outside the windows of Joy Brashear's office at the Courier-Journal. Below, the street was jammed with cars headed to a Jim James concert at Louisville's grand and ornate Palace Theater.

"So now we're wondering if Edgar or Carter Clayton IV, of the bourbon Claytons, might be mixed up in any disputes or reheated vendettas that could inspire murder," Laurel said.

"This is still about the Taylor murder?"

"And still off the record."

"Well," Joy said, this time sitting in a normal office chair, not bouncing a ball, not tapping her foot, but staring at Laurel with intense, pharmaceutically-enhanced focus. "For starters, you already know that the Claytons are a household name with respect to bourbon distilling. But you may not know that they're *also* huge liquor distributors, meaning Paul Taylor was a potential competitor."

"I didn't think distillers could also be distributors," Trey said. "Isn't there still some screwball old Kentucky law about that?"

"There is," Joy said, shifting her laser beam gaze to Trey. "The infamous three-tier system, held over from the 1930s. It's why Kentucky distilleries, wineries, and breweries can't sell direct to grocery stores or restaurants. It all has to go through a distributor. It discourages entrepreneurs and screws the existing distillers, winemakers, beer brewers, restaurants, stores, and customers by limiting our choices and making everything cost more. It's why a six-pack of craft beer is $12. It's why most restaurants serve the exact same handful of boring wines year after year. In my opinion, the only people who benefit from the existing system are the distributors and their political stooges. It's protectionism."

"Sounds like something the French would do," Trey said. "But if the system is so ridiculous, why is it still the system?"

"Lobbying. Campaign contributions. God knows what. This is just my conjecture, mind you. So far, my evidence is circumstantial. The people involved aren't very forthcoming with me," she said with a devilish smile.

"So then how are the Claytons both distillers *and* distributors?" Laurel asked.

"The rules don't apply to the uber-wealthy, Laurel. You know that."

"How does it work in this particular case?"

"Using shell companies in Delaware and the Bahamas, and probably with the help of some campaign contribution-influenced looking the other way by certain state officials, Edgar Clayton's father, Carter, owns a controlling interest in a company called Redbud Wine and Spirits, Incorporated. One of the small handful of distributors that are allowed to operate in the state of Kentucky. So, on paper at least, Edgar Clayton's bourbon distilling business is a different company. But everybody knows old man Carter runs both companies. He just scratches the right backs."

"Corruption being used to get around rules that only exist because of other corruption," Trey said.

"Something like that," Brashear said.

"I should go into lobbying," Laurel said.

"You and me, both," Brashear said. "It's where all the money is. And I'll tell you something else. That old man, Carter, is a bona fide viper."

"Meaning he's cold-blooded enough to kill someone to suppress potential competition from a new distributor?"

"Well, I'm no headshrinker. But for my money, that guy is capable of anything. I don't know if you already knew this, but in the late 60s, Carter had a very public affair with a local paraplegic Vietnam War hero's wife. Bragged about it all over town. And he's an unrepentant bigot. Has quite the reputation as an internet troll. Likes to get on news and social media sites and post inflammatory anti-black, anti-Jew, anti-immigrant, anti-gay comments just for the fun of it. All under pseudonyms, of course."

"Good to know," Laurel said. "We'll try to look as white and straight as possible if we have to go interview him."

"A very good idea."

"What about his son, Edgar? Is he a creep too?"

Brashear shook her head. "Actually, he seems like a decent enough guy. A loser, but a kind loser. Doesn't seem all that enthusiastic about taking over the family business. Most of the time it looks like he doesn't know whether to check his ass or scratch his watch."

"There's another southern expression for you, Trey," Laurel said.

"Could just be that Edgar has a fool's face," Brashear added.

"How about Benjamin Clayton?"

"Benjamin Clayton. Huh. Isn't he Carter's estranged nephew or something?"

"Or something."

Brashear thought for a second, then shrugged her shoulders.

"So you haven't heard any rumblings about Benjamin being Paul Taylor's shadow partner in the distribution business? About him being Taylor's financial backer?"

"Afraid not. In fact, now that I think about it, I always heard Benjamin was more or less broke."

THIRTY-TWO

"Hey, you know what?" Trey said as they left the building. "This day is done. Let's clock out and go do something."

"What kind of something?"

"Go out somewhere."

"I was going to go to the range. Shoot a few courses of fire with my alley cleaner," she said, referring to her short-barrel Remington 870 shotgun.

"It's quarter to nine. The range is closed."

"I have a key."

"Of course you do." He looked at her. "Let me ask you something. Is this your job, Laurel, or is it your whole identity?"

"Hey, now."

"I'm serious. Life is short. You should be out there living it up. Not sitting in butt sweat-smelling Ford sedans, surveilling other peoples' crappy lives every other night, and then hiding in your depressing little condo."

"Depressing?"

"You live in a town that's on the edge of exploding onto the national scene, like Portland and Seattle were in the 1990s. And it's all right here waiting for you to reach out and touch it."

"What are you talking about?"

"I'm talking about Louisville and all of its musicians, artists, restaurateurs, brewers, craft distillers, entrepreneurs. Young people reviving grand old spaces into galleries and bars and music venues and whatnot. Making things happen. Let's check it out."

Laurel gave him a long look before answering. "So where would we go?"

"Anywhere. Where do you normally go?"

"I don't."

"Well, I'm not much of a dancer. But we could go see some music. Have you ever been to that semi-secret place that's in a cave down the street from

Headliners Music Hall? The Workhouse Ballroom, or whatever?"

"Never heard of it."

"It's this crazy thing. Owners of the house on the lot above it were working on their property when they found this old door in the ground. They opened it up and found a big, underground chamber. Nobody knows how old it is or what it was used for."

"Maybe it's where Peepaw hid his Confederate gold."

"The owners cleaned it up and turned it into an intimate, funky, underground concert venue."

"Literally underground."

"Yeah. And a good local band is playing there tonight. Frederick the Younger. They have a cool, very original sound. Or if you like classic stuff, Emily's Garden and Electric Garden are both playing at Zanzabar. They're both awesome. We should go."

"It's been a long day, Trey. I'm tired."

"Don't give me that crap. You were going to go to the range and shoot your shotgun."

"But tomorrow we have to—"

"Come on, Laurel. Life is passing us by."

She gave him a hard stare. "It wouldn't be a date. You understand that."

"Well, obviously."

*****

They stood on a dark stretch of Lexington Road, next to a stone wall cut into a sloping and forested hillside. In the middle of the wall, a drab steel door looked as if it would give access into the hillside itself. They could hear music playing on the other side of it. Trey gave the door a couple of hard knocks and it opened to reveal the glowing, arched interior of the cavernous Workhouse Ballroom. A band—presumably Frederick the Younger—was playing at the far end of the chamber. The space resembled an aging cave of an old European winery or cheesemaker. The air smelled of damp stone, sweating bodies, and incense.

"Get you a drink?" Trey shouted over the thumping music.

"Double Knob Creek with one ice cube."

"You're such a badass."

Laurel stood close to a wall in the back half of the space, feeling unsure of what to do with her hands. She put them in her pockets.

As Trey waited in line for their drinks, out of an unexpected sense of protectiveness, he kept looking back to check on her. And in reading her body language it occurred to him—not for the first time—that even though she was a self-assured ass-kicker while on the job, she was socially awkward. Out from behind the hard façade she wore as a detective, she looked like a fish out of water. Fearful, even. It was probably a big part of why she was alone. He wondered where her fear came from.

Regardless, when he went back and stood by her after getting their drinks, she seemed her relatively relaxed, normal self. She smiled a lot, which warmed his heart. They took turns entertaining each other by picking people out of the crowd and guessing what they were thinking based on their facial expressions: *That singer is hot. —Does my breath stink? I think maybe my breath stinks. —If my boyfriend keeps sneaking peeks at that slut in the tube top, I'm going to wait until he falls asleep tonight and then take a pair of scissors and....*

At one point, when they were at the bar ordering another round, Trey even got Laurel to laugh out loud. A hipster bartender was trying to convince her to try a new, small-batch bourbon instead of going with her usual Knob Creek. When she asked the bartender if he really thought it was better, Trey jumped in with the smart-ass comment, "Don't insult him, Laurel. He has a beard and a man bun. What more qualification as a bourbon expert does a guy need?"

After her laugh at the bartender's expense, Laurel acquiesced, then watched as the man placed one large cube of ice in her glass and filled it part way with a generous pour of a deep amber spirit. She parted her lips and held the glass to her nose, taking in its complex profile of aromas, then took a sip. To draw out the flavors, she swirled it all around in her mouth and smacked her lips as she swallowed, doing what bourbon legend Booker Noe of Jim Beam called the Kentucky Chew. It was excellent. Turning to thank him for pushing her to try something new, she found that Trey was staring at her with a flushed face and a stupid but adoring grin. *Uh-oh.*

Two rounds later, Laurel's fears were realized.

"Hey, Laurel," Trey said. "Even just once, have you ever been with—"

"Trey."

He paused, blinking slowly. "What?"

"Get ahold of yourself."

"What do you mean?"

"You're drunk."

"A little. But we're just talking here." He held up his hand and, slowly, clumsily, made a pinching gesture with his thumb and index finger. "I just want to know if you have ever, even just a little tiny bit, ever even just considered—"

"Trey!" she half shouted. "Just stop talking."

At last, Trey seemed to take note of her darkened face, her warning tone. He gave her a long look through scolded puppy dog eyes, but kept his mouth shut.

*****

When the show ended after 1 a.m., they spilled out into the balmy night with the rest of the concertgoers. Not ready for the evening to end, they sat on a low stone wall alongside Lexington Road.

"I don't think I should drive," Trey said.

"No, sir."

"Hey—we should have a Lyft car take us to that Dasha Barbour's chicken place you were raving about."

"It's 1:15 a.m., Trey. They're closed."

"Oh, yeah. How about White Castle, then?"

"Yuck."

Trey took a deep, happy breath and turned to face Laurel. "Wasn't that a great show?"

"I liked it. Very much. Thanks for convincing me to go."

The stupid but adoring grin reappeared on Trey's face. His gaze dropped to Laurel's lips and settled there. He seemed to just barely lean toward her.

"But I'm bushed," Laurel said, standing up. "Let's get some sleep."

With that, they called it a night, leaving Trey's car where it was parked and taking separate Lyft rides home.

THIRTY-THREE

Wanting to prep her favorite prosecutor for an eventual search warrant or cell phone records request, Laurel decided that they should pay a visit to Commonwealth's Attorney Seth Greenberg to get him up to speed on their investigation. To get to Greenberg's building on Liberty Street, they had to circumnavigate a march in support of professional athletes who refused to stand during the national anthem, along with a sizable counter-protest following just behind. There was a lot of shouting back and forth between the groups. Traffic was backed up for blocks in every direction.

Making it to the building at last, they got into the elevator. "Seth is a great prosecutor," Laurel said. "A pit bull in the courtroom. But he's eccentric. Still lives with his mother. Acts a little bit like an old grandpa, even though he's only like 50 years old."

"What's that supposed to mean?"

"He can be a little pedantic. Unintentionally condescending."

"I can handle it. You should meet *my* grandpa. Every time I see him, he wags his finger at me and reminds me that smoking is a filthy habit."

"I didn't know you smoked."

"I never have."

"Ah. You'll do fine then."

"He's 50? I thought all prosecutors hung it up at age 35 and went off to make the big bucks as litigators for private law firms."

"Seth is a true believer."

*****

"Seth!"

"Laurel, sweetheart! Come in, come in," Greenberg said as he dug through one of several foot-tall stacks of case files sitting on the windowsill of his cluttered, claustrophobic office. He had a bushy head of wiry salt-and-pepper hair and wore a wrinkled, coffee-stained dress shirt with the sleeves rolled up. A pair of reading glasses clung to the end of his nose, and he peered at the detectives over the tops of the frames.

"Your office smells musty," Laurel said.

"A pipe ruptured in the ceiling and flooded us out last week," he said with an amused smile. "That's why you saw those big industrial fans in the hallway. We're still drying out. What a mess. Who's your youthful partner?"

"Allow me to introduce Trey Hewson. The first of his name. Detective extraordinaire, lord of the seven kingdoms, *et cetera, et cetera.* Sorry we're late. Got stuck on the far side of the protest."

"Ah, yes. The protest. Sometimes I think that all protests ever do is to cause traffic jams that make normal people hate the protesters."

"Martin Luther King might disagree with you there, Seth."

He smiled.

"You going to any Derby parties this week?" she asked.

"I'm invited to one. I don't want to go. I hate parties. I'll probably go anyway. I don't like being home alone either."

"You're an introverted extrovert."

"My mother is nagging me to go. Thinks I might meet a new lady friend."

"Doesn't she know you're married to your job?"

"Ha. At least it's an indoor party, so I won't have to worry about the crazy weather."

"Crazy weather?"

"Severe thunderstorms, maybe tornados, rolling in on Friday. Cup of chamomile tea, either of you?"

"No, thanks."

"Russian tea? San Pellegrino? Carrot juice?"

"No."

"Are you hungry? I think I still have some of my mother's apricot hamantash cookies left over from Purim. They're in that blue box on the shelf right behind you."

"Wasn't Purim like five weeks ago?"

"They're still good. It isn't smart to let your blood sugar run low, Laurel— especially in your line of work. You can get tired and shaky."

"We're fine, Seth."

"Blurred vision, in extreme cases. You don't want that if you have to handle your gun."

"We're good."

"Have one. Don't hurt my mother's feelings."

"Seth!"

"Okay, okay," Greenberg said, plopping down in his chair. "But you really should have one."

The detectives took seats on the opposite side of his desk.

"So what's new, sweetheart?" Greenberg asked, taking up a pad and pen. "I'm up to my eyeballs in purse snatchers, perverts, and drunken frat boys crashing their daddies' BMWs. Please say you're bringing me a nice juicy homicide."

"Two homicides, Seth. And our shortlist of suspects includes members of an old money horse farm family and an old money bourbon family."

"Music to my ears! You know what? It never ceases to amaze me how much awesome debauchery and weirdness there is with the old money class of Kentucky."

They filled Greenberg in on the details of their progress. But they didn't mention either the out-of-bounds orders involving the Duke and the Barnstone people or the pilfering of the case files. Like the detectives, Greenberg was at least partly at the mercy of political masters, and he would be obligated to report such peculiarities up his own chain of command—which Laurel figured might lead to further obstruction of their efforts, or worse. They'd fill Greenberg in on the dirt once they'd gathered more information or were ready to ask for warrants.

"You catch some colorful cases, Laurel. Remember that one where the drug dealer tried to sew up his own scrotum after catching a bullet in the gonads?"

"Do I remember?"

"Silly question. Anyway, thank you for this. Now go build me a homicide case."

THIRTY-FOUR

Just as they crossed Muhammad Ali Boulevard on their way from Seth Greenberg's office back to the Homicide Unit, Laurel spotted a lanky man walking down a sidewalk. He wore a hooded sweatshirt with the hood up over his head—despite the heat—and dirty jeans that hung down so low that half his boxer shorts were exposed.

"Oh! There's Speedy."

"Who's Speedy?" Trey asked.

"Hit the lights."

Trey switched on the dashboard police lights as Laurel gave a loud honk of the horn, prompting Speedy—who was no more than 20 feet in front of them—to nearly jump out of his shoes, stare at the flashing lights, and frown.

"Speedy," Laurel shouted out the window.

"Oh, man. Laurel," he said, looking relieved. "You gonna give me a heart attack, man."

"Just messing with you. But hey, meet me around the corner real quick."

"Alright."

Laurel circled the block, giving Speedy time to get down the side street without anyone seeing him—thereby avoiding any possible accusations that he was a police informant.

Speedy—alias for Stuart Runyon—was a perennially homeless 30-year-old skateboarder and heroin addict for whom Laurel had a soft spot. He was born in the eastern Kentucky coal mining town of Pikeville. His parents died in a car accident when he was three, and he was dumped on unenthusiastic, substance abusing distant relations in Louisville. Things went downhill from there. He'd been in and out of the city's free recovery centers nearly every year since he turned 17. But he refused to give up on himself. In Laurel's eyes, he was a very decent man who, despite his struggles, had a big heart.

The detectives pulled their car into the truck bay of a vacant warehouse just as Speedy walked up. He got in the back seat unbidden.

"Hey, Speedy. How are you?"

"Oh, you know, Laurel. Fighting the good fight."

"Haven't seen you in a while."

"Yeah, man. I was back in inpatient."

"Sorry to hear that."

"It's all good now. Three months clean."

"That's great. How's that going?"

"Ah, well, it's hard, man. Day to day. You know."

"Yeah."

"You need a tip?"

"We're working the shooting by 11th and Broadway."

"I heard of it. But I don't hear nothing about it. You know what I'm saying?"

"No rumors? Like things going wrong with one of the regular stickup guys maybe? Or somebody with some kind of beef?"

"No, man. Nothing. I mean, like, not a thing."

That, in and of itself, was telling. If the killing had involved any of the people who usually made trouble within a 10-block radius of Bacchus Distribution, Speedy would have heard about it. He was plugged in in that part of town. And word travelled fast on the street.

Laurel gave Speedy a $20 bill anyway.

"Hey, thanks Laurel. You the best, man."

"You know what I'm going to say."

"Don't worry. I ain't gonna buy no dope with it. Cigarettes, maybe," he said, smiling a broad smile that was missing several teeth. "And I need a new hat."

THIRTY-FIVE

After checking in at their office, Laurel and Trey headed for the address provided on the registration for Edgar Clayton's Cadillac Escalade. They drove along River Road—a country road with vast parks and tree-lined pastures on one side, and the broad, brown Ohio River on the other. Around three miles from downtown, they turned onto Longview Lane and entered the exclusive Glenview neighborhood—a hamlet of huge estate homes, many of them built in the 1800s by Louisville's rich elite, many of them perched on a forested bluff overlooking the river. The narrow lane was flanked by tall oak and maple trees. It crossed a small creek before climbing from the floodplain up onto the bluff. There, the forest opened onto large, cleared pastures and long driveways leading off to various estate properties. The detectives took one such driveway, winding across a hillside dotted with dogwoods and weeping willows, until it led to a stately, three-story mansion of whitewashed brick and tall windows with black painted shutters and doors. It had quite a number of chimneys and dormers protruding from its roofline. A covered porch and white-columned colonnade ran the entire length of the front of the house. Laurel guessed it had at least 10 bedrooms. Unlike the manor house of Barnstone Farm, it was well-maintained. The grounds were immaculate, the paint fresh and bright. The majestic seat of a still-flourishing family empire.

On a flat area of lawn at least an acre in size, a small army of Hispanic workers was stringing lights in the trees and erecting the second of two large white tents for Carter Clayton IV's annual Kentucky Derby after-party—one of the oldest, grandest Derby parties in the city. In addition to a handful of Hollywood stars, it drew a large number of regional politicians and titans of industry—all for the ostensible purpose of raising money for disabled veterans in the Louisville area. But Joy Brashear had told Laurel and Trey that the party was more about Carter Clayton's vanity, his social standing, and his desire to curry favor with local powerbrokers.

They parked the Taurus in the circular drive, adjacent to a tall and imposing front door which stood at the top of a wide flight of cut limestone stairs. As they ascended to the door, Laurel turned to see that the house had a commanding view of the Ohio River stretching all the way to downtown.

"Hey, Laurel," Trey said, pointing at the surface of the porch. Something small, metallic, and circular was embedded in the middle of the cut stone semicircle in front of the door. The detectives knelt down for a closer look. It was a coin stamped with an image of Lady Liberty encircled by the words *Confederate States of America—Twenty Dollars.* It looked like it was made of gold.

"I thought Confederate money was all paper," Trey said.

"That's largely true. And I happen to know for a fact that the Confederacy did not produce gold coins."

"How in the world do you know that? And don't tell me you learned it in the Sacred Heart honors program."

"I used to moonlight as a security guard at the Louisville Numismatic Exchange down on 3rd Street. A very cool place. They taught me all about rare coins."

"So you're saying this Confederate gold coin here doesn't exist?"

"Or isn't supposed to. Then again, the Confederacy did control the New Orleans Mint after Louisiana seceded from the Union in 1861. Despite what the history books say, maybe they did manage to crank out a few gold coins of their own. Or maybe the Carter Clayton side of the family had this one custom-made and put here to taunt the Lucian Clayton side of the family, playing on the old rumor about the gold discovery." She rose to her feet. "Let's get into character. Remember what Joy told us. We're supposed to look as white and straight as possible."

"People can't look whiter than we do unless they're dead."

Laurel took hold of a heavy gargoyle door knocker and gave it three good knocks. The sound echoed from within such that the detectives could tell the entry hall behind the door was vast. After an age, the door opened six inches. A middle-aged, forlorn looking Hispanic maid in an antiquated black and white uniform peeked through the gap.

The detectives held up their badges.

"Hello there," Trey said. "We're looking for Edgar Clayton."

Without so much as a nod, the maid closed the door in their faces.

"Should we knock again?" Trey asked.

"Give it a minute."

A moment later, the door reopened, again only a few inches. This time, an old man with angry eyes peered through the gap.

"Good afternoon," Trey said. "We're looking for Edgar Clayton."

"The hell are you?"

The detectives presented their badges without uttering a word.

"Not here," the old man said.

"Are you Carter?" Laurel asked.

"The hell you want?"

"As my partner said, we're looking for Edgar."

"Why?"

"To have a word with him."

"About what?"

"We're just trying to clear something up, and we think he might be able to help us out."

"Don't play coy with me, woman. What's this about?"

"Just a routine police matter."

"Fine. Be vague. Edgar isn't here. He's at work. And I don't have time for your insolence. So why don't you leave us taxpayers alone and go do your job where it counts, over on the West End, where all the crackhead welfare porch monkeys are shooting each other every day." He grinned an evil grin. "Then again, who cares if they do?" And with that, he closed the door in their faces.

Laurel and Trey looked at each other. "Did he really just say *porch monkeys*?" Trey said. "I haven't heard that one since the 80s."

Laurel was smiling.

"What is it?" Trey asked.

"Carter is the old man I saw at Churchill Downs walking with the big guy in the black Glock baseball hat."

"You're kidding."

"Nope."

"So now what?"

"Let's pay a visit to the Clayton Distillery. You heard the old bigot. Young Edgar is at work."

Before leaving, they each took another look at the mysterious gold coin embedded in the porch.

THIRTY-SIX

The sun was just peeking out from behind a tall column of dark, purple-gray clouds as the detectives turned off a remote country road and onto the long drive of the Clayton Bourbon Distillery. It was situated on the northeastern edge of Henry County, near the village of Port Royal—home of National Humanities Medal laureate Wendell Berry, the esteemed novelist and poet. It was a collection of grand, old, rough-cut limestone masonry buildings perched on a grassy hillside above the meandering Kentucky River, which, a century earlier, was the favored shipping route for barrels of Clayton bourbon.

"It's beautiful here," Trey said. I'd love to buy some land and build a cabin in a place like this when I retire. Have a big fire pit. A barn I could refurbish classic cars in. Maybe a trout pond." He took a deep breath of the fresh country air blowing through his open window.

"Retire? Don't you read the news, Trey? Our state retirement fund is billions in the red. You'll be working for the man until the day you drop dead. Maybe longer."

"Thanks for ruining my daydream."

"Sorry."

"Maybe Edgar will give us a tasting of his Peepaw Clayton 21-year-old. You can't even find it in Louisville liquor stores anymore."

"It really isn't that big a deal."

"Wait—you've *had* it?"

"I got a bottle as a gift back when it was a semi-sane $85. Before the Clayton media blitz and engineered shortages drove the price up to $800."

"What it's like?"

She shrugged. "It's good. Smooth. But honestly, I don't think it's any better than Woodford Reserve, which is $30 or $40 a bottle. It isn't $760 better, that's for sure. That being said, you have to hand it to the Clayton marketing people for being able to drive a price like that."

"Well, it's still cool to think that they've been making Peepaw Clayton out here since the 1800s. I mean, aside from during Prohibition."

"See, that's another part of it."

"Part of what?"

"You want me to ruin this for you too?"

"I won't know until you tell me."

"It's the Clayton's marketing genius again. This particular distillery only reopened in the late 1990s. It had been in mothballs since 1920. Rotting. Its roof caved in. And guess what? The recipe for Peepaw is less than ten years older than the iPhone."

"No. Hold on. I thought Peepaw was 100 percent authentic, original family recipe old-time bourbon."

"That's because you bought into their marketing department's 100 percent authentic baloney. Regular old Clayton bourbon—which is mass-produced rotgut—is made down in South Louisville, in a cinderblock building that has all the charm of a General Motors factory. The Claytons resurrected this place out here in Port Royal as part of an effort to refine their image. To go with the charming stories of how they can trace their lineage back to pioneer days or whatever. You hear the name Peepaw and you picture a place like this, don't you? Lovely stone distillery perched above a slow-moving river, surrounded by immense pastures of pristine bluegrass? Maybe some wise, old, white-haired Southern gentleman farmer sitting on the porch in a hickory rocking chair, wearing a linen suit and smoking a pipe while the Oompa Loompas make bourbon using his 150-year-old secret family recipe."

"A Catahoula hound sitting next to him?"

"Exactly. But you know as well as I do that Carter 'Peepaw' Clayton was a social climber and scoundrel—maybe even a Confederate deserter and murderer—who lived in the city. And Carter IV is a washed up womanizer and internet troll who lives in Glenview. So with respect to the image being pushed here, you're looking at bourbon Disneyland. It isn't real."

"I had to ask, didn't I?" Trey said. "It's like you just told me there's no Santa Claus." He stuck his nose out the window and took another sniff of the fresh air. "It's still beautiful."

"It certainly is. My favorite thing about these resurrected distilleries is the way air smells in those big old rickhouses," Laurel said, gazing at one of the massive, seven-story stone barns in which thousands of oak barrels of bourbon sat aging on dusty, shadowy racks built of stout wooden beams. "I love to go inside them, close my eyes, and just breathe through my nose. Damp limestone, earth, charred oak and bourbon vapor," she said, her gaze unfocused, her mind half lost in distant memory. "Anyway," she said, snapping out of it. "Getting back to business, let's keep things low-key again. Our first priority is to get Edgar to commit to stories about where he was on the evenings of the Taylor and Cervantes murders."

They parked the Taurus in a small lot of crushed limestone gravel and made for a small, low stone building—more a cottage—that had a cutesy sign pointing to it that said *office*. Laurel didn't bother to knock. In a front room that took up at least a third of the entire cottage, a slight man with perfectly styled hair and a fitted lavender shirt sat at a modern, shiny ebony desk that clashed with the old country character of its surroundings. He wore wireless earbuds.

"Looking for Edgar," Laurel said loudly, in case the man was listening to music.

Without a word, the slight man pointed a thumb at an open doorway behind him and went back to whatever he was doing on his computer. Laurel and Trey passed through the door into the next room. There, at a similar ebony desk and also wearing wireless earbuds, sat Edgar Clayton—heir to the Clayton Bourbon empire. A framed promotional poster for something called the Ultra Festival of Electronic Dance Music in Ibiza, Spain hung on the wall behind him. There were two other framed posters for different years of the same event hung on two of the other walls. They each featured images of sweaty, shirtless muscle men and half-naked young women with fluorescent makeup dancing under multicolored lights and laser beams.

"Help you?" Edgar said, looking up and pulling out his earbuds.

"Are you Edgar Clayton?" Laurel asked to mask the fact that they'd already looked up his DMV records and knew what he looked like.

"Yes."

"Hi. I'm Laurel, and this is Trey. Sorry to bother you. We're detectives with the Louisville Metro Police Department."

"Oh, wow. What can I do for you?"

"It's a quick thing we're hoping you can help us out with," Laurel said. "We have to go down a long list of people who were seen in the general area of a crime the other night down in Louisville. Gotta check boxes next to each name saying we asked everyone this and that. It won't take more than a minute or two."

"Sure. Happy to help. What was the crime?"

"Just another shooting in the West End. Some overzealous Neighborhood Watch do-gooder probably wrote down your car license plate number as you passed through the area. They don't really keep us in the loop on the details of these things. They just tell us to go down the list and collect statements. So here we are, 50 miles from Louisville, to ask our standard questions."

"Oh. Okay. Well, whatever."

Edgar's face and body language confirmed Laurel's first impression of his driver's license photo. He looked somehow disappointed with life despite his relatively young age. His downturned eyes were dark and baggy, and there was a sad poutiness to his mouth. His shoulders slumped forward and his arms hung down in the posture of the defeated. To Laurel, he looked disengaged and depressed. As if he was going through the motions because it was expected of him. An altogether unexpected demeanor for a man who led a life of privilege beyond most people's wildest dreams.

"First, can you tell us where you were between 9 and 10 p.m. the Sunday before last?"

"Sunday before last. Huh." He hesitated. "Oh, yeah. My family has a horse getting ready to race on Derby Day. A 3-year-old named Carbonado. Beautiful black colt. You should bet on him. But you didn't hear it from me. Ha-ha. So anyway, as far as I can recall, I was down at the backside stables at Churchill Downs."

"What were you doing there?"

"Just sort of tooling around out of personal interest. Absorbing it. I don't serve any real function down there. Don't know a damn thing about horses, to be honest. My father's the horse nut of the family. He's always buying interests in horses. Loves to rub elbows in the winner's circle suites and all that. Still, it's awesome on the backside this time of year."

Edgar was talking quickly.

"You got to Churchill Downs when?"

"A bit after 8 p.m., if I remember right."

"Why so late?"

"It's quiet at that hour. Peaceful. A nice time to stroll the barns."

"How did you get there?"

"Drove."

"Was anyone with you?"

"No."

"Anyone at Churchill Downs who can vouch for you being there?"

"When I first arrived, the folks working with our horse saw me."

"Only when you first arrived? Not later?"

"I doubt it. I mean, not that I know of."

"How late were you there?"

"Oh, I stayed for, I don't know, less than two hours. I would guess I was there until about 9:45. Something like that. But my memory isn't what it used to be."

"And again, nobody was with you later on, maybe strolling the backside with you?"

"Not that I recall."

"Or in your car when you left?"

"Nope."

"And where did you go from there?"

"Home."

"Straight home?"

"I think that I...." He paused. "Oh, wait. I stopped at a store."

"Which one?"

"I don't know what it's called. It's a little corner grocer on South 3rd Street, right by Churchill Downs."

"Do you recall what you purchased?"

"Uh...cigarettes. Box of Twinkies. Hand sanitizer."

"How long were you there?"

"Maybe, like, 10 minutes. I don't know."

"How did you pay?"

"Cash," he said without the slightest hesitation.

"What route did you take home?"

"Oh, let's see. Got on I-65, by U of L there. Took that to I-71, then got off on Brownsboro Road."

"Have you heard the name Javier Cervantes?"

"The jockey who was murdered."

"Did you know him?"

"No. Heard about it on the news."

"Never met him?"

"Not that I know of."

"And where were you the Friday before last, between 8 and 10 p.m.?"

Hearing this, Edgar sat quiet for a moment. "Friday before last? I mean, I'll have to think for a second. Well, I guess I was at home. Yeah. I was at home watching golf on ESPN."

It was beyond Laurel how anyone had the patience to watch golf on television.

"You didn't go anywhere?" she asked.

"I don't think—oh, wait—I went for chicken. That's right."

"Chicken?"

"Yeah, I had a craving for fried chicken. So I drove to the city and got some."

"Where?"

"Indi's."

"Extra spicy, I hope?"

"Of course," he said, now smiling.

"It's the best, isn't it?"

"It's so good."

"What time was that?"

"Let me think. I guess I left home at maybe 8:30."

"Which Indi's?"

"The one on Broadway."

"Bit of a rough location, isn't it?"

"It's the closest Indi's to my house."

"Pay with a credit or debit card?"

"Cash," he said, again without hesitation.

"And then?"

"I went home and ate it."

"Anyone else with you?"

"No."

"What about your father? Was he at home?"

"Yes, but he goes to bed at like 8. I'm sure he was asleep before I went for chicken."

"Have you ever heard the name Paul Taylor?"

"No."

"Not even from the news?"

"I don't think so. No."

"Okay. One last question. Do you own a handgun?"

"I do."

"Caliber?"

".45"

"What make and model?"

"It's a Colt 1911."

"A classic."

"Need to see it?"

"No. Is that your only gun?"

"I inherited an antique double-barreled shotgun. Don't even know if it still fires."

"Okay. Thank you. We appreciate your cooperation."

*****

"He may be smarter than he looks," Laurel said once they were back in the car and headed for Louisville.

"I was thinking that myself," Trey said. "For one thing, he was faking that he was surprised to see us. The old man called and told him the police wanted a word. He'd mentally prepped himself."

"Yes. The question is why."

"And he probably guessed that we had some video footage. That we might have seen him coming and going from the general area of each murder. So his alibis put him in the vicinity of each, with plausible explanations, so that we wouldn't catch him in a lie."

"Stopping at a corner grocer or at Indi's chicken would take five or 10 minutes, right?" Laurel said. "Which is probably about all the time he and an accomplice would have needed to string up Cervantes's body in his garage just down the block from that corner grocer, or to draw out and gun down Paul Taylor at his liquor warehouse near Indi's. And, of course, he says he used cash, so we can't trace the transactions—or lack thereof. Clever."

"Assuming he's guilty."

"Yes, well. He did lie about not having anyone with him in the Escalade at Churchill Downs, didn't he? Now why would he do that?"

"Because the other guy is his life coach, and he's embarrassed about having one?"

"Anything's possible."

"Do you think the other guy in the Escalade is the one who owns the P226 that shot Taylor?"

"I reckon we'd better find out."

*****

As they drove back to Louisville, Trey called Indi's fried chicken restaurant on Broadway, as well as the only corner grocery on South 3rd Street anywhere near Churchill Downs. Though both businesses had security cameras, having not dealt with crimes on the nights in question, employees had already purged the relevant digital video footage from their respective systems to free up memory space for new recordings. However, as the detectives reached the eastern outskirts of the city, Laurel's cell phone gave a chirp indicating that she'd received a message.

"Open that message for me, Trey, will you?"

"What if it's private and embarrassing?"

"Just open it."

He did. "Uh…."

"What?"

"It's from a number with a blocked ID." That often meant it was from another law enforcement phone. "It's a photograph."

"Of what?"

"Of you."

"Huh? Let me see that." She took a quick glance. It was a photo of her, standing in the living room of her condo in a bath towel with her back to the camera. It was taken from outside her window at night. From *just* outside.

"What's that all about?" Trey asked.

Laurel exhaled. "It's a warning. A threat."

Sure enough, her phone received a second message. It was text. All it said was, *Back off or else.*

"How unoriginal," Laurel said.

"You have to report this."

"To whom?"

"I don't know. The union?"

"What are they going to do?"

"Protect you."

"How? And from whom?"

"They could at least note that you're receiving threats, so that if someone tries to set you up to come after your badge, there'll be a record."

"I think the best protection we can give ourselves right now is to crack this case."

"No, the best protection would be to quit this case. But I know you too well to bother suggesting that."

"We had better watch our backs."

"You think?"

THIRTY-SEVEN

The next morning, Laurel and Trey were back in the old-moneyed Glenview neighborhood, albeit on the extreme far side of it from where Carter IV's mansion was. This time, they were parked under tall oak trees on a weed-free, crushed stone driveway that led up to a well-maintained Tudor-style cottage. Laurel guessed that the cottage had once been the carriage house to a grand Tudor mansion that stood maybe 100 yards away, at the far end of a tulip-lined walkway. She wondered whether the mansion had, many years ago, served as the seat of Lucian Carter's side of the family.

"Why don't you take the lead on this interview," Laurel said.

"You sure I'm ready?" Trey asked, deadpan. "Sure I can handle it?"

"Afterward, I'll tell you all the places where you screwed up."

The front door opened before the detectives even reached it. In the doorway stood a slender man with styled hair, wearing a yellow pastel button down shirt over robin's egg blue shorts embroidered with small horses.

"Ben Clayton?" Trey asked.

"Benjamin. What can I do for you?"

After the usual introductions and vague explanations of their purpose for being there, Benjamin led the detectives into his cottage where they sat on distressed leather chairs in front of an empty river rock fireplace. The interior was small but cosmopolitan—devoid of the gaudy brass fixtures, floral print wallpapers, and red painted rooms common to so many older Louisville homes. Benjamin had taken out the original ceiling to open up the attic space, and had knocked walls out between the small kitchen, dining, and living rooms to give the common area an open, bright, and airy feel.

"I was beginning to wonder whether anyone was ever going to ask me any questions," Benjamin said.

"Why do you say that?" Trey asked.

"Well, I assume this is about Paul."

"Yes."

"I was Paul's partner."

"We know."

"No, no. Well, that too. But what I'm telling you is that I was his *partner*."

"I see."

"We broke up a month ago, just before our two-year anniversary."

"Who initiated the breakup? You or him?"

"He did."

"Did he say why?"

"Told me he found someone that he wanted to be with more than me."

"You don't know who that *someone* was?"

"No clue."

"Were you angry?"

"No."

"Bitter?"

"A little bit, sure. Sad, mostly."

"You don't sound too upset. Especially considering that he was just killed."

"I'm taking Xanax, and I've been on Lexapro for weeks."

"Prescription?"

"Want me to get the Walgreens bottles for you? They're in the bathroom."

Trey shook his head. "Needless to say, we'll need to rule you out as a suspect."

"Of course."

They spent the next few minutes getting Benjamin's explanation of his whereabouts on the nights of the Taylor and Cervantes murders, along with names of a half-dozen people who could verify his story. They would check the veracity later. Laurel was confident that, unless Benjamin was the most cold-blooded actor she'd ever come across, he hadn't been involved in either of the killings. His responses to their questions seemed altogether genuine and honest.

"Did Paul's wife, Mimi, know the extent of your relationship with him?" Trey asked.

"Hard to say. I only met her a handful of times. I mean, I'm sure she'd figured out that her marriage to Paul wasn't what she thought it was. But I don't know that she pieced together my part in the whole situation. Then again, that creep she hangs around with—what's his name, Chad—he definitely suspected that I was gay right from the start. Always looked at me like he wanted to try to kick my ass. That would have been funny. I have a black belt in Krav Maga."

"Can you think of anyone—anyone at all—who might have wished Paul ill will?"

At this, Benjamin's face betrayed regret. "I can't tell you anything specific."

"What can you tell us?"

"Bear in mind that I don't have anything concrete to base this on. But I long suspected Paul of working some sort of scheme. Something that wasn't on the up-and-up."

"With respect to what, exactly?"

"Getting licensed."

"As a liquor distributor?"

"Yes. From the state government. Normally, it's quite an ordeal. Some say it's impossible."

"And so you think that, in an effort to squeeze a distribution license out of the state government, Paul may have been using tactics that angered someone?"

"Yes."

"Someone dangerous?"

Benjamin nodded, looking profoundly sad despite the mood-lifting medications flowing in his veins.

"What gave you that idea?"

"When we firmed up our plans to start the business—to start Bacchus Distribution—I told him how hard it would be to get licensed. I offered to help fund the effort. Pay for, you know, lobbying and so forth."

"With what funds?"

"Well, that's a bit of a story in and of itself. As you can see, I don't exactly live a luxurious lifestyle. But I stumbled into the cryptocurrency thing at just the right time. Turned a few thousand bucks into a small fortune."

"Lucky you."

"Yes, well, as they say, money can't buy happiness."

"But Paul didn't take you up on your offer to fund his efforts?"

"He did not."

"And yet he was able to get a distribution license from the state."

"He was. God knows how."

Trey took a breath. "Benjamin, do you have even the slightest shred of suspicion of anyone at all? Maybe a potential competitor? A state official? An acquaintance? A family member?"

Benjamin thought about it. "I'm sorry. I really don't."

"How is your relationship with your Uncle Carter?"

"My relationship with Carter? There is no relationship. Incidentally, he was my father's cousin. I don't think that makes him my uncle, does it? God, I hope not."

"He's hostile to you?" Laurel asked.

"To put it mildly, yes."

She waited for more, letting the implication sink in.

"I see what you're getting at," Benjamin said. "But I think it's the wrong track. I really do. I haven't so much as seen Carter for at least 10 years. He's practically a recluse, except for when he hosts his big Kentucky Derby party. I doubt he could have any clue of my business or private affairs." Benjamin leaned back in his chair. "Don't get me wrong. Carter is mean as a snake. But as much as I'd like to see the old man go down, I don't think he's crazy enough to murder anyone just for the sake of stifling competition. He already has more money than God."

"What about his son Edgar?" Trey asked.

"I ran into him at a dance club downtown, I don't know, maybe five years ago. Once at the Glenview post office before that. I hear he's in charge of the distilleries now."

"Know who he runs with?"

"No idea. Sorry. But if you want to learn more, you might try talking to Carter's daughter Magnolia. She's actually quite nice. Must be the milkman's kid. I have her number. We bump into each other from time to time at gallery openings and so forth. She hates Carter more than I do. But she has more interaction with him too. I imagine she knows something of his affairs through her brother Edgar."

The conversation went dead.

"Is that it?" Benjamin asked.

"I suppose," Laurel said. "Actually, Mr. Clayton, out of simple curiosity, I have to put a question to you."

"Yes?"

"Having come into money with your cryptocurrency windfall, why would you try to establish a business in such a challenging sector? Why liquor distribution, when you know the difficulties? Why not real estate or franchising or something—anything else? Why not take your money, cut the cord, move to California, and reinvent yourself?"

"I'm the last of my line, detective. Liquor is my heritage. My blood. My family name. Until, that is, we were humiliated and cheated out of it, years and years ago, by Carter's side of the family."

"So, what then? Getting back into liquor will somehow redeem your side of the family?" *And spite old Carter,* Laurel thought, *in the latest salvo of a pointless, generations-old vendetta.*

"I know it sounds silly in today's world. But I genuinely believe that there's honor and meaning in a family name. At least where I come from. My name *is* bourbon. I'll be damned if my legacy is going to be that I stood by and let my branch of the family tree wither and die without dignity. That I stood by and let our history fade away. I may be the last of us. But when I go, at least our name will mean something again."

THIRTY-EIGHT

It turned out that Magnolia Clayton's massive, turreted red brick house—the one Perry Clark described as *a crumbling monstrosity of a Queen Anne*—stood on Magnolia Avenue, barely five blocks from the Homicide Unit offices in Old Louisville, so the detectives stopped in on their way back from Benjamin's.

"Magnolia's house is on Magnolia Avenue," Trey said. "How weird is that?"

"I'll say it again, Trey. Nothing gets by you."

The yard wasn't landscaped with the usual manicured boxwoods and hostas that decorated most of the yards of upper-crust Louisville. Instead, the well-tended flowerbeds were bursting with purple bearded iris and white primrose. Yet the small front lawn was overrun with weeds. The open front windows of the first and second floors were covered from within by blue and white Mandala tapestries that stirred in the gentle breeze. The closer the detectives got to the front door, the more they could smell sandalwood incense.

"Why don't you lead again on this one," Laurel said. "Women Magnolia's age love talking to handsome young men like you."

"Oh, please."

"I'm half-serious. I bet you'll have an easier time establishing rapport with her than I would. Say something nice about her hair or clothes or whatever."

"Get real."

"Middle-aged women feel invisible. It'll go a long way, I'm telling you."

Their knock was answered by a tanned, muscular model of a man wearing nothing but denim bib overalls. His hair was black, curly, shiny, and longish. His bulging, hairless pectoral muscles shined as if they'd been waxed and oiled. His look reminded Laurel of any number of romance novel covers. She wondered whether he was Magnolia's kept man.

"Good morning," Trey said. "Mister?"

"Raúl."

"Raúl." *Of course*, Trey thought. *Of course your name is Raúl.* "Is Magnolia home?"

"She is in studio," Raúl said with an accent Trey couldn't place.

Raúl led them through a front room decorated with little more than a consignment shop couch and several 30x40 inch canvas prints of penises, past a bare-bones kitchen equipped with ancient appliances, to a former dining room that had been converted to a studio. Two large empty easels stood to one side. Canvasses bearing plein air paintings of tree-lined pastures and slow-moving rivers leaned against one of the walls. Two of the other walls were decorated with more of the large prints of penises. In a far corner, reading something at a small desk, sat Magnolia Clayton—estranged middle daughter of Carter Clayton IV.

"Can I help you?" Magnolia asked, standing up and taking off her red-framed reading glasses. Like Raúl, she was barefoot. She wore a simple black shift dress.

Trey, struggling to ignore the giant penis prints, made the introductions.

"Thank you, Raúl," Magnolia then said, dismissing her resident Adonis. "Can I offer either of you a cup of tea or a French press coffee or anything?"

Trey gave Laurel an eager look. But Laurel responded with a polite no-thank-you before Magnolia led them out to a trio of powder blue Adirondack chairs that circled a small zinc-iron table in the backyard.

"A female detective," Magnolia said. "How interesting. I imagine it's challenging to work in such a male-dominated profession."

"Oh, I do alright, I suppose."

"I like your dress," Trey more or less blurted at Magnolia. Laurel, standing behind Magnolia as she sat down, rolled her eyes at him.

"I, eh—thanks," Magnolia said. "Well, I'm sure you're eager to get to the point."

"Did you know a man named Paul Taylor?" Trey said, forgetting the usual preamble.

"Paul Taylor? I don't think so. Is he an artist?"

"He was a liquor distributor."

"Was?"

"We're investigating his murder."

"Oh. And how on Earth did your investigations lead you to me?"

"We're in that preliminary investigative phase where we're casting a wide net. Your family is, of course, prominent in the world of bourbon."

"My *family*, yes. Not me."

"No?" Laurel said.

"No. As I'm sure you've noticed, I'm a woman. And my father, who sits on the throne of the exalted Clayton Bourbon empire, is a misogynist, sexist pig. A man who considers his own daughters a waste of parenting. Second-tier members of the family. In fact, I'm sure that if my late mother hadn't been such a devout Catholic, my father would have had her abort my sisters and me."

"Wow," Trey said, earning himself another eye roll from Laurel.

"Yes, wow. We were just speedbumps in his quest for a son. I'd say you can corroborate that with my older sister, Violet. But years ago, in a deep depression I blame on my emotionally abusive father, she killed herself. I'd say you can corroborate it with my younger sister, Zelda. Zelda with the genius IQ. But after a needlessly traumatizing adolescence that I again blame my father for, she developed a severe case of schizophrenia. Now she lives at Central State Hospital, off and on, and usually thinks her name is Teetee."

"Do you keep in touch with your father?"

"Through his lawyer, and only when absolutely necessary. He is not a part of my life."

"How familiar are you with his business activities?"

"Not very. I mean, I hear a bit now and then. But as for the details of day-to-day operations, I don't know a thing."

"What about your younger brother, Edgar?"

"The golden boy? He runs the distilleries now, at least on paper, so he knows more than I do. But he has no business sense. Still, my father designated Edgar heir to the throne. And why? Because Edgar is a man. In name, anyway." Magnolia cracked her knuckles. "Wait—do you think my father or brother might have something to do with this Paul Taylor person's murder?"

"We're not at liberty to discuss the details of active investig—"

"Oh, wow. You do. It's okay. God knows, I'd love to see my father take a fall. Maybe I can still help."

"Yes?"

"Edgar and I aren't what you'd call close. But we're civil to one another. And he means well. I don't think he has it in him to kill anyone. At the same time, he *is* a confused and easily manipulated man-child. My father's marionette. Simple enough to let my father lead him into deep water."

"How deep?"

"Deep enough where he might be surprised to find himself an accessory to something terrible."

"Your father is rather old to be—"

"The person you want to look at is Barton Rill."

"Barton Rill?"

"My brother-in-law."

"Violet's widower?" Laurel asked.

"No. Zelda's husband. According to official records, anyway. A walking pile of meat animated by a greedy little brain that's incapable of feeling empathy or guilt. A bully. An ambitious redneck loser. I know that's something of a contradiction in terms, but it fits him."

"Ambitious as in he wants a piece of the Clayton Bourbon empire?" Trey asked.

"Exactly. He married my sister when she was 19, knowing full well that she was in a downward spiral of mental illness. Since her initial commitment at Central State Hospital—which, mind you, was 16 years ago—he has been to visit her a total of eight times, even though she has spent more time in the hospital than at home. I checked Zelda's visitor's log myself."

"Is Zelda hospitalized now, or is she home with Barton?"

"In the hospital. She hasn't been home in almost six months. Barton doesn't want her around. Whenever she comes home, he looks for any excuse to have her recommitted. Probably hides her medications, for all I know. And yet he's been able to set himself up as my father's right-hand man. That tells you something about how little my father cares about Zelda—or any of the rest of us."

"You said Zelda has a genius IQ?" Laurel asked.

"Scored 161."

"How did she end up married to a guy like Barton Rill?"

"God knows. I mean, I guess she was aching for affection that she wasn't getting from my father. So that made her vulnerable. The usual story of how girls end up with creeps, right? And I suppose her grasp on reality was somewhat compromised by the time Barton came along. But it's still hard to fathom." She shook her head. "Anyway, as I was saying, Barton is my father's fixer. His goon. He takes cash to the people who my father wants to influence, then reminds those people—subtly or not so subtly—of the favors they owe when the time comes. And he chaperones Edgar. Rides shotgun for him."

"Meaning what?"

"Meaning he makes sure Edgar stays on the rails. Doesn't get pushed around by his suppliers or customers. Gets him out of jams. Doesn't let him get caught after crashing his car at 4 a.m. on his way home from a dance club while high on cocaine and ecstasy. Pretends to be his friend. That sort of thing. Barton is Edgar's shadow."

"What does Barton look like?"

"Tall. Maybe 6-foot-3. Chubby. Sort of muscular. Mostly bald."

"Does he wear baseball hats?"

"Always. Baseball hats and jeans. Except when he's delivering money or threats for my father. Then he wears a tie and an undersized blue blazer that make him look like some sort of 1970s country club buffoon from *Caddyshack*."

"Does he own a gun?"

"Several, I'm sure. He's one of those guys who puts NRA stickers all over his truck and is just sure that Hillary Clinton and her fellow devil worshippers are going to break into his house and take away his toys. He even has a Marine Corps bumper sticker. But he was never in the Marines. It's pathetic."

"You know a lot of detail for someone who wants nothing to do with these people."

"Yes. Well. I suppose I still gawk at them like I would a big traffic accident."

*****

"Was that Raúl guy straight out of Hollywood Central Casting, or what?" Trey asked as Laurel drove them back to the office. "The independent, middle-aged woman's exotic love slave cliché."

"Hey, you're the putz who's dating Fake Boobs. Talk about cliché."

"We aren't dating."

"Whatever. You asked her on a date."

Trey raised his palms in surrender. "So you think Barton Rill was maybe the other guy in the Escalade at Churchill Downs?" he asked.

"I think we should take a good look at him. I'll run him on NCIC and whatnot."

*****

When Laurel got to her desk, she found a note once again summoning her and Trey to the office of Detective Sergeant Isaiah Turner. She grabbed Trey on her way.

"What's up, Sarge?" she asked as they entered.

"I'm about to ruin your whole day," he said.

"What is it now? We haven't bothered the Duke or the Barnstone people at all."

"It isn't about them. It's about the Claytons."

"You've got to be kidding me."

"I wish I were. Hands off. Orders from on high. Apparently Carter Clayton sits at the right hand of God in this town. Simply put, you can still work the case, but you can't touch the Claytons."

"Are the orders coming via Mecklenburg again?"

Turner's long face and silence answered the question for her. She wondered what could have corrupted a seemingly decent cop like Mecklenburg. Then she decided not to tell Isaiah about the threatening text message. At least not yet.

"Look, Laurel, just let it go. You have your third shot at a sergeant's promotion coming up. You deserve that promotion. You've deserved it for a long time. This town needs detectives like you. So keep your head down and your mouth shut. Go along to get along. Just for now."

"You sound like a TV show."

"Be that as it may, you know as well as I do that you can't beat the political machine."

"Is that some sort of veiled threat?"

"Not from me. But things have been made clear."

"If my promotion is blocked a third time, I can take it to the union."

"Sure you can. But you know that some jackass in the chain of command will just concoct a story of your insubordination, or bust you for having had a beer on city premises at the department holiday party even though everyone else—including all of the LMPD majors—drank beer there too. They *will* find a way to bust you. And me. You know the game. Plus, you have to consider how a black mark in your file might impact, you know, other aspects of your life. Plans you might have," Turner said, doing his best to make covert reference to

Laurel's interest in adopting a child, not knowing whether she'd ever communicated her interest to Trey. "Plans that may already present an uphill battle given your private…your situation."

"The Claytons are probably involved in two separate homicides," she said. "You're telling me we're never going to close these cases."

"You don't know that for sure."

"We're close, Sarge."

"The decision's been made."

"Give us 24 hours."

"No."

Laurel shook her head. "I'm going to take up a collection for you, Isaiah."

"A collection?"

"Yeah. So you can get that backbone transplant surgery you've needed for so long."

"Laurel, you're a great detective. But you need to learn when a fight is unwinnable. Plus, I have two kids in college. A mortgage. Three car payments."

"This is crap."

"Don't shoot the messenger. And think about it. I'm black. You're a woman. And a…."

"What's that supposed to mean?"

"It means they're always watching. A few of them are probably even looking for an excuse to pounce and say, *See, I told you so.*"

"I thought that just meant we had to be better than them."

"It does."

"This isn't better, Isaiah. It's worse."

Laurel's face was flushed and her limbs were taut. She visualized pulling Turner's computer monitor off his desk and throwing it through the window.

"Come on, Laurel," Trey said, gently placing a hand on her shoulder. "I'll buy you a milkshake at Dairy Kastle and you can give me dating advice. I promise I'll listen this time."

"Hell, take her for beers at O'Shea's, on me," Turner said, reaching into his pocket to pull a $50 from his wallet. "You two can take the rest of the day off. Full pay."

THIRTY-NINE

Back in the car, Trey couldn't help asking, "So what's the deal with your sergeant's promotion? You've been blocked?"

"Twice."

"Why? Have you ever been sanctioned?"

"Never. And I have all the right stats."

"So why did someone block you?"

"They don't have to give you a reason until the third time, so I don't know. Could be I've ruffled a few feathers over the years. Could be someone in the chain of command is a misogynist. Could be someone doesn't approve of my sexuality. Your guess is as good as mine."

But in the back of her mind, she was certain it was because of the dust she'd raised over the investigation she was ordered to drop years earlier. The one involving the entitled son of the gas station magnate. Her mind drifted back to the unhappy memory once again, and it made her that much angrier. Worse, she once again wondered whether her decision to stay with LMPD—to devote so much of her life to her work—had been a huge mistake.

"That sucks," Trey said.

"Huh?" she said, shaken from her reflections.

"That they blocked your promotion. It sucks."

"Well, if they block me a third time, I'll take it to the union."

Trey started the car, but held off on shifting into drive. "Can I ask you something?"

"No."

"What's it like working in a profession that's dominated by straight white males?"

Laurel turned to face him. "Do you have any idea how exhausting that question is?"

"Exhausting?"

"Imagine if, all the time, people were asking you what it's like to be you. How do you even begin to answer that? Do you have any idea how nice it would be to never be asked that?"

"I don't understand."

"How could you?"

*****

Halfway to O'Shea's, Laurel had Trey detour to Goss Avenue.

"Where are we going?"

"Let's have a quick coffee and think about things before we surrender to the drink."

They pulled to the curb in front of Bean Roasting House & Cafe. Entering the old building with its high front windows and bright interior, they were greeted by the aroma of fresh coffee. They each opted for a cup of the custom Big Dog blend, black, and took a table in the back where they could speak privately as a batch of raw coffee beans tumbled in the drum of the café's nearby roaster.

"Oh, baby," Trey said, taking his first sip. "That's velvety."

"Velvety?"

"Glorious. But enough about the coffee. What's on your mind?"

Laurel gave a curt nod. "We're close to the finish line on this case. We're closing in. Would you agree?"

"We *were* close. Yes. Why?"

"Aren't you tempted to finish the job?"

"Well, I mean, orders are orders."

"We were already stretching orders by talking to people who are working with Barnstone Farm."

"Yeah, okay. But I get the feeling you're going to suggest something a little, like, crazier."

"Let me ask you something. Have you ever experienced anything like this before in your career? This level of outright interference?"

"We've all had people call us with favors to get their neighbor off the hook on a speeding ticket or whatever, right?"

"We're talking about two homicides here, Trey."

"Right. So, no, I've never had anything like this happen. But I haven't been a homicide detective for very long either. What are you getting at?"

"The writing is on the wall. LMPD has some serious rotten apples. Rotten apples near the top."

"I guess it probably does."

"That's not good for us. Not good for our colleagues. Not good for our city."

"No, it's not."

"Don't you feel compelled to do something about it?"

Trey held his palms out. "What can we do? Like Turner said, we make a stink, they demote or fire us. End of story."

"*Or* we could close this case, hand it off to Greenberg for indictment, and then quit before they know what happened."

"A race against time."

"Sure. But I mean, really—what's keeping us in this job? Our magically disappeared state pension fund? Stay in this job and we'll be selling hot dogs at Cardinal Stadium when we're in our 80s."

"How would you pay your bills while you look for another job?"

"With savings."

"You have that kind of money saved?"

"I always keep a stash of what I call 'screw you' money."

"Screw you money?"

"Yeah. So if I need to leave my abusive significant other, quit my job because of my boss's constant sexual harassment, or, case in point, quit because of departmental corruption, I'll have the financial wherewithal to do it. I can tell them all, *screw you. I'm out of here.* And I know I'll be okay."

"Ah. Smart."

"So let's think outside the box, Trey. Let's dream up some clever way to trap these sons of bitches. How can we resist taking a shot at it? We could expose the corruption."

"Maybe we could—maybe we couldn't. But what's the point? These people are untouchable. And even if they aren't, what's going to happen? They get reprimanded before everything is swept under the rug and forgotten? Or, for the sake of argument, let's say, best-case scenario, they get fired and sent to prison—which, by the way, is a pipe dream. Then the mayor just replaces them with the next ball-playing, corrupt, scumbag yes-men waiting in the wings. You know the game."

"Maybe you're right. But if that's the way it's going to go, then I don't want to work for these people. I'd rather go down fighting, and maybe take a few of them with me."

"If it's futile? Why? Why put yourself through that hell?"

"Trey, why are you a cop?"

"I don't think that's a fair way to—"

"Are you a part of this community or not? Don't you have any chips on the table?"

"Did you learn to wield guilt like that at Catholic school?"

"Really, though. In this era of ever more liars and cheats, don't you want to help hold the line? Help flush out the establishment crooks? I mean maybe, if we're lucky—if we're really, really lucky—we can even leave the world in a little bit better shape than we found it in. Who else is going to do it?"

"Yeah, but...."

"But what?"

"I'm not sure about...."

"You're not sure about what? Spit it out."

Trey shook his head and looked at the ceiling. "Oh, man." He took a deep breath and let it out slowly as his gaze dropped to meet Laurel's own. "Alright, Don Quixote. What's your plan?"

Laurel smacked her palms on the table. "Okay. Turner said we can still work the case, but we can't touch the Claytons, right? So we can't run any Claytons on NCIC without risking that someone in management will see our queries on the log and deduce that we've disobeyed direct orders. Given the anonymous texts to my phone and the suspicious timing of Isaiah's orders, we have to assume someone is watching us. So let's not do anything that will provoke the hidden dragon until we're ready to make a finishing move."

"Right. So what can we do?"

"Watching our backs, let's go give Barton Rill a sniff. Technically, he isn't a Clayton. So technically, we aren't being insubordinate by taking a look at him. And remember, Magnolia told us that Barton is Edgar's shadow. I have a feeling about that guy."

FORTY

That evening, Laurel ran Barton Rill on NCIC to discover that he had two priors for assault that pre-dated his marriage to Zelda Clayton and, presumably, the prosecutorial immunity privileges he probably enjoyed by virtue of being Carter Clayton's son-in-law and stooge. His DMV photo revealed an acne-ravaged, pockmarked face with a thick brow ridge and dark eyes. Nobody ever looked good in a DMV photo. But Rill's was particularly bad. He was an ugly man. And he was, without a doubt, the big guy Laurel had seen wearing a black Glock baseball cap and walking with Carter Clayton at Churchill Downs.

*****

Just after sunset, the detectives sat in their Taurus a few doors down and across the street from Barton Rill's dilapidated camelback house in Louisville's Germantown neighborhood. Trey was taking periodic looks at it through a pair of high-powered binoculars while Laurel kept an eye on the street. There was a bright yellow Ford Mustang GT parked in the narrow driveway. It still had dealer plates.

"For being the right-hand man to Mr. Moneybags, Carter Clayton, Rill sure has a crap house," Trey said, squirming in his seat. "Paint is peeling. Yard is full of dandelions. Concrete front steps have a huge crack going right down the middle of them."

"Carter must be tight with his money."

"Rill's going to feel like a giant sucker if Carter's will turns out to leave everything to the Klan or whatever."

"And yet Rill owns a brand new, expensive, impractical car," Laurel said.

"Maybe it was a gift from Carter for doing him a favor. Some dirty work."

"Some very dirty work."

"You think Carter might have given him money for a Legion Series .45

caliber P226 too?"

"It wouldn't surprise me. Any new activity?"

"Not that I can see," Trey said, squirming in his seat again. "Television is still on. He's probably passed out in front of it."

"You got ants in your pants?"

"I'm fine."

"Diarrhea? What's wrong?

"I burned myself this morning. It's starting to itch."

"How'd you burn yourself?"

"Don't worry about it."

"Come on. What happened?"

"I was eating a breakfast Hot Pocket on the couch. I was really hungry, so I grabbed it out of the microwave, sat down to watch ESPN for a minute, and bit into it before it cooled down. A bunch of molten cheese squirted out the back end and fell on me."

"Fell on you where?"

"Why don't you just leave me alone?"

"Trey, come on. Fell on you where?"

"You know where."

"But wait," Laurel asked, now grinning from ear to ear. "How did the molten cheese get on your privates?"

"I told you. It leaked out the back of the Hot Pocket."

"No, no. I mean, did it burn you all the way through your pants?"

"No."

"So you were...."

"Naked, Laurel. I was naked. Yes. Happy now?"

"Of course you were. You were *stark naked* on the couch, watching ESPN, eating your microwaved breakfast Hot Pocket. You're a classy guy, Trey. There's no doubt about it."

"You think I should sue the Hot Pocket corporation?"

"And become the laughing stock of the internet? Absolutely."

The headlights of a large vehicle turned onto the street at the end of the block. It was a black Escalade.

"This might be Edgar," Laurel said.

Trey lowered his binoculars and they both watched the Escalade maneuver, with difficulty, to fit into a parallel parking spot. The door opened, and Edgar emerged, just identifiable in the dim glow of a nearby porchlight. He slammed his car door shut, marched up to Rill's front door, threw it open without knocking, and disappeared into the house.

"Huh," Trey said. "Did he look happy to you?"

"No, he did not. Want to sneak up and try to see what's going on?"

"Sure."

They got out of the car and approached the house slowly. They each went to a different edge of Rill's front yard and began to creep toward the windows under cover of darkness. It was another warm night, with fireflies dancing here and there above Rill's weedy lawn. Laurel took position behind a maple tree just off the front window, while Trey stood around the far corner of the house itself. They could hear a loud argument from within. But it was muffled by the structure of the house so that neither of them could make out more than the occasional word. Suddenly, the front door flew open and Edgar emerged once again, yelling, over his shoulder, something to the effect that Rill should have minded his own business. Trey and Laurel each stayed hidden until Edgar was back in the Escalade and driving down the street at reckless speed. Once he was far enough away that he wouldn't spot them, the detectives broke for their own car and jumped in.

"You don't want to stay on Rill?" Trey asked.

"Let's follow Edgar. Something's up."

Trey pulled the car out and pursued Edgar at a strategic distance.

"What do you think that was all about?" Trey asked as they followed Edgar toward the Cherokee Triangle neighborhood.

"Sounds like maybe Edgar wants a longer leash. Sounds like he's had enough of his shadow."

"We should have more than one car for this," Trey said.

"The more people we bring in, the greater the risk of the wrong people finding out that we're still investigating the Claytons."

"Yeah, but single car surveillance increases the risk of detection."

"It'll be alright. Just don't get too close to him. It's dark. We have that in our favor."

Trey grinned. "Did you get a look at Barton Rill?"

"No. I couldn't see much of the inside from where I was."

"He was shirtless."

"So?"

"He has man boobs."

"Man boobs?"

"Pectoral muscles that have gone to flab. To the point where he needs a bra."

"Good to know, Trey. Good to know."

*****

Edgar eventually slowed to a proper speed, which made tailing him easier. He wound through the Highlands, across Bardstown Road, and down to the corner of Dundee and Highland avenues. There, he parked alongside the brick wall of the vast, hauntingly beautiful Cave Hill Cemetery.

The detectives pulled over well up the road and watched as Edgar got out of his car, climbed a small tree next to the wall, and jumped over it, into the cemetery.

"What's wrong with the main entrance?" Trey asked.

"It's closed at this hour."

"Then why not wait until tomorrow? What's he up to?"

"Let's go find out."

They gave Edgar a brief head start, then ran down the street and followed his route up the tree, over the wall, and into the cemetery. Dropping to the ground, they were greeted by a landscape of exotic, ornamental trees that lined a curving drive. In between the trees, rows of gravestones led off in every conceivable direction. Some looked new. Most looked old. Many were large and ornate, bearing sculptures of angels, crosses, or obelisks. Some were small and plain.

It took the detectives a moment to spot Edgar making his way through the darkness.

"Hang back a bit," Laurel whispered. We don't want to spook him. And watch out for the security patrol."

With the help of bright moonlight, they tracked Edgar through the cemetery. After circumventing a small pond, Trey spotted him sitting on the ground maybe 200 yards away. They slowed their approach, making their way across a sea of graves arranged in a wide semicircle. The night air smelled of honeysuckle and cut grass. Frogs could be heard croaking all around them, the sound distinct against the white noise backdrop of a city that went on buzzing just outside the cemetery walls.

Once they were within about 50 yards of Edgar, they took up positions behind a couple of the larger headstones in the area and studied him through binoculars. He was sitting cross-legged, his shoulders slumped, with his back to them. He appeared to be sitting directly in front of a modern granite headstone that was flush with the ground. It marked a fresh grave, its red clay soil rising in an unsettled mound. Edgar had a bottle in his right hand. To Laurel, it looked like a whiskey bottle.

Over the next few minutes, Edgar sat there, looking sad and broken even from behind, taking occasional drinks from the bottle. Twice he wiped the back of his hand across his eyes as though drying tears. Then he got to his feet, muttered something that neither Laurel nor Trey could hear, tipped the bottle, and poured some of its contents on the grave. At this, Laurel heard Trey gasp. She turned and gave him a searing look. But Trey was too busy to notice, staring through his binoculars, his mouth hanging open in an expression of horror.

Edgar took one more long drink from the bottle, brushed off the back of his pants, and started back along the same route he came in by. As soon as he was a decent distance away, the detectives broke cover and ran to the marker to discover that it was Paul Taylor's grave.

"What in the world?" Trey said.

"I don't know, but what was with that gasp back there?" Laurel said. "He could have heard us, you moron."

"Sorry about that. But he was pouring 21-year-old Peepaw Clayton bourbon on the ground, Laurel. On the ground! It still makes my heart ache."

"Let's go. We don't want to lose him."

"He's driving drunk."

"Possibly."

"Aren't we obligated to pull him over?"

"It would blow our cover, maybe get us fired, *et cetera, et cetera.*"

"Not sure how I feel about that," Trey said as they headed back to their car, careful not to overrun Edgar. As they jumped back over the wall, they could see the taillights of Edgar's Escalade as he made his way back down Highland Avenue. The detectives raced for their own car to resume their pursuit. Once underway, Trey asked the question that was on both of their minds.

"Why is Edgar Clayton moping around at Paul Taylor's grave?"

FORTY-ONE

"There he is," Laurel said, having spotted the Escalade a block down Baxter Avenue, headed for downtown. Edgar led them out of the Highlands, across the NULU neighborhood, then on through Whiskey Row—one-time home of the bourbon industry—with its Victorian-era storefronts. The streets were thronged with people, out on a pleasant, warm night, enjoying the pre-Derby buzz. But Edgar kept going, leading the detectives to the very western edge of the business district where he at last turned down a steep street toward the Ohio River, then parked. The detectives passed the same street and pulled to the curb on Main, where they could watch Edgar in the rear and side-view mirrors. Edgar got out, walked down the hill, turned right onto Washington Street, and disappeared from view. The detectives jumped out and tailed him. Just as they turned onto Washington—which was more of an alley than a street—they saw Edgar disappear through the back door of a narrow, old brick building that shared walls with the buildings to either side of it. As the door closed, the detectives walked up for a closer look. Though its steel frame was dinged up and grimy, the door itself was bright green and recently painted with a high-gloss finish. It was plain and windowless. There were no signs to indicate what was behind it. Not even an address number. It was illuminated from above by an inadequate, bare lightbulb that hung at an odd angle in an old-fashioned porcelain fixture. Just above the heavy-duty doorknob was a 10-digit cypher lock. The detectives both stared at the buttons. No sound came from within.

"Crap," Trey said. "Now what?"

"Now we stake out this door."

They took a walk all the way around the block, checking to see if there was a front entrance up on Main Street through which they might be able to gain stealthy access to see what was going on inside. But the doors on the front of the building were locked tight. The detectives peered through the windows, but all was dark and quiet. The interior appeared to be in a state of disrepair or initial renovation. Whatever the case, there was no visible activity on the first floor, nor any light emanating from the higher floors overlooking Main Street.

They moved the Taurus to a spot down on Washington Street where they could keep an eye on the mysterious green door. And there they sat, for more than an hour. In all that time, nobody came out. But other people did go in. At least 20, in fact. Men and women both. Most in their 30s and 40s. Laurel tried to pin down some sort of defining quality about them, but couldn't. She hated the word *normal,* so she instead thought of them as unremarkable. Well dressed—perhaps expensively—but unremarkable.

"Do you want to follow one of these people in?" Trey asked.

"Not until we have some idea of what this place is. Of what's going on behind that door. Plus, unless the place is super crowded, Edgar would see and recognize us."

*****

Over the following hour, they grew bored and stiff.

"Do you have any good jokes?" Trey asked Laurel.

"They're all old."

"Like you."

"I can tell you an interesting story about this neighborhood."

"Yeah?"

"Ever hear of Bloody Monday?"

"No."

"On election day in 1855, mobs of anti-immigration fanatics attacked Louisville's German and Irish businesses, neighborhoods, and churches."

"Well," Trey said, "those Germans and Irish just don't share our values, Laurel. They steal our jobs and corrupt our women. Oh, wait—I'm Irish."

"During the ensuing riots," Laurel said, "a Catholic priest—who happened to be a co-founder of our St. Joseph Orphanage—was stoned to death. And just west of where we sit right now, up on Main, an entire block of row houses was set on fire by one of the anti-immigration mobs. Anyone who tried to escape the flames was gunned down in the street. Somewhere between 20 and 100 men, women, and children were shot or burned to death."

"Damn, Laurel. Couldn't you have just told me an old joke or two?"

Just then, Trey spotted a face he recognized in a group of three entrants.

"Hey," he said. "See that guy in the hipster fedora that's about two generations too young for him?"

"What about him?"

"Isn't that what's-his-face, the vegan pizza franchise king? From the TV commercials?"

"Yeah. I think you're right."

"Buddy of mine in the 8th Division used to moonlight as his driver. Said the guy has like three Ferraris at his mansion out in L'Esprit. Said he's a total jackass."

"He's rich," Laurel said. "And so is Edgar. Maybe the green door leads to some sort of millionaires club or secret society."

*****

They took turns napping until, just after 2 a.m., the green door opened and several dozen people emerged, including Edgar. Some of the people were arm-in-arm. Some were visibly intoxicated or perhaps on drugs.

"Trey, wake up."

"Eggs and bacon? Hot coffee?"

"Everybody's leaving," she said, watching as Edgar headed for his car.

Then, all of a sudden, and as though he knew exactly where and when to find Edgar, Barton Rill appeared out of nowhere and stepped up until he was toe-to-toe with Edgar.

"Man boobs at your 2 o'clock," Laurel said.

"Huh?"

"Barton Rill. Right there in front of Edgar."

"Where the hell did he come from?"

Rill seemed to be shouting at Edgar. But all Edgar did was smile a silly, detached smile. Then Rill backhanded Edgar, hard, across the face."

"Whoa!" Trey said as he sat up. "Did you see that?"

"I did."

After an odd delay, Edgar put his hand to his smacked cheek, then touched his fingertips to his lips. He burst into tears, stepped around Rill, and disappeared around the corner, walking toward his car.

"Edgar might be high on ecstasy," Trey said.

"At the very least."

As Trey gathered his wits, he spotted another face he recognized. "Laurel," he said, pointing.

"Who am I looking at?"

"The guy in the white loafers."

"Holy Toledo."

It was Senator Riley McKittrick.

FORTY-TWO

Shortly after 4 a.m., Laurel woke from another troubling dream. She'd been struggling against an endless flood of people at an extremely crowded airport, trying to make a flight with seconds to spare. But for all her desperate, frantic striving, she'd only lost ground, being forced in the wrong direction, away from her gate. In the end, she'd watched her plane back out and taxi away, leaving her behind.

She sat up in bed—breathing hard, heart pounding, anxiety washing over her—her mind once again grappling with that familiar unwelcome question. *Is this all there is?*

It was the second time it had happened in less than a week. A new, unhappy record. She wondered whether it was a byproduct of her anger over the political interference with her investigation. The sense that all her hard work was being rendered worthless, her integrity meaningless.

It took her a good twenty minutes to climb back out of the rabbit hole of her anxiety, and another hour to come down from the anger that took its place. She was tempted to pour herself a huge bourbon, but managed to hold off. It was nearly dawn by the time she fell back to sleep.

FORTY-THREE

After a very short slumber, Laurel swung by Plehn's Bakery to grab jelly donuts for Trey. She parked in a spot downwind of the bakery's vent fan, and the second she opened her car door, the smell of frying donuts enveloped her, making her mouth water. But as she got out of the car, she had a sudden sense that she was being watched. Making a quick scan of the nearby vehicles, a familiar face caught her eye. It was Empire Builder's boozy vet, Eldon Ridgeway, sitting in his maroon Pontiac Grand Am across the street, apparently focusing on his cell phone. She wondered whether he'd been following her. Whether he might be the one who'd sent her the mysterious, threatening text message. He didn't appear to be eating donuts. Then again, a box of donuts could be sitting next to him on the passenger seat.

With half a mind to march up to his window and ask him what he was doing, she walked into the bakery as nonchalantly as possible, as if she hadn't seen anything—electing to wait and see what his next move would be. But by the time she came back out with her box of donuts, he was gone. She called in his license plate to learn that his home address was within a few miles of the bakery. It wasn't exactly close. But it wasn't out of the realm of possibility that Ridgeway would be found there. It was, after all, an enormously popular bakery. She decided that crossing paths with him was probably a coincidence. Still, she resolved to keep a closer eye on her rearview mirror for the rest of the day.

*****

The detectives met at the office to run a records check on the owner of the building that the green door led into. Though the green door, which was on Washington Street, didn't have an address number, the building had long sides and went all the way through the block to Main Street, so they searched ownership records associated with the building's Main Street address. Curiously, the entire building turned out to be owned by Persona, Inc.—a big health insurance company that owned several buildings in the downtown business district.

"I'm guessing the members of the mysterious green door club—senators and millionaires though they may be—are technically squatters," Laurel said, "and that Persona has no idea they gather there in the dead of night."

"I wonder what they're up to."

"Let's go back down there and see if we can get in through the Main Street entrance during business hours."

"Why not just knock on the green door on Washington Street?"

"Trey, it's an unmarked steel door with a serious cypher lock located on a quiet back alley. Whatever is going on in there, the people involved want privacy. Even if someone answers the door, they aren't going to let us in without a search warrant."

*****

Soon, they were back at the front door to the building, on the Main Street side. The door was still locked. It was still dark and quiet inside.

"Any bright ideas?" Trey asked as Laurel peered through a dusty window. But just then, a young woman carrying a cup of coffee happened by.

"Can I help you?" she asked.

Laurel produced her badge and credentials, covering her name with her index finger. "Hi there. We're just answering a burglar alarm call. Probably a false alarm. Mice setting off a motion sensor or something. But we're obliged to check."

"I haven't seen the workers at this place for more than two weeks. But there's a side door from our building you can use if you'd like."

"That would be fantastic."

"No worries. Follow me."

She led them into the adjoining building which housed an architectural firm. Part way down the long main-floor corridor, she turned left into a short spur hallway that led to a small, modern fire door that had been cut through the old red brick.

"It's such a cool old building over there," she said as she turned a deadbolt lock and opened the door. Beyond it, there was another door—a wooden door with nothing but a round hole where the knob was supposed to be. The woman pushed it open. "Persona promises they're going to preserve its old character in the renovation. But every time their people seem to start working in earnest, they pause for another month or two. Maybe they're having permitting issues with the city. Anyway, I'll leave both doors open and you can let yourselves out if that's okay."

"Perfect. Thank you."

The detectives stepped through the doorway. The main floor was littered with sawhorses, extension cords, and five-gallon cans of some sort of primer or sealant. While in disrepair, the interior retained vestiges of the building's glory days—traces of a bygone era when aesthetics were still as important as functionality in architecture and design. There was elaborate trim work, wide-plank hardwood flooring, high ceilings, and tall windows. Polished up, it would be a thing of beauty.

"I don't see any sort of burglar alarm system," Laurel said. "Do you?"

"Nope. Looks all clear."

"Let's see if we can find a stairwell to the lower level," Laurel said.

They walked down a narrow hallway lined with tall office doors. The doors each had transom windows above them, like the classroom doors of old American schools.

In the very rear of the building, they looked out another set of tall windows, down onto the buckling sidewalk of Washington Street. They were directly above the green door. To their immediate left, there was an interior door to what could have been a closet. Laurel tried the antique knob. It was locked. She took firm hold of the knob and shook the door from side to side in its frame. Satisfied that there was enough flexibility, she pulled a pocket knife from her jacket, flipped it open, and went to work on jimmying the latch bolt free of the strike plate.

"Trey, take hold of the knob and pull the door toward its hinges, would you?"

Trey did so, and, as Laurel put a little pressure on the inside edge of the latch bolt, it came free and the door popped open.

"That was easier than I thought it would be," Trey said. "Did you bend your knife?"

"Nah. It's good."

They each took small but powerful flashlights from their pockets, turned them on, and peered inside. The door opened onto a tiny landing at the top of a steep and narrow set of dusty stairs that descended into cobwebbed darkness.

"Watch your footing," Laurel said. "Don't go stepping through any rotted wood. I don't have time to be taking you to the ER to get your already-burned scrotum stitched up."

"Thanks for caring."

Taking it slow, they descended the stairwell, Laurel taking the lead, testing the soundness of each step before putting her full weight on it.

"I hate spiders," Trey mumbled, keeping his head ducked, his arms tight against his body, in a futile effort to avoid touching any of the dusty cobwebs. "Do you think there are black widows down here?"

"Thousands of them."

"I hate you."

They emerged on a lower floor that they guessed was level with Washington Street, one floor below Main Street. It was nothing more than a derelict storage area, the entire floor wide open from wall to wall. The ceiling consisted of exposed joists, pipes, and antique knob-and-tube wiring. There was a haphazard scattering of discarded pint-size whiskey bottles on the dusty floor. The air smelled of staleness and mildew.

"Look at this," Trey said, shining his light on the foundation. It appeared to be constructed of nothing more than river rock embedded in crumbling mortar. "What on Earth holds these old buildings up?"

"Magic."

"It's a good thing you don't have earthquakes in this part of the country."

"No earthquakes? I take it you've never heard of New Madrid."

"Should I have?"

"It was a town on the Missouri-Kentucky state line that was wiped off the face of the Earth in the 1800s by an earthquake that was so powerful it changed the course of the Mississippi River."

"Then let's not stay in the bowels of this old place any longer than we have to."

They found a brick vault-like structure that appeared to enclose a stairwell leading down from the green door to a sub-basement level that was even deeper than the floor on which they stood. Laurel thought it looked like something that would have led to an underground, Prohibition-era speakeasy. But there was no way to access the stairs from the floor they were on. It seemed the green door was the only way in.

"Did you bring a crowbar?" Trey asked. "Maybe we can pull out a few bricks and squeeze through a hole to the stairwell."

"You're a detective, Trey. Not Indiana Jones," she said, turning her flashlight toward the far end of the space. "Look down there." She was shining the beam on what appeared to be a bank of old, multi-pane windows that were painted over with black paint.

"Why would there be windows down there?" Trey said. "It's a floor below Main Street. What's the view of? Dirt?"

But Laurel was already walking toward them, flashlight in hand, kicking stray pint bottles out of her way. Once at the far end of the space, she examined the windows carefully, then tapped on the glass, listening to the sound. She took her pocket knife out once more and began to scrape at the black paint covering the glass.

"What are you doing?" Trey asked.

"There's something behind here. An open space."

She scratched out a peephole. The space beyond the window was dark, so she scratched out a second, larger hole for her flashlight and looked in.

"What can you see?"

She backed off to give Trey a look. It was a cavernous space, with high, cut stone walls and a floor of poured concrete as big as two tennis courts. Laurel guessed that the painted windows they were peering through must have, at one time, been those of an office that looked out over a factory or warehouse of some sort. The floor—which was at least thirty feet below them—sloped to a large, manhole-sized drain in its center. At eight more or less equally-spaced positions across the floor sat large objects of varying shapes and sizes, each covered by a black sheet. There was a path of dampness leading from one of the covered objects straight to the large floor drain, as if the object had been washed recently. Another black sheet covered an object that protruded from one of the walls. The only things that weren't covered by black sheets were several large oil paintings that hung on the walls. Given the distance and darkness, they were somewhat hard to see. But Laurel could tell they were macabre, to say the least. One appeared to be of a giant, winged demon devouring the body of a naked woman it had in its clutches. Another was a portrait of a shriveled old man with no eyes—just black pits where his eyes were supposed to be—holding a candle that burned a red flame. Another depicted a naked man who looked an awful lot like Elvis Presley, nailed to an upside-down cross, his body bleeding from innumerable small slashes. Suspended above the space were two massive, ornate, wrought iron chandeliers that looked to have been salvaged from the ruins of a vampire's castle.

"I must get the name of their decorator," Trey muttered.

"Is your place feeling dated?"

"It could use some sprucing up."

"I suppose neo-Transylvanian is as hip a style as any."

After they each took a good, long look, they stood back, perplexed.

"A sewing club?" Trey said.

"Ha."

"Devil worshippers?"

"I suppose it's possible. But it seems too fantastic to believe."

"Maybe Persona's CEO is the Prince of Darkness."

"Well, Persona *is* an HMO, right?" Laurel took one more look through the peephole. "What do you think is under those black sheets?" she asked.

"Goat heads. Candles. Pentagrams. Oh, wait! I'll bet it's card tables! This is an illegal gambling place."

"Gambling place? You mean *casino*?"

"Gambling place, I say. A big-money, members only gambling place that caters to millionaires and high officials."

"Big money gamblers with a taste for satanic art?"

FORTY-FOUR

That night, at around 1 a.m., the detectives returned to the Main Street side of the vacant Persona Health Insurance building. When the coast was clear, they popped the front door open with a screwdriver and a little bit of pressure toward the hinges—a task made easy since, when they left earlier in the day, Laurel had stuffed the latch-bolt hole with wadded up paper until the latch bolt just barely held the door shut. Closing the door behind them, they made their way to the back stairwell and descended to the abandoned lower level. They could hear the moan and pound of some sort of techno music as they crossed the dark space to the holes they'd scraped in the blackout paint of the widows. They could also hear screaming.

Peering through their peepholes with mini binoculars, they were treated to the spectacle of an S&M club running full steam. The room was aglow with the soft light of red-shaded floor lamps and dozens of burning candles. The black sheets had been taken away to reveal leopard print chairs, red velvet couches, and other nice pieces of furniture upon which men in black tie and women in beaded and fringed Roaring Twenties Art Deco dresses sat drinking cocktails or smoking cigarettes in long cigarette holders. In a far corner, a naked man wearing nothing more than a ball gag was bound, hand and foot, to a large x-shaped rack constructed of black wooden beams that were bolted to the floor. A woman in a red latex suit was lashing his back with a flogging whip of braided leather tails. At a nearby table, a man was dripping hot candle wax onto the naked butt cheeks of a woman who was hooded and held face down by leather restraints of the sort one might expect to see in a psych ward. On yet another table, a woman was cranking the wheel of what appeared to be a medieval rack torture device, while the arms and legs of an emaciated man wearing a codpiece were being pulled in opposite directions. The onlookers, dressed in their fine formal attire, were gathered in rough circles around each pleasure-slash-torture station, watching the action with expressions ranging from those of boredom to amusement to arousal. Some of them were glassy-eyed and looked as if they might fall asleep standing. Some stood and watched with superhuman focus and intensity. The gaze of others flitted here and there with rapid, birdlike movements. To Laurel's eye, this meant they were probably on various club drugs—benzodiazepines, ecstasy, cocaine, LSD.

High on the wall opposite the detectives' vantage point, a huge purple neon sign bore a pentagram and spelled out, in avant-garde font, "Club Astarte."

"Look at the big pentagram on that neon-lit sign," Trey said. "That's a devil worship symbol for sure."

"No, hillbilly boy. Astarte is the Canaanite and Phoenician goddess of fertility and sexuality. One of her symbols is the pentagram—the star within the circle—representing the planet Venus. Astarte is the deified evening star."

Trey lowered his binoculars and looked at her. "Of course," he muttered. Getting no response, he resumed his observation of the crowd. "Hey," he said a minute later. "That guy with the top hat watching the flogging. Why does he look familiar to me?"

Laurel raised her own pair of mini binoculars, lined up one of the lenses with her peephole, and looked through. The man in the top hat was a good head taller than anyone near him. He wore Prohibition-era tails and leaned on a long, black walking stick. He looked higher than a kite.

"Oh, boy," Laurel said.

"What?"

"That's the mayor's chief of staff. Vernon something-or-other. Fuchs, I think. Vernon Fuchs. Yeah. One of those shifty guys who's always skulking on the fringes at city hall, working the angles. Used to be a back-slapping good old boy big firm lawyer-slash-lobbyist."

"With what law firm?"

"O'Neckless, McSweaty, and VanOverdressed, PLLC."

"Good one. How high is he on the ladder at city hall?"

"He's the mayor's right-hand man."

Trey exhaled. "Things just keep getting weirder."

Laurel continued to scan the room, looking at each face, committing each to memory as best she could. Her eyes found their way to a single wooden post that was bolted to the concrete floor just below their viewing window. There was a naked man chained to it, a neck cuff holding him in a sort of low, submissive kowtow such that his head was only a few inches off the ground. A semicircle of other naked men in black leather masks stood around him, each holding what appeared to be cattle prods. They were taking turns electrocuting the chained man, making him yelp and squirm. Amidst the clothed onlookers, Laurel spotted Edgar Clayton. He was holding an empty martini glass. Unlike his fellow spectators, he looked sullen.

"Tally ho," Laurel said.

"What?"

"Target at your 10 o'clock, low."

"Oh, Edgar, my man. What would your black-hearted bigot of a father say if he knew you were here paying special attention to the gents and their private parts?"

"I don't think he'd be terribly pleased," Laurel said, zooming in and snapping photos with her smartphone.

Trey lowered his binoculars again, taking a moment to reflect. "So, like, seeing what we're seeing here, and considering Edgar's little crying session at Paul Taylor's grave, do you think it's possible that Edgar Clayton is the man Paul Taylor dumped Benjamin Clayton for?"

"I'd say that's a reasonable theory."

Trey looked mystified.

"What is it?" Laurel asked.

"Now Edgar Clayton is gay."

"I'm sure he was gay before now."

"You know what I mean. Edgar Clayton is gay. Benjamin Clayton is gay. Paul Taylor was gay. Perry Clark is gay. You're gay. For all we know, Senator McKittrick is gay. Everyone is gay. This is, like, Vice President Pence's worst nightmare."

"Unless he's secretly gay."

FORTY-FIVE

"I have to say, I think it's kind of disturbing," Trey said as he drove Laurel home to her condo.

"The S&M club? You're a homicide detective. Don't be so delicate."

"I don't mean the mere existence of the club or whatever. I mean, I get that a few people out there have different fetishes. I happen to have a weird thing for colossally-breasted women wearing bib overalls. But torture? The mayor's chief of staff? A state senator? A bunch of our local millionaires and captains of industry? Really?"

"Have you ever *not* known power to go hand-in-hand with weirdness?" Laurel asked.

"George W. Bush and Barack Obama both seemed pretty normal. For presidents, anyway."

"Please. You have no idea what kind of crazy stuff those two have in their basement freezers. Stacks of heads. Body parts. Human breast milk. Who knows?"

"Thanks for putting my mind at ease."

Laurel took a deep breath. "Let's stop for a beer," she said. "My mind is too spooled up to go straight to bed."

"Wait, *you* want to go out? The queen of lameness?"

"You trying to talk me out of it?"

"What's even open this late?"

"The Back Door, off Bardstown Road. Old joint with ice cold beer and pool tables."

"The fundamentals."

*****

Laurel offered to drive Trey home afterwards, so as soon as they got to the bar, he gulped down a couple cold pints of IPA from his home state of Oregon. Midway through his third, he started getting a little silly. What had started off as their fifth evenly matched game of pool was quickly degenerating into a route by Laurel.

"Care to make it interesting?" Laurel asked.

"Now that I've had a bunch of high-alcohol beer on an empty stomach? No thanks."

"You don't even have to do anything. Give me challenges."

"Fine. Bounce the six ball off the far edge and sink it in this back corner pocket."

"What do I get if I do?"

"You won't make it."

"That's not what I asked you."

"Five bucks."

Laurel lined up and made the shot.

"Damn," Trey said. "That was a great shot."

"How about this?" Laurel said. "If I run the table from here, you pick up the bill."

"There're still nine balls on the table."

"Do we have a bet?"

"You're not going to make nine shots in a row."

"So you're saying we have a bet."

"Fine. You're on. For the bill."

"Two ball, side pocket," Laurel said before sinking it. "Welcome to school."

Laurel was already lining up to take a shot at the eleven ball when Trey said, "Are you hustling me?"

"Would I do that to you?"

Trey seemed to give the question a great deal of thought. Then he let it go. "So, tomorrow morning—what—do we go pick up Edgar and put the thumb screws to him?"

"Not quite yet. I have one more duck to get in the row. Seven ball, corner pocket." She sank the shot.

"You think we'll be able break Edgar eventually?"

"If we get his phone location records. No question. His father's a homophobe and hater of all things non-WASP. Edgar is either gay or bisexual. We have photographic proof. And even though Edgar probably hates his father, he also probably doesn't want his father to see photos exhibiting his sexuality. There's always that part of us that wants to please our parents, right? Or at least not disappoint them. Even if they're creeps."

"Speaking of which, can I ask you a personal question?"

"What do I always say?"

"You always say *no*. But how old were you when you came out?"

"Nineteen."

"How did your parents take it?"

Laurel gave him a look. "Not well."

"How not well?"

"How not well? They asked why I couldn't have waited until they died before coming out."

"You're joking."

"No."

Trey shook his head. "How could any parent say that to their own child?"

"That's easy for someone of our generation to say," she said, lining up another shot.

"Still."

"The church they happened to grow up in seems to give the Book of Leviticus more weight than the New Testament. Leviticus says homosexuality is evil, plain and simple. How do you get someone to reconsider what they think of as the word of God?" She shrugged.

"But your child is your child."

"You have to look at it from their perspective."

"I don't know how you can be so understanding."

Laurel sank another shot. "What am I going to do? They're my mom and dad. Anyway, I think they're starting to come around."

"I hope they do. They have every reason to be proud of you."

At this, to Trey's horror, Laurel teared up. Frozen in place, he deliberated giving her a hug. But then she took a deep breath, wiped her eyes on her sleeve, and sank the eight ball.

FORTY-SIX

Back at the offices of the Commonwealth's Attorney, the detectives filled Seth Greenberg in on where things stood. Laurel figured it was worth a shot trying to get Greenberg to give them a warrant for the records of Barton Rill and Edgar Clayton's cell phones so that they could better nail down their locations on the nights of the Taylor and Cervantes murders. But Greenberg wasn't buying it.

"Sweetheart, you don't even know who their cell phone service providers are yet."

"That's easy to fix," Laurel said.

"You don't know that either of them own the type of handgun that was involved."

"We have video of Edgar's car near both murder scenes, and the timing matches up."

"But as you mentioned, with respect to Rill, your Churchill Downs security video only shows shadows. You can't see whether or not it's Rill in the passenger seat of Edgar's Escalade. And you have no footage whatsoever indicating that Rill might have been anywhere near the Taylor crime scene."

"The evidence is circumstantial. But there's a lot of it. Rill is Carter Clayton's fixer. And at the center of this whole affair we have an astonishing commonality in the involvement of a number of our key players with the secret S&M club behind the mysterious green door on Washington Street. That's no coincidence. Give us Edgar, at least."

"I can't. But I'll give you a hamantash cookie. In the blue box behind you."

"Come on, Seth."

"For heaven's sake, have one of my mother's cookies. They're really good."

"Seth!"

"Go get me a murder weapon."

"Sure. Why hadn't I thought of that?"

"Reach into your bag of clever detective tricks."

"We're asking for cell phone location records, not an arrest warrant," Trey said. "What's the big deal?"

Greenberg turned on him. "The big deal? Listen, my neophyte friend. Any ethical judge will toss *all* the evidence you get from a cell phone records search if you don't have probable cause. Fruit of the poisonous tree, *et cetera, et cetera*. You know this. It's an absolutely fundamental rule of your work." Greenberg took a breath. "You don't think I'd love to bust these creeps? You ever hear of the Altamont Club?"

Trey gave a curt nod.

"Did you know that Clayton Carter IV was on the executive board of the Altamont Club in the early 1960s when my soft-spoken, kind, humanist, five-foot grandfather applied for membership there and was *denied* for no other reason than his being Jewish? Denied, even though he was a highly respected federal court judge? You don't think I'd love to see an old snake like Carter on TV wearing an orange jumpsuit and handcuffs? Of course I would. But Carter is a heavyweight donor to every re-election campaign that matters, which, in our imperfect world, means we have to tread lightly, dot every *i*, and cross every *t*. We'll cross the Rubicon when we have enough spears, so to speak. And, I guarantee you, I'll be riding in the vanguard with a huge smile on my face. So don't try to guilt me into making a decision we'll all regret. Go do your job."

"You're going soft in your old age," Laurel said.

"I'm not that old. Anyway, deep down, you still love me."

"Well, obviously." Laurel paused. "Seth, listen—don't let anyone know we were here discussing this case, alright?"

"Are you in some sort of trouble?"

"I'll fill you in later. Just keep it under your hat."

"Laurel."

"Look, you have to trust me. I'll fill you in later."

FORTY-SEVEN

Central State Hospital—formerly known, in certain less-enlightened eras, as the Central Kentucky Lunatic Asylum and the Central Kentucky Asylum for the Insane—was a psychiatric hospital situated near the town of Anchorage in a quiet pocket of eastern Jefferson County. Like so many psychiatric facilities the world over, its history included heartbreaking periods of underfunding and overcrowding. Indeed, though initially built to accommodate 1,600 patients, by 1940, it housed more than 2,400. And while the facility had long since been modernized and its services vastly improved, the grounds were still littered with the innumerable unmarked graves of mentally ill people who'd been abandoned there by their families—their names lost to history.

The name of the nearby town—Anchorage—had always struck Laurel as odd. There was no port. No sea, major lake, or navigable river for miles around. Certainly nowhere a ship would drop anchor. Regardless, it was beautiful. If she ever had to be committed to a psychiatric hospital, she figured it wouldn't be a bad place to end up.

While the original twin-spired brick hospital building had looked like a haunted Bavarian castle, the modern facility had the pleasant and unimposing look of a small community college campus. There were flowering trees and wide walkways lined with low-rise buildings.

It took a bit of explanation and pleading, but the detectives were, after a quick policy and procedure briefing, led to a common room with couches, chairs, tables, and tall windows looking out over a wide pasture bordered with stately oaks. There, sitting in a chair and reading a book, sat Zelda Rill—formerly known as Zelda Clayton. Often known to her schizophrenic self as Teetee. Last name unknown. She was the only one in the room.

"You have visitors, Teetee," an orderly said. "These people are police detectives. I'll leave you to it," he said to Laurel

Zelda didn't look a day over 30. It seemed that hospitalization agreed with her. The only thing that gave her away as a patient was her hospital-issued slippers. Aside from those, she wore a navy blue shift that had a similar cut to the black one Magnolia wore when they'd interviewed her. Laurel guessed that Magnolia was the one who bought Zelda her clothes. She was glad someone on the outside was looking out for her.

"Hi, Teetee. I'm Laurel. And this is Trey."

"Nice to meet you," Zelda said in a lively, girly voice as she rose from her chair. "Am I taking a test today?"

"No. No tests. We're just hoping you can help us solve a puzzle."

"I'm good at puzzles. I did a 3,000-piece puzzle of the Great Barrier Reef last week. It only took me five hours."

"Well, then I'm afraid this puzzle won't be much of a challenge for you. It's more of a memory puzzle."

"What do you mean?"

"It's about your husband, Barton, and where he keeps things."

Zelda stared at them blankly.

"You remember Barton?"

"Barton?" she echoed, looking perplexed as she sat back down on her chair. It seemed, to Laurel, that Zelda had difficulty holding her gaze steady on any particular person or thing. Her eyes—which were an unusual pale blue—moved every couple of seconds, refocusing on something new, as if she were trying to puzzle out where she was and whether her surroundings were at all familiar. She also kept glancing at different parts of the chair she sat in, as if to reassure herself that it was actually there.

"Well, I know you didn't come to discuss *this*," Zelda said, "but I feel compelled to tell you that lately my mind has been preoccupied, really fully occupied, by ruminations on the number three."

"Three?" Laurel said.

"The natural number three. I'm so preoccupied that I don't know if I'll be of much help to you discussing anything else. I can't seem to stop thinking about it."

"Why do you think that is?"

"The doctors say it's because of my illness. But maybe it's because few numbers have so many facets. Think about it. Three follows two and precedes four. But that's neither here nor there. In my opinion, the quality worth focusing on is that, even though you think of three as being third, it's actually many different things. It's the *first* odd prime number. It's the *second* factorial prime. It's also the *fourth* Fibonacci number. So, in a sense, the number three is first, second, third, and fourth, depending on your point view."

"I hadn't thought of that."

"See? It's one of the reasons I've been so preoccupied. It's funny how one thing can, quite naturally, be many things."

"I see your point."

"Even the puzzle I did, of the Great Barrier Reef? It didn't have 1,000 pieces.

It didn't have 2,000 pieces. It had 3,000. Coincidence? Maybe. Or maybe synchronicity. Synchronicity in the Carl Jung sense, I mean. You've heard of Carl Jung? C.G. Jung? The Swiss analytical psychologist? Born June 26, 1857? Refined theories of individuation—the process of discerning the so-called self from your individual conscious and unconscious components?"

"Actually, Teetee, we were wondering about where your husband, Barton, keeps his handguns," Laurel said in the gentlest possible voice.

Once again, Zelda stared at them, seeming not to comprehend the question.

"Do you remember your sister Magnolia? She told us Barton had guns. We were just wondering where he kept them."

"There are three of us sitting here talking, even. Oh—and today is the third of the month! See?"

"Yes, I see," Laurel said. With her heart aching for Zelda, and sinking over the fact that the interview was going nowhere, her gaze dropped to her shoes.

"You don't think I have control of my thoughts," Zelda said, suddenly looking and sounding quite desperate. "I know because I can hear *your* thoughts. I really can."

"I believe you."

"Your partner is in love with you even though you're a lesbian."

Trey focused on keeping his jaw from falling open.

"I suspected as much," Laurel said. "Can you blame him?"

"No, I can't. I...." She paused, and for a fleeting moment, her restless eyes locked on Laurel's. "I want to help you."

"I know."

"It's just that I have trouble...." She let her statement hang unfinished. Her eyes resumed their frequent shifting.

"Teetee, is there anything at all that you can tell us about the guns?" Laurel asked.

"I'm not sure what you mean. But do you know what else just occurred to me? Even the holy trinity has three parts. The Father, the Son, and the Holy Spirit. Three divine entities in one God. Think about *that*!"

Laurel stood. Trey followed suit. "It was nice to meet you, Teetee."

All at once, Zelda seemed agitated. Her eyes darted here and there even more quickly than they had before. Her hands gripped the armrests of her chair so tightly that her knuckles turned white. Laurel watched her, waiting for more. But Zelda remained silent. Laurel and Trey turned to leave. However, just as they reached the door, and in a slower, deeper voice, Zelda said, "Detectives."

When they looked back, Zelda had fixed them in a now rock-steady gaze. Her face had changed. The energy was gone. She looked weary. Like someone who carried the burden of knowing too much.

"I remember something," she said, her voice listless, the words labored.

"Yes?" Laurel asked.

"Barton keeps a gun in his nightstand." She smiled a sad, weak smile.

"Thank you, Teetee."

"Zelda," she said.
Laurel bit her lip to keep from tearing up.
"Thank you, Zelda. You take care now."

FORTY-EIGHT

It took Laurel all of about 10 seconds to come up with a plan for finding out what cell phone service providers their suspects used. She decided to target Rill first. From Central State Hospital, she and Trey drove back to Rill's house to stake it out. Soon enough, he popped out his front door and took off in his yellow Ford Mustang. He led them down to an old Louisville watering hole called the Magnolia Bar and Grill—known to locals as the Mag Bar—where, to the detectives considerable surprise, he met Edgar for lunch. Apparently, they were letting bygones be bygones. Or something like that.

"Let's see if we can't kill two birds with one stone here," Laurel said, placing a call that would set her plan in motion. She reached out to a friend and off-duty female police officer, Kendall Tate, and asked her to swing by the Mag Bar. When Kendall got there, on Laurel's instruction, she went inside, rolled right up to Edgar and Barton as they sat drinking beers at the bar, and pretended to be having trouble hearing someone on her phone. She turned and complained to them about her poor cell phone reception. She asked them if they had the same provider that she did. They said no, told her the provider they both used, then each checked their own reception to confirm that it was good. Tate noted the make and model of their phones, then left the tavern to report back to Laurel.

To Laurel's delight, it turned out Edgar and Barton both had models of smartphones that came equipped with an operating system that allowed for historical movement tracking by recording the host phone's GPS coordinates. This was something that some brands of phone didn't yet allow for. It meant that, once Laurel and Trey could get a warrant, the company that created the operating system on Barton and Edgar's phones would be able to tell the detectives exactly where they'd been on the nights of the murders—assuming they'd had their phones with them. Otherwise, the detectives would have had to depend on cell tower data dumps to approximate Edgar and Barton's locations on the nights in question.

As soon as Kendall left, Laurel's own phone rang. It was Sergeant Turner. "What are you up to, Laurel?"

"What am I up to? Grabbing a burger with Trey at the Mag Bar."

"So I can rest assured that you haven't been pursuing anything having to do with the Claytons?"

"Why do you ask?" He didn't answer. "Is someone telling you that we've been questioning Edgar or Carter Clayton or their cronies? Because we haven't." Technically, that was true.

"I just don't want to see anyone drop the hammer on you, Laurel. You're good people. Good police."

"Don't worry about me, Isaiah. And I promise, cross my heart and all that, we haven't bothered Edgar or Carter since you gave us the hands-off message. We have enough to do already."

The second she hung up, Laurel got another text message on her phone. Again, it was from a number with a blocked ID. She looked at it, then showed it to Trey. "Check this out."

It said, *Back off. Final warning.*

"You get this two seconds after Isaiah checks up on you?" Trey said. "What are the chances? The person pressing Isaiah to keep you on a short leash has to be the same person sending you these texts."

"Probably," she said, looking up and down the street, seeing if any of the nearby cars struck her as familiar.

"Laurel, you have to take this to somebody."

"We can't go to Isaiah, or he'll know we've been disobeying orders."

"The union then. Like I said before, at least it would establish a history of you being messed with. That could help cover your butt if anyone tries to set you up."

"Maybe."

"I have the union rep's number programmed in my phone." He took his phone out and dialed it. "Here," he said, handing it to Laurel.

It only rang twice before the rep picked up.

"Bill Richards," the man answered.

"Hello, Bill. Are you the union rep?"

"That's me."

"My name is Laurel Arno. I'm a detective with violent crimes. I've had a couple of things happen over the past few days that I think I should put on record with you guys."

On the other end, silence.

"Hello?"

"This is Laurel Arno?"

"Yes, it is. Did you hear what I just—"

"I'm sorry. I can't get involved with this."

"I beg your pardon?"

"I can't get involved."

"I haven't even told you what it's about yet."

"I'm sorry."

Laurel paused to consider the implications. "Has someone approached you about this already?"

"Look, I have young kids. I'm sorry," Richards said.

"Did someone threaten you?" Silence. "Is there anyone there I can talk to? Anyone at all?"

"I'm really sorry."

Richards hung up. Trey was already staring at her. "That didn't sound good."

"It wasn't." She could feel her initial surprise and twinge of fear giving way to anger. The anger worked its magic on her mind—got her wheels turning, sped up her thoughts. "You know what, Trey? Screw this. If these sons of bitches are going to turn up the heat on us, I say we turn up the heat on them. Let's get devious."

FORTY-NINE

Laurel, Trey, and Speedy sat in the unmarked Taurus, parked half a block down the street from Barton Rill's dilapidated shotgun house once again. They'd already established that Rill was at home watching TV.

"Speedy," Laurel said. "You got a place to take cover tomorrow when the crazy weather comes rolling in?"

"Crazy weather?"

"There's a tornado watch tomorrow."

"Oh. Well. Shelter where I'm at has a good basement."

"Good," Laurel said. "Stay close to home tomorrow. Until the storm passes."

"Man, don't worry about me, Laurel."

"Alright. So you understand the plan here?"

"When do I get my hundred bucks?"

"As soon as we're done. If you don't blow it."

"Ha!"

"You understand the *whole* plan?"

"Laurel, man. Relax. I got it."

"Is there any part of it you aren't sure about?"

"Naw, man. Long as Officer Trey's car is where you say it's at, it's all good."

"Okay. Just remember, it might take us a little while to spring you free, so don't panic."

"It's cool, man. Long as I got air in there. So now what?"

"Now we wait until this creep leaves his house and the coast is clear."

"Coast is clear," Speedy said with a dry-throated sort of giggle. "You sound like Bugs Bunny Looney Tunes."

"Bugs Bunny Looney Tunes?"

"Yeah, man. *The coast is clear*, and shit. Like something Bugs Bunny would say."

*****

After most of an hour, they spotted Rill coming out his front door. He crossed his weedy lawn, jumped in his Mustang, and sped off.

"Alright," Laurel said. "We don't know how long he'll be gone, so we had better get the show on the road here. You ready?" she asked Speedy.

"Sure, man. Ready to rock."

"Pull up your hood and pull the strings tight to hide most of your face. Be careful."

"Laurel, you got to relax, man. I'm a pro at this sort of thing."

"Oh, no—don't say that."

"Just messing with you."

"Okay, funnyman. We'll see you on the other side."

With that, Laurel and Trey did a quick scan of the area, making sure nobody was around to see Speedy get out of their car. Then they sent him on his way. As Speedy got closer to Rill's house, he started to run. He turned up the walk, ran to the front door, reared up and started kicking it with the bottom of his dominant foot.

"Oh, crap," Trey said, after Speedy's fourth kick. "Maybe Rill has a serious lock."

But just as Trey finished voicing his worry, the door gave way in a shower of splintered wood. Speedy was in.

"Go?" Trey asked.

"Go."

Trey pulled the car onto the street, floored it, and roared the half block down to the curb in front of Rill's house, where he deliberately hammered the brakes to make a screeching racket. Trey jumped out, drew his gun, and ran into the house while Laurel radioed that they were in pursuit of Caucasian male—fitting Speedy's very general description—after witnessing a possible drug deal. She paused after giving the name of the street and block number, then added that the subject had just broken into a private residence. She gave Rill's address, then got out of the car to cover the front of the house. Now it all depended on Speedy. Laurel hoped he lived up to his nickname.

To her relief, she heard the sound of shattering glass coming from the rear of the house. Then Trey came out the front, gave Laurel a subtle but reassuring nod, shouted "he went out the back," and took off in pretend pursuit. Laurel heard sirens approaching from two different directions. She jumped back in the Taurus and sped away, as if to cut off Speedy's escape on the other side of the block.

*****

Half an hour later, one of the patrolmen who'd responded to their call had already committed the bulk of the official version of the incident to paper. According to his report, Laurel and Trey, while driving back to the Homicide Unit offices in Old Louisville, happened to witness a possible hand-to-hand drug deal on Shelby Street—in an area considered a known open-air drug market— and had initiated pursuit after the subject spotted the detectives, noticed their undivided interest in him, acted furtively, and then bolted. The subject had sprinted down the CSX railroad tracks, turned onto Goss Avenue, then turned again into a residential neighborhood where he broke into a house in a probable effort to hide. Realizing the police were still in pursuit, the subject escaped by smashing out a back window, fleeing across the backyard, and then jumping the fence into an alley that split the residential block. At that point, pursuing officers lost contact. While in pursuit, a patrol officer did, however, recover a handgun— a .45 caliber Sig Sauer P226 Legion Series—that the subject probably dropped in the backyard of the house as he crawled through the broken back window in order to escape. It wasn't yet known whether the subject had already been carrying the gun, or whether he'd found it in the house he'd broken into. More information to follow.

The unofficial version of the incident would, of course, read very differently. After breaking in, Speedy had gone straight to Rill's bedroom and thrown open his cheesy black pressboard nightstand to find the gun right where Zelda "Teetee" Clayton said it would be. Speedy picked it up with a bandana, careful not to get any fingerprints on it since his were already in the system. Once Trey entered the house, Speedy waved it at him to show he'd found it, then smashed a chair through a back window and made his staged escape, dropping the gun in the back yard just as Laurel had instructed. After cutting through yards across the middle of two blocks, then crossing the CSX railroad tracks again, Speedy found Trey's Buick parked in a vacant lot in front of a partially demolished warehouse, behind high, overgrown bushes. There, he got in the already-unlocked trunk. He closed the trunk, turned on a small battery-powered lantern, and went to town on a huge bag of M&Ms—his favorite candy—that Trey had left there for him. Once the so-called crime scene was buttoned up, Trey walked a few blocks to recover his car, drove across town to a predetermined spot—a quiet alley that didn't have any known security camera coverage—let Speedy out of the trunk, and gave him $100.

"You want some M&M's, man?" Speedy asked Trey.

"They're all yours, brother. See you around."

FIFTY

"Turns out the house is owned by Barton Rill," Laurel said as she and Trey sat side-by-side in Seth Greenberg's office first thing the next morning. "His fingerprints are all over the gun. In fact, they're the only finger prints that were found on the gun. And, to top it all off, an expedited analysis established that the gun is a match for the one that killed Paul Taylor."

"Wouldn't you know it," Greenberg said. "And you just happened to witness this quote-unquote drug transaction in broad daylight in a known open-air drug market—or, as you cretins like to call it, a hotspot."

"A textbook hand-to-hand. I have to give Trey credit there. He has sharp eyes."

"Oh, I'm sure. And Trey didn't think it was, by chance, just a couple of old buddies shaking hands?"

"Seth, please. We're seasoned professionals. We have that cop's sixth sense for these type of things."

"So your subject bolts, and you pursue. And then, against lottery ticket odds, your quarry runs straight to Barton Rill's house and breaks into it. Barton Rill, who just happens to be Carter Clayton's henchman."

"Sometimes you get lucky," Laurel said.

"And you chase him into the house and out the back of the property, knowing it was legal for you to do so because of the *hot pursuit* exception to the requirement for a warrant."

"Always mindful of the law."

"Then you get an expedited analysis of the gun. One of the fastest I've ever heard of, in fact."

"Friend in the lab owed me a favor."

"And you thought to yourself, hey, why not burn that valuable favor on a low-priority drug deal case?"

"Don't put off until tomorrow what you can do today, Seth. That's my motto."

"That's Ben Franklin's motto."

"Whatever."

"What did the other subject look like?"

"Other subject?"

"In the hand-to-hand drug deal."

"Oh, *that* other subject."

"There wasn't a description in the report. What did he look like? You know what? Never mind."

Greenberg went quiet, turned in his chair, and looked out his window.

"Are you going to give us our cell phone records warrant now?" Trey asked.

Greenberg gave him a sharp look. Then he leaned back in his chair and said to the ceiling, "For I know that after my death you will surely act corruptly and turn aside from the way that I have commanded you. And in the days to come evil will befall you, because you will do what is evil in the sight of the Lord, provoking him to anger through the work of your hands."

"Pardon?" Trey said after a moment's silence.

"The words of Moses himself, dressing down the stubborn Levites who carried the Ark of the Covenant. Deuteronomy 21:29."

"Ark of the Covenant?" Trey said. "As in *Raiders of the Lost Ark*?"

"The very same."

"Didn't know you were religious," Laurel said.

"I'm not."

"What an odd thing for you to quote," Laurel said with a straight face. "Now, about Clayton and Rill's cell phone records. I think it's safe to say that we have probable c—"

"Yes, yes. I'll sign off." Greenberg gave each of the detectives another hard look. "But don't ever do this again."

"I'm sure neither of us know what you mean," Laurel said.

"Right. Just don't do it again."

"Can I have one of your mother's cookies?"

"No."

FIFTY-ONE

Greenberg helped the detectives by putting the fear of God in the cell phone service provider representative's heart, getting the poor sap to send them the phone location data ASAP. It was usually a very slow process. But within an hour, to their utter amazement, they had it. And sure enough, a quick analysis showed that phones registered to Edgar Clayton and Barton Rill had pinged their locations to within a few yards of Bacchus Distribution and Javier Cervantes's backyard on the nights of each of the murders.

*****

The detectives headed for their car, planning to drive east, back out to the Clayton Distillery. It was sunny, but the hot air was sticky and still.

"Pre-storm air," Laurel said as they got to the car. "Heavy with moisture."

"It's so sunny and clear," Trey said. "I can't believe a bunch of nasty weather is supposed to be coming at us this evening."

*****

"Listen, Trey," Laurel said once they were in the car and rolling. "Things are going to start moving fast."

"Works for me."

"Also, we're not going to take Edgar to the Homicide Unit."

"Because we don't want Isaiah to know we've arrested him yet?"

"Exactly."

"He's going to be pissed."

"Not if we bring him a corrupt CID major on a silver platter."

"If."

"Trey, all our chips are already on the table. Win or lose, we're all-in. So let's take Edgar to the 5th Patrol Division. I have friends there who can help us arrange things quietly. We have to get all our ducks in a row before Isaiah or anyone else up the chain of command finds out what we're up to. We're going to have to be ready to move quickly, before the powers that be can obstruct us again—or flush both of us down the toilet."

"What about Rill? It's his gun, after all."

"We wait on Rill. Edgar is going to be the easier target. I feel it in my bones. Let's get Edgar to turn and rat out Rill. If we're lucky, maybe we can even get him to hand us his own father."

*****

They pulled Edgar Clayton over on a quiet stretch of Kentucky Route 193 near Port Royal, less than half a mile from the distillery, as he was on his way to pick up an order of biscuits and gravy at the country store. Laurel read him his Miranda rights as Trey slapped the cuffs on and did a standard pat down for weapons.

"I didn't do anything," Edgar mumbled. "I really didn't."

"You'll have a chance to explain," Laurel said. "Right now, we're going to take you to our office. Then we can talk."

"Wait—I want to talk to a lawyer."

"We'll get that all squared away for you once we get to the office. In the meantime, again, you're under no obligation to talk to us. But I will say this, Edgar. Once we get to the office, I urge you to listen to what we have to say before you make any decisions. You don't have to say a thing. Just hear us out."

And with that, Laurel stuffed a bewildered Edgar in the back seat of the car while Trey moved Edgar's own car off the state route and onto a side road where it would be more or less out of sight of anyone driving to or from the distillery.

*****

After fingerprinting him and filling out the initial arrest paperwork at the 5th Patrol Division station, they put Edgar in an interrogation room for safekeeping. Trey bought him an Ale-8 soda from the vending machine while Laurel grabbed files from the trunk of the car. A couple minutes later, they met back at the door to the interrogation room.

Trey pointed to the stack of file folders in Laurel's arms. "That's gotten big all of a sudden."

"The stuff relevant to our case is only in the top two folders. I built this big stack with a bunch of other random crap to make it look like we have tons of evidence. If you go through it, you'll find my utility bills, a manual for my new washing machine, and my aunt's recipe for peanut butter cookies, among other things."

"Good trick."

"You ready?"

"Gung-ho."

As they entered, they found Edgar slumped in his chair and looking altogether miserable.

"Here's your soda," Trey said. "It's nice and cold."

"I think I want to talk to a lawyer."

"We can arrange that," Laurel said, assuming an authoritarian voice, slapping the big stack of files down on the desk as she and Trey sat down. "But if we go that route, it permanently closes off a lot of options for you. So, for your own sake, right now I'd really, really encourage you to just hear what we have to say. Like I said before, you don't have to talk. But just hear us out." Edgar stayed quiet, so Laurel went on. "By way of putting things into context here, you're being charged with two counts of murder, along with a handful of lesser crimes related to you lying to us. Murder, of course, is a capital offense, with each count punishable by life imprisonment without parole, or even death. However, as you probably already know from watching *Law & Order*, when suspects cooperate, we can go easy on them. The commonwealth's attorney who is prosecuting this case is a very reasonable man. He can knock charges down. He can recommend leniency to the court, and the court will heed him. But someone is going to pay the price for the lives of Javier Cervantes and Paul Taylor. It's just a question of who."

Edgar held his palms up. "Wait. I really think I need to—"

"Now hold on, hold on. Hear us out. We know about you and Paul Taylor," she said, leaving her statement vague.

Edgar looked like he was going to be sick.

"Did your father know about that?" she asked, standing up. "About you and Paul?" Laurel waited. "I guess it doesn't matter. But something that does matter is that you mislead us, Edgar. You lied to us. Repeatedly, in fact."

Edgar looked as if he were about to protest again. But Laurel held up her index finger while Trey pulled a bunch of glossy 8x10 photos from the topmost file folder. He set the first photo on the table. Laurel pointed at it.

"Edgar, this is your Escalade at Churchill Downs on the night Javier Cervantes was strangled to death."

"I already told you—"

"Matter of fact, your car is backed up to the very stall where Cervantes was working that night. And this," she said, turning over the next photo, "is you and your accomplice loading Cervantes's body into the back of your car. Now, you told us that, that night, you stopped by what you described as a little corner grocer on South 3rd Street, right by Churchill Downs for—what was it Trey?"

"Cigarettes. Box of Twinkies. Hand sanitizer."

"The funny thing is, the only corner grocer on South 3rd anywhere near Churchill Downs has no records of such a combination of goods being purchased on the evening in question."

Edgar tried to speak. "Maybe they made a mist—"

"Wait, there's more. You also told us you hadn't known who Javier Cervantes was until you heard his name on the news. And yet, according to our cell phone tracking friends at the phone company, you were on his property at 112 East Greenfield the same night he was murdered. Behind his house, in fact. Back by the garage. What an extraordinary coincidence, Edgar."

Edgar had nothing to say.

"Now, shifting gears a bit, this," she said, flipping over another picture, "is a photo of your Escalade near Broadway and 11th on the night of Paul Taylor's murder."

"Like I said, I went to get—"

"To get fried chicken at Indi's. Yes. We remember. But what you didn't tell us was that, as our phone company friends have further confirmed, you turned off of Broadway, drove down 11th, and stopped in front of Bacchus Distribution at 9:09 p.m. Bacchus Distribution happens to be Paul Taylor's warehouse. Maybe you were just looking for a quiet place to eat your fried chicken while it was hot. But the weird thing is, that's also the exact time at which Shotspotter caught the sound of gunfire in the 800-block of South 11th Street."

"What's Shotspotter?"

"Haven't you heard? Louisville has a system of listening devices all over the city that can triangulate the exact location of gunfire. It even records the sound. Cutting-edge stuff, Edgar. Makes our job so much easier." She gave him a confident smile. "Now then, another interesting thing is that you were observed weeping at Paul Taylor's grave in Cave Hill Cemetery the other night—even though you told us you had no idea who he was. But perhaps even more interesting," Laurel said, ready to tempt Edgar with the bait, "is that Taylor was shot to death with a gun owned by your brother-in-law, Barton Rill."

Laurel waited.

"I need to call my father."

"Sure. Sure, no problem." She reached into the file folder, pulled out seven more photos, and arranged them in a line on the table. They were photos of Edgar at Club Astarte, his gaze transfixed on the semicircle of naked men who were holding cattle prods and electrocuting the other naked man whose neck was chained to a wooden post. "You know what?" Laurel resumed. "Maybe we could talk with you and your father here together. That would save time. Two birds with one stone."

Edgar was quiet, staring down at the photos, looking horrified. Terrified.

"Should we give him a call and get him down here?" Laurel asked. "The phone is at your disposal. Just say the word."

Edgar was speechless. Laurel softened her voice.

"It's lonely, isn't it—living a secret life?" she said, turning and staring into her own eyes in the reflection of the one-way observer's window. "So lonely." She sat back down at the table. "Then again, maybe your father knows. Maybe he's proud of you anyway."

Edgar cringed. Closed his eyes. "I hate him," he mumbled.

"Pardon?"

"I *hate* him."

FIFTY-TWO

"I take it you don't want to call your father just now," Laurel said after half a minute of tense silence in the interrogation room.

Edgar was staring down at the photos again. Or rather, staring through them.

"Edgar, tell us what really happened," Laurel said, her voice taking on a note of sympathy. "Look, with just the evidence we've already told you about, a Kentucky jury is going to be sizing your arm up for the needle. Don't let it come to that. Don't throw your life away. We can help you. But you have to tell us what happened."

"It wasn't me."

"I believe you. When I look at you, Edgar, I don't see a killer. But from an objective standpoint, the evidence is airtight. It's damning. Convince us."

He remained silent, but appeared to be considering Laurel's request.

"Politically, we understand your father is somewhere to the right of Hitler. By that, I mean I could see him really blowing his stack over you and Paul," she said, observing a clenching in Edgar's jaw. "I could see him losing his mind, to be honest. I could even see him ordering his lackey, his goon, Barton Rill, to get Paul out of the picture. To remove the threat to his business. To remove what he saw as a stain on his family honor."

At this, Edgar glanced at the detectives, looking half-furious, half-heartbroken.

"I could also see Rill dragging you along, perhaps unwittingly, to tie you to the crime," she said. "To make you a de facto accomplice—the getaway driver. After the fact, maybe you wanted to go to the police. But then Rill convinced you that the police would never believe you now that your car had surely been caught on video near the crime scene. Plus, there was a plausible motive given your competing business interests—not to mention your, shall we say, nontraditional and perhaps intensely emotional personal entanglements with

Paul. Rill told you the police would lock you up and throw away the key. And it wouldn't have been an unreasonable thing to believe. After all, our justice system is far from perfect, right?"

"Yes," Edgar muttered.

"Yes?"

"Yes! Yes! You're right. All of it. Yes, Barton tricked me. Yes, Barton killed Paul for my father. Yes, Barton killed the jockey, Cervantes."

Trey thought he felt his heart skip a beat. Then Edgar broke down, sobbing.

*****

"Okay, okay," Laurel said, after giving Edgar a chance to compose himself. "Let's start at the beginning."

"The beginning? Ha. The beginning. Well, then." Edgar took a breath and wiped his eyes and nose with a tissue Laurel had given him. "It begins with my father. My father hates the other side of our family. Has always hated them, for a bunch of stupid reasons."

He paused, looking lost in memory, so Laurel fed him a line. "One of those reasons being that your distant cousin, Benjamin, wanted to get back into the liquor business?"

"Sure. Benjamin has wanted to get back into bourbon for years. His side of the family was a big part of it once. Started the Clayton brand, matter of fact. But my father, who has powerful friends, was always able to block Benjamin's efforts. He didn't want the competition. Didn't want anyone to even know Benjamin's name. Basically wanted Benjamin's side of the family to die off, poor and unacknowledged. It's insane. My father carries around this hate that's too strong to even wrap your head around. Because of some stupid, ancient, never-ending family feud."

"And because Benjamin is openly gay?"

"Yes. My father is a major homophobe. Thinks Benjamin is a disgrace. Didn't want anyone to know there was a gay man in his extended family. That the Clayton name was *tainted by Benjamin's filth*, like he said one time. I guess it was a threat to our family's stellar reputation," Edgar said, his voice rising.

"Carter sounds like a charmer."

"Then he found out that Benjamin was the one behind Paul's attempt to start up a distribution business. That Benjamin was advising him. Funding him. He was furious."

"Isn't Carter a recluse, except at his own Derby Day party? How did he figure all that out?"

"He had Barton spy on Benjamin sometimes. Follow him around. Dig into his affairs. That's what led him to Paul."

"When was all this?"

"Maybe three months ago."

"Three months? Odd that Carter would wait until last week to have Paul killed. Or did something else set him off? Something more recent?"

"Well," Edgar said. His lower lip trembled.

"He found out about *you* and Paul."

Edgar nodded.

"When?"

"I don't know. I only first met Paul at a bourbon industry New Year's Eve gala. He was the first man I.... Anyway, my father has Barton spy on me too. Babysit me. Pretend to be my friend. I'd managed to hide my sexuality from them for a long time."

"But then he saw you with Paul?"

"Yes. Barton followed me to a sort of social club that I took Paul to."

"Club Astarte?"

Edgar looked at her. "How...." He paused, then gathered himself. "Yes. At Club Astarte. Barton couldn't get in, of course. You have to be a member. There's a $25,000 initiation fee. And then it costs $10,000 a year. Barton doesn't have that kind of money."

"Was Paul a member?"

"No. He was my guest. Elite-level members can buy guests a one-day pass."

"So how did Barton see you there?"

"Saw us come out the exit with an audience that was still partly dressed in bondage gear. It's against club secrecy rules. To exit in costume, I mean. Hardly matters now. Barton saw me. Confronted me. At first, I managed to convince him that I was there out of a purely heterosexual taste for bondage. Then, as I was walking away, Paul walked up and wrapped his arms around my waist. He'd been inside getting dressed. Hadn't seen the confrontation. Didn't know any better."

"And Barton saw this. Saw Paul wrap his arms around you."

"He must have."

"Why do you say that?"

"Because he told my father."

"Told your father that you and Paul were together?"

"Yes." Edgar's lips moved as if he were subconsciously annunciating something—as if he wanted to say more. Laurel and Trey waited. "My father is one of those people who can tell himself something is true that he knows isn't, but he believes it anyway. There's a word for that."

"Delusional?"

"That's it. I mean, like, things happened when I was younger. Things...." He paused. "Anyway, my father always said I'd grow out of it. Probably convinced himself that I had. But I've just been playing a role. My Clayton Family role."

"What makes you think Barton told your father?"

"First," he said, his voice grave, "because the Friday before last, Barton told me his car had a dead battery and that he needed me to drive him around to run errands for my father. Like you said, he's my father's errand boy. Always kissing his ass. I'm sure Barton dreams of what he'll get in my father's will. Anyway, next thing you know, he has me turning off Broadway, onto 11th, parking right in front of Paul's warehouse. He told me to wait in the car. Told me he had to hand-deliver a letter to the owner, but said nothing about knowing who Paul was. So I didn't say anything either. Played dumb. Then Barton went to the front door, rang the buzzer, and waited for Paul to come out. Paul didn't know who Barton was, so he had no reason to fear him." Edgar's voice had grown tight. The pace of his speech had quickened. "Anyway, somehow Barton convinced Paul to come outside. Then Barton drew his gun. Paul, he tried to run...."

Edgar broke down again, burying his face in his hands. Laurel gave him a minute before resuming.

"Barton shot Paul," she said, gently.

Edgar nodded, his face still in his hands. Then he looked up. "Shot him in the back as he tried to run away. Then, when Paul fell, Barton walked up and shot him in the head."

Edgar needed another minute to gather himself. Then he went on to describe how Barton had convinced him that if he went to the police, he'd be arrested for murder—or at least as an accomplice.

"But you had second thoughts," Laurel suggested. "Then, two nights later, when you were both in Carbonado's stall at Churchill Downs, it came up again."

"We argued. I told him the police would figure it out. He told me to keep my mouth shut if I didn't want to go to prison for the rest of my life. Or worse."

"And then you emerged from the stall."

"And that jockey, Cervantes, was standing there staring at us with big, terrified eyes. It was obvious he'd overheard our conversation. As we walked away, Barton said we had to make sure Cervantes didn't tell anyone. So we hid in the Barnstone stall. Empire Builder's stall. Waiting for Cervantes to come back."

"Barton pressured you to go along," Laurel said in as sympathetic a voice as she could muster.

"Barton said he'd take me down with him if I didn't. I wasn't thinking straight. I was still out of my mind over Paul. Plus, I'd been drinking."

"So the two of you waited for Cervantes."

"He came back to the stall after an hour or so," Edgar said, breathing hard. "Barton jumped him." Edgar shook his head as if trying to purge the memory.

"Barton jumped him, and then?"

"Got a rope around Cervantes's neck before he could shout for help. Lifted him off the ground with it. The man struggled, kicking in the air, trying to reach back and get hold of Barton's head. But he couldn't get any leverage. He looked so scared. It was horrible. So horrible. After a bit, Barton lost his balance and fell to the ground on top of Cervantes, then just held him there while the man' eyes bugged out and his head turned purple."

"And then?"

"Then Cervantes stopped kicking." Edgar took a breath. "Once Barton was sure Cervantes was dead, he told me to go get the Escalade and back it up to the stall. We got Cervantes's driver's license out of his wallet to find out where he lived. Then we wrapped his body in a tarp, loaded it in the car, and took him home. We strung him up in his garage to try to make it look like a suicide. I knew it wouldn't work. Even then, I wanted to go to the police. Barton said the cops would never believe me. But here I am anyway."

"And you think your father actually told Barton to kill Paul?"

"He did."

"Maybe Barton did it in on his own initiative, to curry favor with your father."

"No. Once it got back to my father that I was thinking about going to the police, my father called me and said that if I ratted them out, I could consider myself out of the family."

"*Them*, meaning Barton and himself?"

"Yes. The order to kill Paul came from my father. He told me he did it to protect the family name from my degeneracy. He's gone insane." He looked at Laurel. "Where does it come from, detective? Where does such insane hatred come from?"

"I don't know, Edgar. I surely don't."

Edgar wiped the tears from his face and set his hands palm-down on the table. "I'll do whatever you want. Sign anything you want. I don't care anymore."

"Let's get your statement down in writing."

"If it will get my father out of my life."

"It's the right thing to do."

Edgar's expression lost focus. "You know," he said. "Paul was the only person in my life who I ever really thought...." But his voice trailed off and he never finished his statement.

FIFTY-THREE

"I want to run a theory by you, Trey," Laurel said, as they sat in a nearby cubicle while Edgar sobbed in the interrogation room. "An attempt to fill in a few blanks. Tell me if there are any parts of it that don't make sense."

"Fire away."

"While at Club Astarte one whip-cracking evening, Paul Taylor recognizes Senator McKittrick among the attendees. Seeing an opportunity, Taylor sneaks in a camera and takes some covert photos that dear old Mrs. McKittrick wouldn't want to put in the family album."

"Or videos."

"Sure. Photos or videos showing the good senator thoroughly enjoying Club Astarte's unconventional entertainments. Soon thereafter, Taylor uses them to blackmail McKittrick into getting a distribution license granted to Bacchus. Next thing you know, Carter Clayton finds out that Taylor had been granted a distribution license and blows his stack. Making things worse, with an eye toward getting Edgar booted out of Carter's will so that he could inherit the whole of the Clayton bourbon empire, Barton Rill spills it to Carter that his son is not only gay, but is in a relationship with his new upstart competitor in the distribution business, Taylor. From there, we more or less know what happened."

"Yeah," Trey said. "But don't forget that Senator McKittrick might have had his own set of Club Astarte blackmail photos. Photos he could use as leverage to squeeze a major political favor out of the City of Louisville—via the mayor's pervert chief of staff—in the form of orders that we lay off the case. And in the form of an LMPD insider's efforts to destroy evidence."

"Unless it was just a matter of Carter using his history of campaign contributions to call in that favor. Yes. Those are the twists."

"But what about the orders to lay off the Barnstones and other upper-crust horse racing people? How does that fit in?"

"Crazy as it seems," Laurel said, "I think we have to assume that those orders were the consequence of separate pressure coming from different people who were worried about something else entirely—something that doesn't have anything to do with our murders."

"Separate conspiracies? Hard to believe."

"It only takes one bad apple, as they say."

"Then let's find that apple and throw it in the trash."

"You should say that with an Arnold Schwarzenegger accent."

*****

They took Edgar's sworn statement, along with all their other evidence, back to Seth Greenberg, who promptly prepared affidavits supporting their request for arrest warrants for Barton Rill and Carter Clayton. Greenberg had the judge sign off in her chambers to reduce the risk that the wrong person might overhear their discussion and alert the suspects.

With arrest warrants in hand, Laurel placed a quick call to Rill's cell phone as they made their way out of the courthouse.

"Hello?" Rill said, sounding irritated.

"Good afternoon. This is United Parcel Service. I'm trying to reach Barton Rill."

"What do you want?"

"We have a Next Day Air parcel for you that requires a signature. Are you at home, sir?"

"Yes."

"Our driver can be there in the next 30 minutes, if that's convenient for you."

"Sure. Whatever."

"I'll inform the driver. Thank you for using UPS." She hung up and looked at Trey. "Green light."

"You know there's a tornado watch in effect this afternoon, lasting until 10 p.m.?"

"How appropriate."

"Do we wait on arresting these guys?"

"Because of the weather? No. This train is already rolling. We don't dare stop now."

FIFTY-FOUR

The detectives called in a request for a special reaction team—SRT for short—a heavily armed unit that specialized in dynamic entries and high-risk arrests. They also called for several regular patrol units to secure a perimeter. They all rendezvoused at a predetermined staging point on a quiet street behind the Monnik microbrewery, a scant half mile from Rill's home. The SRT guys rolled up in a matte black beast of an armored vehicle called the BEAR—or, as Trey liked to call it, the bread van from Hell. Trey popped the Taurus trunk open so that he and Laurel could access their gear—handguns, ballistic vests, utility belts, extra magazines, handcuffs, pepper spray, and telescoping steel ASP batons. The SRT guys wore full black body armor and Kevlar helmets with ear mikes. They carried either .223 caliber rifles or MP5 submachine guns. One of them held a large metal battering ram for breaching the front door. The regular patrol officers carried short-barrel Remington 870 shotguns, as well as their standard issue .40 caliber Glock G22 semiautomatics and Tasers.

Laurel briefed them on their target, emphasizing that Rill had been known to possess firearms. She also gave them a basic description of the layout of the house and yard. Then she asked the SRT guys for an extra MP5, explaining that she wanted to be first through the door.

"You sure you want to do that?" one of the SRT guys asked. "We're happy to clear the house for you."

"I'm sure. I used to be in SRT."

"You were in SRT?" the man asked, his tone respectful, but his question laced with implicit doubt.

Trey thought that Laurel's jaw tightened just perceptibly at the man's question. She stared at the man for a moment, then gave a curt nod.

"Okay," the man said, handing Laurel an extra submachine gun. "Your case. Your target."

"Meet back here at Monnik for beers on me, right after we drop Rill off at the sally port," Laurel said, using the unofficial name for the secured prisoners' entrance to the jail downtown. "Alright. Stay frosty. Let's roll."

*****

Laurel and Trey rode in the BEAR with the SRT unit. They pulled over at the end of the alley that ran behind Rill's house so that two of the SRT guys could jump out and run down the alley to cover the back door. Once the patrol units were in position at the ends of Rill's street and alley, the SRT driver rolled the BEAR up to the curb in front of Rill's house. The entry team spilled out the back of the vehicle with weapons out and approached the front door. It didn't look like it had been fully repaired since Speedy kicked it in. Reaching it, the team stacked up with Laurel in the lead and the officer with the battering ram standing to her right. The team nodded in readiness. Then Laurel pounded on the door.

"Police. Open the door."

Without waiting for an answer, she stood back and the officer with the ram broke the door down with one swing. The entry team ran forward, each officer focusing on a different zone, each with their guns out and up. Laurel spotted Rill, in nothing but boxer shorts, standing in his narrow hallway.

"Hands in the air! Hands in the air!" she shouted, aiming her submachine gun at his chest. Rill raised his hands. As Laurel neared him, he jumped to his side, through the open door to the bathroom. As Laurel ran to the bathroom doorway and began to step through, it slammed shut, hitting her in the nose so hard that it started to bleed.

"Son of a bitch," she muttered, looking furious. "He isn't armed. Call an ambulance," Laurel said as she handed off her gun.

"Are you hurt?" Trey called from behind the SRT guys.

"It's not for me," she said, pulling her expandable ASP baton from her belt and whipping it to full length with one fluid swing of her arm. Then, before Trey could even begin to annunciate his fear that Rill might have a gun hidden in the bathroom, she reared up, kicked the bathroom door in with the flat of her foot, and sprang forward with two of the SRT guys following her, shouting, "Get on the ground!" Rill had been at the bathroom window, trying to raise it in a futile attempt to escape. Seeing Laurel, he turned and raised his fists to fight. But in a flurry of moves so quick that Trey, watching from the doorway, wasn't even sure what had happened—and before either of the SRT guys could even get around her to help—Laurel had Rill pinned face down on the tile floor. His right arm was broken. Clearly a compound fracture. He was screaming in pain even though Laurel limited her handcuffing to the wrist of the unbroken arm, locking it to a sturdy iron pipe protruding from the base of the bathroom's ancient radiator. Then she stood up, brushed herself off, took a breath, and gave him his Miranda warning.

*****

In addition to the broken arm, it turned out Rill had a broken collarbone, two chipped front teeth, a four-inch laceration across his forehead, and a possible concussion, leaving Trey wondering at how thoroughly Laurel had beaten the snot out of him in what couldn't have been more than five seconds. The lesson being, don't slam a door on Laurel's nose or resist arrest.

Trey stood slack-jawed and impressed. Still, something about how it went down nagged at him a bit. Brought an unsettled feeling to the pit of his stomach. Why had Laurel insisted on being first through the door? The SRT guys practiced or did this sort of thing damned near every day. It made sense to leave it to them. Also, there was something about her fight with Rill that bothered him. As far as her use of force was concerned, nobody would fault her for using her steel ASP baton on a murder suspect who was fighting arrest as Rill was. But there was something about the ferocity of her attack that struck him as perhaps just exceeding what was necessary given the circumstances. As if she maybe—just maybe—struck Rill with her ASP one more time than she really needed to. He thought back to when Laurel's jaw seemed to tighten as they were suiting up with the SRT guys, then couldn't help but wonder whether she might have a bit of a chip on her shoulder.

*****

Having secured the house, the officers put Rill in belly chains instead of standard behind-the-back handcuffs because of his broken arm.

"I'm sorry, but it looks like we're going to have to ride in the ambulance with Chuck Norris Junior," Laurel said to the SRT guys, gesturing toward Rill. "We'll have to get those beers another time. I won't forget."

"Hey, shit happens," one of the officers said. "No worries."

As they waited for the ambulance, Laurel asked to borrow one of the regular patrol officer's mobile data terminals. Getting hold of it, she entered her own ID and password, then ran Rill on NCIC. In truth, she'd run his name on NCIC just after their interview of Magnolia Clayton, and thus already knew all she needed to know about his record. She was doing it again to hopefully set off internal alarms with anyone who might be watching for such queries.

As the detectives rode in the ambulance with Rill, they ran through a preplanned conversation that emphasized how important the seizure of Rill's P226 handgun was to their case—how critical it was for linking Rill to the murder of Paul Taylor.

"You know, our case is only solid because we have the gun," Trey said to Laurel, as if thinking out loud, making sure Rill heard him. "We'd never get a conviction without it."

Just inside the hospital door, Rill demanded the right to a phone call. Suppressing a smile, Laurel drew Rill's own cell phone from her pocket—having, quite against normal procedure, purposely brought it along for Rill's potential use.

"You get one call," Laurel said, handing him his phone. "Better make it count."

Given that Rill wasn't a flight risk—being, as he was, thrashed and chained to a gurney—they walked out of earshot so that he'd feel comfortable discussing sensitive matters with whomever he called. After about 10 minutes, Rill hung up. Laurel walked over and took the phone back from him.

They watched as hospital staff rolled Rill away on a gurney, flanked by two LMPD officers. Then Laurel took a look at Rill's still-unlocked phone to observe that his most recent call was made to a number labeled "Carter."

"That's it then," Trey said. "The trap is baited and set."

FIFTY-FIVE

In the early evening, in a vacant conference room, Laurel and Trey sat at a table covered with take-out containers of food from Hammerheads. There were tender smoked ribs, duck meat tacos, smoked cheddar grit cakes in hollandaise, and French fries cooked in duck fat and sprinkled with truffle oil. Across from them sat Detective Sergeant Isaiah Turner, now up to speed on the case and on board with Laurel's plan. At the end of the table, Trey's laptop screen was split to show two separate live images that were being recorded via small security cameras Trey had stuck to the sides of smoke detectors protruding from the ceiling. One was of the hallway that, just outside the door of their conference room, led to the nearby secure evidence room. The second was of the evidence room itself—covering, in particular, the shelf on which a Sig Sauer P226 .45 caliber handgun marked as evidence for the Taylor case sat in a sealed plastic evidence bag.

"Take it easy, Ken doll," Turner said to Trey, watching him stuff another cheese grit cake in his mouth. "You eat any more of those things, you'll be constipated for a week."

"Never been an issue for me."

"Gentlemen," Laurel said, pointing at the screen. A man was walking down the hall. But he didn't go to the secure evidence room. Instead, he turned and went down a perpendicular hallway. "Never mind."

"Not that I'm not loving this feast, but do you really think someone will take the bait?" Trey asked Laurel.

"I do. I just hope they do it before our arrest warrant expires."

"And you don't think we'll just end up catching poor Stuart Donnelly the janitor again?"

"No. Think about it. It will have to be someone who can access the secure evidence room. Someone official."

"They could just give Donnelly the keys."

"And trust him to get the all-important gun? Not at this point, I think."

*****

As it turned out, they only had to wait another 15 minutes before another man appeared on the screen.

"Sarge, look," Laurel said.

As the man's face passed the hallway camera, it became clear who he was.

"Dale," Turner said, shaking his head. "Oh, Dale."

"You still sound surprised," Laurel said. "Even after the jacked up orders he's been handing down to you."

"Didn't want to believe it, I suppose."

"You also sound oddly sympathetic."

"We go way back," Turned said. "To the academy, actually. He was a good guy. His wife died of a brain aneurism a couple of years ago, leaving him with two young twins."

They watched Mecklenburg unlock the evidence room, step inside, then close and lock the door behind him. The action moved to the other side of the split screen of Trey's computer. They watched as Mecklenburg searched the evidence shelves, twice stopping to reference a scrap of paper he held in his hand that probably told him where he'd find what he was looking for. After a moment, he reached up to the highest shelf and grabbed the sealed evidence bag containing the P226 handgun. He placed the gun in a large paper grocery bag he'd drawn from his coat pocket and unfolded. Then, the gun safely wrapped and obscured, he went back out the door.

"Give it a minute to make sure he exits the building," Turner said as they watched him disappear down the hall.

*****

They caught up with Mecklenburg in the parking lot as a strong breeze and darkening western sky threatened a hard rain—or worse.

"Dale!" Turner shouted. "Hey buddy."

"Isaiah. How are you?" Mecklenburg said with less enthusiasm, noticing that Turner was flanked by two detectives he knew to be working the Taylor murder case.

"What's in the bag, Dale?" Turner asked.

"Pastrami on rye."

"Yeah. Look, here's the deal, my friend. We can cuff you right here, right now, in the parking lot in front of all your colleagues. Or we can be civilized and go inside to discuss your options."

"What are you talking about?"

"Dale, we have you on video. The thing is, that isn't even the real gun. It's a ringer. Laurel bought it with her own money, at Kentucky Gun Co., down in

Bardstown."

"I always wanted a P226 anyway," Laurel said. "Great gun."

"You know the score, Dale," Turner said. "Cooperate, or don't cooperate. The choice is yours. But, out of respect, we'd rather not embarrass you here in public."

"Why did you take the gun?" Laurel asked.

Mecklenburg gawked at her, then looked to Turner. "Isaiah, I don't.... Can't we work something out, maybe just this once?"

"Sorry, Dale."

"My kid—my son. He has blood cancer. He's only five. Please."

For a moment, all was quiet.

"The gun, Dale," Laurel said again, this time softly. "Why'd you take it?"

"His lips moved soundlessly. He clenched his fists, then relaxed them. At last, he mumbled, "I just...."

"Pardon?"

"I just follow orders."

As they all knew, the only people above Mecklenburg in the LMPD chain of command were the deputy chief, the chief himself, and then, of course, the mayor's office.

"So who *ordered* you to take the gun?" Turner asked. "Where did the order come from?"

Mecklenburg had gone mute.

"From Vernon Fuchs, the mayor's chief of staff?" Laurel asked.

Hearing the name, Mecklenburg gave her a surprised glance that told her all she needed to know. It was the chief of staff. A guy who liked to dress in 1920s formal wear, get drugged out, and watch people being whipped, burned, and electrocuted at underground sex clubs. So the corruption went at least as high as the mayor's right-hand man.

After a bit more prodding, Mecklenburg followed the detectives back into the building where they put him in an interrogation room—on the opposite side of the table from what he was used to.

"Did you see the look on Mecklenburg's face when we confronted him in the parking lot?" Trey asked with a huge smile as they prepared to question the fallen LMPD major. "That was priceless." He tried to give Laurel a high five but she left him hanging.

"Don't revel in human weakness, Trey. His little boy is sick. There are pressures on him we can't even fathom. Pressures that probably made him vulnerable to whatever carrot or stick his superiors used to nudge him across the line."

Laurel doubted that Mecklenburg would give them a statement, let alone a confession. But it didn't matter. They had all they needed on him. They had the statement from the janitor, Stuart Donnelly. They had the video. And they had a respected homicide sergeant and two detectives as firsthand witnesses. Plus, they could subpoena phone records probably showing that, just after taking a call from the hospitalized Barton Rill, Carter Clayton had called Vernon Fuchs. Eventually, the Commonwealth's Attorney would cut a deal with Mecklenburg, and he'd provide the other half of the progression of orders leading from Carter Clayton's call to Fuchs, down to Mecklenburg's attempt to steal the gun out of evidence. Mecklenburg would certainly, rightly, lose his job. But he might, if he was very lucky, avoid a long prison sentence. Regardless, the bad apples in LMPD and the city government would, at last, be tossed out with the garbage.

FIFTY-SIX

The late evening sky was unusually dark and menacing, composed—from horizon to horizon—of heavy, ever-changing clouds that bore an odd green hue. A powerful, moisture-laden west wind was blowing leaves and other bits of debris sideways through the air.

After once again driving the picturesque tree-lined road that led up the bluff, Laurel and Trey arrived at Carter Clayton IV's massive Glenview mansion, with its immaculate grounds and sweeping view of the Ohio River. There was now a small bandstand and a portable dance floor set up alongside the two large tents erected for the next day's Derby after-party. The unsecured door panels of the tents were flapping in the wind. The dance floor was flanked by clusters of large Peepaw Clayton bourbon barrels that, standing on end, appeared to be arranged so as to serve as small tables for the partygoers. Each cluster of barrels had a large silver vase of red roses for a centerpiece. But the wind had already blown half of the roses to the ground.

"Where are all the party workers?" Trey said.

"It's evening. I imagine they went home. They have all day tomorrow to make final preparations."

Laurel wondered if they planned to serve the Peepaw Clayton 21-year-old bourbon at the party. Probably. Right along with Kobe beef, beluga caviar, and chilled Dom Pérignon. What an extravagant life some people led. But Laurel also wondered whether the guests truly enjoyed themselves at the famous Clayton Bourbon derby party. Wondered whether their pleasure was tainted by the knowledge that it represented Carter's prepayment for future favors. That it was a self-serving prop for his ego. That Carter saw them not as friends but as assets.

As they rounded the last curve of the drive, the detectives found a white panel van parked at the foot of the stair that led to the impressive porch with its embedded Confederate gold coin of questionable provenance.

"He has a visitor," Trey said.

"Call in the license plate."

Trey did. Half a minute later, they learned the van belonged to Central State Hospital.

"Zelda?" Trey said. "Hard to imagine she'd have any interest in visiting her father."

"Your parents are your parents. It's hard to cut that cord, no matter the circumstances."

"Or maybe it's a court-mandated visit. Part of some shared guardianship type of thing."

"Not my province, I'm afraid. All that matters is that Zelda is probably in there, along with whoever brought her here from the hospital. So I think we should bag Carter right away. Don't want to give the old snake time to turn this into a hostage situation."

"You don't want to wait for our backup? Rueff and the two patrol units are only five minutes out."

Given Carter's age, they hadn't thought it necessary to call for the SRT.

"No, let's make this quick," Laurel said. "Look at the sky. Weather is about to hit hard."

They got out and ascended the steps. Taking another quick glance at the mysterious gold coin at her feet, Laurel gave the heavy gargoyle door knocker a couple of loud knocks, shouting, "Police! Open the door!" Just as she did, they heard a distant tornado siren coming to life, its haunting wail echoing across the area, reminiscent of the London Blitz.

"Oh, crap," Trey said. "Do we take cover?"

"Let's grab Carter first. Then we can shelter inside."

Laurel tried the door. It was locked. After a second loud knock—also unanswered—the detectives stood on the porch looking at each other.

"Now what?" Trey said. "We don't have an entry ram."

Laurel looked around, her eyes locking on one of the concrete planters that held rose bushes to either side of the door. "Let's put that thing through one of the windows."

Each taking a side and lifting it, they found it couldn't have been more than 70 pounds. Not too heavy. But enough to do the job.

"It'll be easier if you just let me do it, Trey said, taking it from Laurel. He walked over to the nearest window, lifted the planter high, and launched it through the glass. Shards and wood splinters showered the ground as it crashed through. Standing to the side of the window, using his steel ASP baton, Trey reached over and knocked out a few more pointed fragments of glass that remained in the bottom of the frame. Then both detectives took a quick peek inside. The entry vestibule appeared empty. But just as Trey began to climb through the hole, a close-range shot rang out. Trey staggered backward, fell to the porch, and rolled face-down. Laurel grabbed his legs and dragged him away from the window to cover against the wall. A streak of blood traced his path.

Covering his body with her own, Laurel grabbed her radio mic and began shouting into it.

"Shots fired! Officer down at 7000 Longview Lane! Officer down!"

"Copy, officer down at 7000 Longview Lane," she heard from the radio. "All units be advised…."

Trey hadn't made a sound. Laurel got to her knees and rolled him over, fearing the worst. But he was gritting his teeth as he held a hand flat against the bloody side of his torso, just below the lower edge of his body armor, applying direct pressure to his wound. "Trey!" Her eyes welled up.

"Don't hug me. Boundaries, Laurel."

That almost made her smile.

"Feels superficial," he said, wincing. His face was flushed, his forehead sweaty.

"Superficial? So you're okay?"

"Hurts. But I'm not gonna die."

"Thank God."

Laurel began to stand up, but Trey grabbed her arm with one of his bloody hands. "Laurel."

"What is it?"

"Don't go in alone. Wait for backup." He let go of her arm, leaving a red handprint on her sleeve.

"Trey, his daughter and at least one person from the hospital are in there."

"He could ambush you."

"I can't wait. He's deranged. He might try to hurt his captives."

Trey gave her a hard look. "Right. Okay. Go get him. I'm good. Go."

Laurel gave him a nod, went to the smashed-in window for another quick peek, saw that the entry vestibule was empty, and dove through the hole into the house. Hitting the floor, she rolled behind the nearest object she could use for cover—a marble umbrella holder by the door—and looked around. There was no sign of Carter. A grand foyer had hallways that led off in three different directions on the main floor. A wide marble stairwell led to the second level.

Laurel figured that Carter was hateful enough to use his own daughter and her minder as human shields—assuming he wasn't already disturbed enough to kill them in a murder-suicide. But he wouldn't have had time to get them upstairs. So they were probably somewhere on the main floor.

"Hello?" she shouted. "Zelda? Teetee?"

Despite the roaring wind and distant howling of the tornado siren outside, the interior of the house was surprisingly quiet, but for the gentle metronomic pulse of a grandfather clock that stood against the wall to Laurel's left, next to a huge painting of a black Arabian horse. Laurel stood still, listening for any hint of her target's location. Then, she heard one. It sounded like someone kicking their toe against a wooden baseboard or table leg. It came from her right.

Gun up, she made her way down the right-hand hallway as quietly as she could. Along the way, she passed the open doorways of two rooms—one, a sitting room, the other, a sewing room—taking quick peeks to ensure they were empty. Then, reaching the end of the hall, she came to a closed door.

Standing to its side, behind the cover of a plaster wall, she reached over and knocked on the door.

"Carter! Come out of there. You can't—"

She was interrupted by the clap of Carter's gun firing, and the simultaneous clunking sound of a bullet penetrating the closed wooden door. As the gun fired, she also heard a brief female scream, quickly stifled.

Staying behind the wall, Laurel reached over and threw the door open as Clayton fired off two more rounds through the open doorway. Laurel took a look around the edge of the doorjamb and was able to ascertain that Zelda and a female employee of Central State Hospital were standing arm's-length apart in front of a hardwood desk that Clayton was using for cover, having both been pressed into service, at gunpoint, as human shields. They were in a home library, with built-in shelves full of old hardbound books in all the walls. Carter was crouched down, holding onto the edge of the desk for balance. His gun—which he kept trained on the doorway—was some kind of old revolver. That meant he probably had two shots left—assuming he hadn't reloaded after shooting Trey.

"Carter, drop the gun," she shouted.

"You're trespassing on private property."

"We have a warrant. Drop the gun, stand up, and show me your hands. Now!"

"Go to hell. You should be thanking me for getting rid of another queer for you. Before they take over the whole damned country."

"Drop the gun!" she repeated, taking one more peek. This time, as she looked, she saw the top of Carter's head rock backward as if he were losing his balance. Then his gun hand flew sideways as he reached, without looking, for something to stop his fall. But his hand didn't find anything, and as he fell back, Laurel raced forward until she could see him over the top of the desk. Regaining his footing as Laurel once again shouted for him to drop the gun, Carter swung his arm to take aim at her. In less than a second, Laurel fired four shots into the center of his chest. Carter fell to the floor, dead. As he did, the distant tornado siren wound down and went quiet, the warning canceled.

FIFTY-SEVEN

"You were shot by a .38 caliber, 1962 Smith & Wesson model 14, special long barrel, in case you're interested," Laurel said as a doctor stitched up Trey's wound at the emergency room.

"I'm not," Trey said, laying on his side on the bed. "I'm just glad the son of a bitch wasn't a very good shot. Couple inches to the left and I'd be pooping in a bag for the next few weeks."

In addition to still being in considerable pain, Trey was hugely embarrassed by all the attention and action Laurel's 'officer down' call had brought. Within minutes, dozens—literally dozens of LMPD units had closed off streets to clear a direct route for his ambulance all the way from the Clayton mansion to the level 1 trauma center at University of Louisville Hospital. Television news helicopters had taken to the sky to follow the action. And all for a non-life threatening injury. He felt like a total schmuck.

"Hey," Laurel had said. "LMPD takes care of its own. That's how we do things. So don't sweat it. Actually, savor it. This is your 15 minutes of fame."

"What a thing to be famous for. Crying wolf."

"Trey, you were shot. And anyway, I'm the one who called it in."

"Whatever."

She shook her head and looked at the bank of powered-down monitors next to Trey's bed. "Poor old fool."

"I'm not that old," Trey said.

"I'm talking about Carter."

He gave her a look. "Don't tell me you feel bad for him."

"A little. How could you not? Another scared old man who felt left behind in an ever-changing world."

"Laurel, the guy was a murderer and a total crazy."

"Isolation and ignorance will warp anyone's mind eventually."

"Yeah, well. Maybe he should have gotten out more."

FIFTY-EIGHT

Jockey Buford Gareaux was excited, having been tapped at the last minute to ride a magnificent chestnut colt named Empire Builder in the Pennyroyal Stakes. But it wasn't just the opportunity to ride in a stakes race on Derby Day that had him pumped up. There was something about this horse. In the last two days of exercising, in saddling up minutes earlier back in the paddock, and now as it was walking out to the starting gates, it exuded an aura of uncommon power and potential. Gareaux had been racing for 27 years—most recently as part of the jockey colony at Evangeline Downs, in his home state of Louisiana—and he could count on one hand the number of times he'd been atop a horse that, in that sixth sense intangible sort of way, felt to be of this level of quality and strength. The colt was calm. Self-assured. No newcomer to racing. It was as if the horse somehow *knew* it would own the 10 furlongs of track beyond the approaching starting gate. Knew that it was the class of the field.

Though he was a somewhat jaded old hand, Gareaux still thought there was something special about Derby Day. There was no other event quite like it. Tradition. Grandeur. Pageantry. The crowd alone made it an electrifying experience. 160,000 people. Cheering, roaring, screaming people—most of them dressed to the nines. It was, for one glorious day, the epicenter of the racing world. And what a day. Sun. Deep blue sky. A high of 75 degrees. Light breezes out of the northwest. Picture perfect a mere day after a tornado had touched down less than twenty miles to the north.

The horse had drawn post position 10, which, in a field of 12, wasn't ideal. It meant that Empire Builder would have to run further than nine other horses to reach the finish line. But Gareaux wasn't concerned. If more than a quarter century of racing had taught him anything at all, it was how to sense a winner. Better still, the track's condition was fast—the dirt dry, even, and resilient—which was what Empire Builder favored.

He was nearing the starting gate below the towering white grandstand with its distinctive twin spires. Half the horses were already in. The horse in position six was skittish—so much so that Gareaux wondered if it wouldn't be scratched before the gates opened. But it seemed to calm down just enough as Empire Builder reached its own starting stall at position 10. As the gate closed behind Empire Builder, Gareaux made a last-second check of his helmet strap, stretched his arms in the immaculate cobalt blue silks of Barnstone Farm, and gripped the reins. In a flash, the bell rang, the gates opened, and they were off in a rolling, thundering wall. Beautiful horses and their expert jockeys, each adorned with the brilliant colored silks of their respective farms, flying past throngs of people in seersucker suits, brightly colored dresses, and elaborate Derby hats.

As he entered the first turn, Empire Builder was positioned on the shoulder of the favorite, Travertine, and had already closed to within a length of the leader—a majestic bay named Whirligig, its jockey wearing the purple and yellow silks of Buchanan Stables. Gareaux was hardly having to encourage his mount at all. Empire Builder wanted to win. And yet even from his limited experience working with the horse over the past couple of days, Gareaux could tell that Empire Builder was holding something back, stalking, waiting for the right moment to pour on the fuel. And as they came into the backside straightaway, Empire Builder did just that. The colt's strength was phenomenal, and Gareaux couldn't suppress a smile as, kicking up the dirt, they surged past Travertine and Whirligig and began to expand their lead without letup. By the start of the second turn, the race was theirs.

Gareaux's heart pounded. This was what he'd gotten into racing for. The rush. The adrenaline. The thrill at taking the lead. The roar of the crowd. The blur of color. The thunder of hooves. Feeling the strength and grace of an extraordinary horse. Feeling that almost spiritual horse-rider connection as they flew forward.

They crossed the finish line a full five lengths ahead of the next horse, and Gareaux was over the moon to hear the sudden, notable *absence* of a deafening roar. A clear indicator that few had expected Empire Builder to win, and that even fewer had bet on him. Gareaux hoped it also meant that people would attribute the win, at least in part, to his skill as a jockey.

The lucky few who *had* bet on Gareaux and Empire Builder were making noise, of course. They had a big pot of winnings to share with a relatively small number of fellow gamblers.

As Gareaux looked up to check the results on the tote board, he saw that Empire Builder's as-yet unofficial time was 2:03:20, which had to be close to a Pennyroyal Stakes record. A single tear fell from his left eye and rolled down his cheek.

*****

Gareaux wasn't the only one who was elated. A few minutes earlier, half-astounded that Empire Builder hadn't been scratched from the race despite her follow-up call to Kathy Hammersmith, Detective Laurel Arno had run straight to the nearest betting window from a fantastic box in section 116 that her date, an orthopedic surgeon, had invited her to sit in. There, in the bowels of the venerable, crowded Churchill Downs grandstand, Laurel had hesitated, wondering at the morality of what she was doing. Taking a sip of her icy mint julep as she caught her breath, she reasoned that she'd done everything within her purview to prevent a horse swap. Reasoned that if there really had been a horse swap, a forewarned Kathy Hammersmith would surely have caught it by now. Then she'd put $1,000 on Empire Builder to win, despite the horse's laughable odds. And now, having high-fived, hugged, and kissed everyone standing in the box—including three crotchety old doctors she'd never even met before—she was strolling, with a smile from ear-to-ear, back to the betting window to collect more than $35,000, thinking that the first thing she would do with her winnings was take Trey for a fried chicken dinner at Dasha Barbour's Southern Bistro. Over their meal, they'd reflect on how the risks and struggles of the Cervantes and Taylor cases had been worth it. How their work their hard decisions—had made a genuine difference for their department and for Louisville.

And the public would never come to know that Empire Builder was actually a champion 4-year-old that used to run in Grade I stakes races under the name of Swizzle Stick.

To read
CHASING THE MONKEY KING
by D.C. Alexander
please visit
AMAZON.COM

ABOUT THE AUTHOR

D.C. Alexander is a former federal agent. His debut novel, The Legend of Devil's Creek, was a #1 Amazon Kindle Best Seller. He was born and raised in the Seattle area, and now lives in Louisville, Kentucky. He welcomes your feedback. You can email him directly at:
authordcalexander@gmail.com

GOOD EATS!

If you live in or take a trip to Louisville and want to eat and drink like Laurel, Trey, and your grateful author, try the following, listed in order of their appearance or mention in the story (by the way, the author has absolutely no connection to these places aside from just really liking them and wanting to share):

DAIRY KASTLE
575 Eastern Pkwy
Louisville, KY 40217
(your author recommends the "taco-in-a-bag"—no, seriously—and a butterscotch malt)

SUNERGOS COFFEE
2122 S Preston St.
Louisville, KY 40217

NORD'S BAKERY
2118 S Preston St.
Louisville, KY 40217
(maple-bacon donuts!)

FRANK'S MEAT & PRODUCE
3342 Preston Hwy
Louisville, KY 40213
(go hungry, and get the utterly meat-loaded club sandwich)

WAGNER'S
3113 S 4th St
Louisville, KY 40214

WALACE STATION
3854 Old Frankfort Pike
Versailles, KY 40383
(the chess pie is so good you'll slap your mama)

SAFAI COFFEE SHOP
1707 Bardstown Rd
Louisville, KY 40205

INDI'S FRIED CHICKEN
1033 W Broadway
Louisville, KY 40203
(if you like spicy food, get the extra spicy keel)

ROYALS HOT CHICKEN
736 E Market St
Louisville, KY 40202
(the "apple pie milkshake" is something special, and, if you dare, the
"gonzo" chicken will blow your head clean off with one bite)

DASHA BARBOUR'S SOUTHERN BISTRO
2217 Steier Ln
Louisville, KY 40218
(everything is delicious, but the sweet potato casserole is sublime)

JACK FRY'S
1007 Bardstown Rd
Louisville, KY 40204
(quintessentially Louisvillian, always excellent)

FABD SMOKEHOUSE
3204 Frankfort Ave
Louisville, KY 40206
(ribs!)

MORRIS' DELI
2228 Taylorsville Rd
Louisville, KY 40205
(smoked tuna!)

ZANZABAR
2100 S Preston St
Louisville, KY 40217

THE CAFÉ
712 Brent St
Louisville, KY 40204
(Italian cream cake!)

FANTE'S COFFEE
2501 Grinstead Dr
Louisville, KY 40206

O'SHEA'S IRISH PUB
956 Baxter Ave
Louisville, KY 40204

BEAN
1138 Goss Ave
Louisville, KY 40217

PLEHN'S BAKERY
3940 Shelbyville Rd
St Matthews, KY 40207
(ask for the huge, frosting-covered "yum-yum" donut)

THE BACK DOOR
1250 Bardstown Rd #7
Louisville, KY 40204

MAGNOLIA BAR AND GRILL
1398 S Second St
Louisville, KY 40208

MONNIK BEER COMPANY
1036 E Burnett Ave
Louisville, KY 40217
(the King George brown ale is first rate)

HAMMERHEADS
921 Swan St
Louisville, KY 40204
(your author insists that you get the PBLT sandwich and/or duck fat
fries with truffle oil)

CPSIA information can be obtained
at www.ICGtesting.com
Printed in the USA
FSHW021343091119

9 780578 601274